GIDEON'S REVOLUTION

GIDEON'S REVOLUTION

A Novel

BRIAN CARSO

THREE HILLS
an imprint of
Cornell University Press
Ithaca and London

First published 2023 by Cornell University Press

Printed in the United States of America

Library of Congress Cataloging-in-Publication Data

Names: Carso, Brian F., Jr., author.
Title: Gideon's revolution : a novel / Brian Carso.
Description: Ithaca [New York] : Three Hills, an imprint of Cornell University Press, 2023.
Identifiers: LCCN 2023004160 (print) | LCCN 2023004161 (ebook) | ISBN 9781501771514 (hardcover) | ISBN 9781501771521 (pdf) | ISBN 9781501771538 (epub)
Subjects: LCSH: Arnold, Benedict, 1741–1801—Fiction. | Spies—United States—History—18th century—Fiction. | United States—History—Revolution, 1775–1783—Fiction. | LCGFT: Historical fiction. | Novels.
Classification: LCC PS3603.A7754 G53 2023 (print) | LCC PS3603.A7754 (ebook) | DDC 813/.6—dc23/eng/20230208
LC record available at https://lccn.loc.gov/2023004160
LC ebook record available at https://lccn.loc.gov/2023004161

This is a work of fiction. Names, characters, places, and incidents are either the product of the author's imagination or are used fictitiously, and any resemblance to any persons, living or dead, business establishments, events, or locales is entirely coincidental. In certain instances in which the author makes references to historical events and real persons, those references are made solely in a fictional context.

For Kerry, Owen, and Nathaniel

Let all men know thee,

but no man know thee thoroughly.

Poor Richard's Almanack, 1743

GIDEON'S REVOLUTION

PROLOGUE

Tappan, New York

September–October 1780

1

Yes, I have known spies; more than I ever thought I would. But none were the daring masters of concealment and subterfuge you're thinking about. More often they shuddered at the very idea. I knew a woman in New York, when the city was in the hands of the British. She hung a red towel on a clothesline to signal that a plot was underway to capture a turncoat, and throughout the day, while it fluttered in the breeze, she went about her work with trembling hands. A gregarious tailor I called upon extracted military gossip from his British army clientele, which got passed to Washington's camp. Whenever a cluster of redcoats approached his shop he held his wife and kissed her, unsure if they came to have their breeches fixed or to haul him off to prison. A ring of informants delivered coded messages, as I once did, to a dry goods merchant, who received them with feigned ignorance. He passed the missives to the proprietor of a coffeehouse, who would further them to their destination, and when the merchant returned to his store he would sit in a chair behind the counter, as tired as if he had carried ten sacks of grain.

By some measure we are all spies, of one kind or another. Some play bit parts in grand schemes and swallow the risk like a bitter drug. A few will travel behind the lines to gauge an enemy's strength, or befriend a double-dealing rogue to unmask a secret treason. But I've learned this: that every honest man spies upon himself foremost, to see what hides in his own dark alleys. A bloody war can oust a king, but the skirmishes we fight alone, in silence, also make their mark on the world.

I was a soldier in the Revolution. This would have pleased my father, who measured his worth in the currency of honor. But my mother made me promise to live three score and ten, and she knew the cost of soldiering. In a world in which young breath can expire in a cough, she wrapped her arms tightly around me; but as I grew she would say to herself, just loud enough for me to hear, *I cannot raise an eagle if I treat him like a sparrow.* She raised me to manhood insisting on a middle ground: earn a good name, she told me, but live to see another day, and know that a life sacrificed for honor, though glorified in eulogy, casts a shadow of pity.

When I took up arms, never did I think to be a spy. To live honorably and do my duty: that was my intention, not the thrust and parry of trickery and deceit. To be a spy is to risk both life and honor on a game of dice. I would not do it.

John André was different. He made a bet.

Briefly I knew André, but only as an inquisitor. If anyone had a sporting chance, surely he did; but on a quiet road beside the Hudson River, in the ungoverned territory that neither army claimed, he was abandoned by the good fortune he had known all his life.

When I questioned him, pressing for information about his plot with our treasonous general, I tried to imagine the moment he decided to gamble.

I looked at André, a major in the British army who was now our prisoner, as he sat in a chair beside a small round table.

"Why?" I asked.

He said nothing, but cast a downward glance and slowly shook his head. The galloping menace of the war had simply outpaced him.

2

As Major André struggled to keep his spirits up within the stone walls of Mabie Tavern—a makeshift jail for a single prisoner—a feeling of unease spread throughout the encampment. The enlisted men who gathered around campfires to stare at the flames and think about home were spitting and cursing instead, damning the prisoner and calling for the hangman. The officers I knew were less certain: in their wall tents near the Dutch church, their conversations contained confidential whispers. Inside the brick and stone DeWint house, where General Washington convened his most trusted advisers, a human shadow had descended over the laws of war. Confined in the tavern was a good man of noble character, who in another time would have raised a tankard in merriment with us. The officers who paced back and forth, who heard the strain in the general's voice and watched him squint to read the papers on the map table, were unnerved by the choice they debated: to hold André as a prisoner of war or execute him as a spy.

Even in war there is a protocol among gentlemen, and André was given every accommodation. I knew that Washington sent meals to the prisoner from his own kitchen. The commander in chief permitted André to summon a servant upriver from New York to bring a proper uniform. Even as a prisoner, André had a worldly intelligence and courtly manners that were endearing. Colonel Hamilton, Washington's aide-de-camp, said André had an elegance of mind. Lafayette found the British officer charming, frank, and noble. Major Tallmadge, who supervised André's confinement, told me the prisoner was convivial and polite. Still, there were things that André would not reveal to them about his co-conspirator—our turncoat general—so they sent me to see him because of what I knew about Benedict Arnold, our Judas.

It was the third day of André's imprisonment, in the late afternoon, when I conducted that first interview. A special troop was stationed on the green in front of the tavern, and two soldiers from the Second Light Dragoons stood guard outside the door. Major André rose and greeted me, then offered me a chair, extending what little hospitality he could.

We spoke briefly of the autumn weather, and of amateur theatricals, which I had heard he fancied. Then I asked him what I had come to find out.

"You came upriver as a secret emissary from the British command, to meet General Arnold and receive his plans for treason."

"I was so ordered, and I did my duty."

"It is no small thing for a major general to willfully turn over his command—a strategic fort of high importance—to the enemy."

"It is no small thing. That is true."

"It could have been a trap, to set an ambush against British forces, to draw regiments up the Hudson away from New York, or some other tactic."

"We considered that, of course."

"Then you must have inquired as to his motives?"

Here André became pensive, but only for a moment.

"He lost faith in your cause."

"Did he tell you that?"

"And he disdained the involvement of the French."

I waved my hand, dismissing that explanation.

"Was it for money? What reward had you negotiated?"

"There was a reward, of sufficient size to demonstrate our commitment and gratitude. But it was not for money."

"Then what was the reason?"

"He lost faith in your cause."

I shook my head. We were silent as we regarded each other through the evening twilight.

"I know Benedict Arnold," I said.

"Better than I do, I am certain," André replied.

"Did he betray *you*?"

"In what sense?"

"I suspect he is in the city, drinking wine with your generals. But you are a prisoner, and I regret very much to tell you that our carpenters are looking for timbers to build a gallows."

I saw no reaction in him, and could not tell if his answer was defiant or the recognition of a soldier's complicated duty.

"I know nothing of betrayal," he said.

I had come hoping to persuade, to prod him to resent Arnold's disregard for his safe return to the British in New York. But my jaw tightened with an ire that had bedeviled me for several days, and my thoughts were turning elsewhere.

"Then you do not see it as I do," I said, ending the interview and bidding him a good evening.

Leaving the prisoner and walking to my quarters, I noticed that the soldiers I passed looked at me inquisitively, knowing from where I came, as if my countenance might reveal a clue to how Benedict Arnold—a brother-in-arms, a warrior of such high esteem—could betray us. And I suspected that, like me, they looked closely at one another, and inward at themselves—*especially* at themselves—to discern whether the pestilence of betrayal had infected their nearest neighbor, or, worse still, if it had infected their own ideas and volitions.

To ask such questions—to know the nature of loyalty, and why it is abandoned—was not new to me. Years ago, before I knew anything of the nature of man, I came face-to-face with betrayal. The scene haunts my first memory, which time has made the taproot of my imagination. In it, I am a child with a stick, breaking the crusted ice in the wheel ruts on an empty road. The crystalline pieces reflect the sunrays, and the brittleness of the ice delights me as I follow the wheel ruts, hitting them again and again with my stick, until I am past the crop field and alongside the first big trees of the surrounding forest. As I sense that I have gone too far, I come upon a solitary man standing on the back of a wagon. What little he says puzzles me; he does not want me there, and he tells me to leave. I walk quickly, but around a bend I hesitate and hide behind a tree. I want to go back to him, and I do, walking slowly, head bowed and eyes cast to the ground. When I raise my eyes I see the man jump from the wagon, but he is caught suddenly by a rope around his neck. His body turns toward me, shaking, quivering, and I wait for him to touch the ground. When he does not, when his feet claw at the void below them, I feel the presence of the Devil, who has put every fear known to man in that empty space between the searching feet and the icy ground. Among them, in that emptiness, is betrayal.

3

Every man dies, and rarely is there mercy in it; but the gallows—if it came to that—would be a cruel fate for André. I labored not to think of him swinging from a rope, like the rogues and murderers I have witnessed.

As a young man, taunted by memory and curious to understand my dreams, I rode for half a day to see the hangman take a common criminal named Isaac Frasier. He had killed no one, but was sentenced to death as an incorrigible, and every soul in the crowd seemed to know of his crimes and past punishments. Convicted after a string of burglaries, he'd been given twenty-five lashes. Upon his right hand a "T" was branded with a hot iron, marking him a thief, and his earlobes were cut off, to match his physique to the deformity of his character. Undeterred, he continued his thievery until caught and convicted a second time. Again the whip was laid on him, his other palm was branded, and he suffered the whole of both ears cut off. Still he did not reform, and committed more desperate thievery. He was caught again after stealing a horse.

I witnessed him standing on the scaffold, a man without ears, as a minister addressed him:

"You were born with a soul as full of enmity against God as a toad is full of poison. You have lived now, how many years?"

"Twenty-eight," Frasier said, as I strained to hear.

"And all these twenty-eight years you have been sinning against the Holy God. Ever since you knew how to do anything, you have been guilty of innumerable sins; you deserve the dreadful wrath and curse of the infinite God."

"I am sorry for my sins," Frasier said.

So it went for several minutes, holding the crowd's fixed attention. The minister was then replaced by the hangman, whose face was blackened with soot to hide his identity. When the hemp collar was lowered, the hangman studied Frasier's earless head several times, as would a careful laborer examining the broken handles of a heavy cider jug. He stepped away, and when Frasier fell, the noose held firm.

A man in his dreams can feel the rope on his neck, but I do not suppose he is ever prepared in full measure for his own execution—even a man such as Frasier, for whom it was the culmination of diverse crimes and many punishments. Certainly, the condemned man Paul Moses never gave thought to the gallows, until he sat in a damp stone cell, mostly dark, listening through a small window to the last earthly sounds he expected to hear: child's play, birdsongs, passing wagons, the conversations of commerce, and, shortly after his final sunrise, the work of carpenters nailing planks to form a simple coffin. Moses died for the crime of murder. At a tavern he drank to excess, perceiving insult in all that was spoken and hurling foul curses at everyone present. The proprietor and his burly son wrestled Moses to the door and pushed him hard into the road, leaving him there prostrate. When he regained his drunken senses, and balance enough to stand up, Moses took revenge by striking with a heavy flatiron the next person to leave the tavern. A man named Cook was the luckless patron, who died within hours of a shattered skull.

When he was brought into the sunlight on the morning of his execution, it was clear that Moses had been crying in despair. I was close enough to see his eyes, wet and raw, and sunken in gray caverns that revealed his sleepless nights. His weeping resumed as he was paraded from the jailhouse and saw hundreds of people who stood in wait. At the top of the steps he abruptly turned his head and began sobbing, which after a minute mostly abated when he was directed to face us.

"I pray God that I may be a warning to you all," he said, his speech clear but quivering. A merciful jailer ran a cloth across his face, which dripped with tears and snivel, after which he grew more composed.

"Mind and have care of that sin of drunkenness," he declared, "for that sin leads to all manner of sins and wickedness."

A woman somewhere shouted a condemnation of alcoholic drink, which caused Moses to look at her. Then he resumed:

"When a man is in drink he is ready to commit all manner of sin, until he fills up his cup with the wrath of God, as I have done by committing the sin of murder. As I am a dying man who will appear before the Lord within a few minutes, I beg that you may take notice of what I say to you. Have a care of drunkenness, and ill company . . ."

And so forth, he admonished his audience, until he uttered his last words: *Lord receive my Spirit, I come unto Thee, O Lord, I come unto Thee.* Sadly, for pity had softened the crowd's taste for vengeance, the hangman affixed a length of rope too short for Moses's lean body, and gravity did not snap his neck. His red eyes bulged and he fought for breath, writhing at the end of the rope for an overlong time before dying. A gruff old farmer shouted that the hangman was a failure who couldn't build a crooked shithouse, after which several others joined in yelling vulgar epithets at the hangman, while the corpse was cut down and carted away.

These recollections played in my mind as on a stage. I could not envision André, a dutiful man of noble character, standing on the gallows like a rogue or murderer, with a noose around his neck. He was our enemy in this war, but it filled me with regret that he had gambled with his life and agreed, if only for a day or two, to do the work of a spy, and would face the grim consequence of that decision.

4

A sad resignation was evident in André when I met with him again, on the day before the court of inquiry. A tribunal of six major generals and eight brigadier generals, assembled by General Washington, would hear André's testimony and recommend his fate. André's great hope, as he saw it, was for an exchange of prisoners, that he would be returned to New York for the release of American soldiers held by the British in Charleston. But I knew there was only one man—Arnold—for whom General Washington would give up André, and I hoped that the unyielding protocols of the British army would not be an obstacle to this exchange. These were the only two possibilities that offered any hope to André: Arnold would be surrendered to us, or André would convince the tribunal that he was not a spy. Otherwise, his execution was assured.

"From the moment I was first detained," André said to me, "I have sought to protect only one thing, and that is my honor as an officer and a gentleman."

"But there is no honor in being a spy."

"I have never been a spy, sir."

"But let me review, as I understand it," I said. "Within days after your secret meeting with General Arnold, across the river from West Point, you were to attack our fort, with all its defenses rendered helpless by order of our treasonous general. You had left that secret meeting and were returning to the British in New York, to report to General Clinton and launch the raid, when you were stopped and searched by our militiamen. You were out of uniform, in ordinary clothing, and you had six papers hidden in your boot. They detailed the numbers and locations of troops, the condition of the fortifications, our plans for defense. Do you acknowledge these facts?"

"Yes."

"And the plans were hidden in your boot."

"I grant you," he said, "I did not think anyone would look for them there."

"How did you get the papers?"

"They were given to me by General Arnold, who also suggested that I hide them in my boot."

"You also had a military pass."

"Yes, from General Arnold."

"And it said, *Permit Mr. John Anderson to pass the guards to the White Plains or below it as he chooses.*"

"Yes, that's what it said."

"Your name is not John Anderson."

"No, it is not," André replied, still cordial. "I never intended to disguise my identity. It was written by your general."

"You are mistaken," I said. "He is your general now."

The pass could have saved André, but he identified himself as a British officer to the men who stopped him, for they were close to British lines, and one was wearing the coat of a Hessian uniform. But these men were Americans, and eager for some bounty. When André produced the pass, it was too late. They were suspicious, and they searched him. Finding nothing, they were ready to set him free, until one suggested they search his boots.

In the Dutch church, the court of inquiry heard André's testimony, and at day's end made their recommendation to the commander in chief. The prisoner ought to be considered a spy from the enemy, they said, and consistent with the law and usages of nations, he ought to suffer death. Washington approved the finding and sentenced André to be hanged as a spy two days later, on the first of October.

Yet at the same time, overtures were being made to save André from this vicious fate. General Washington wrote to General Sir Henry Clinton in New York, with an account of the court proceedings and a letter from André. Clinton responded, requesting a conference of representatives to meet at Dobbs Ferry, midway between their camps on the eastern bank of the Hudson. Washington took this as a reason to hope that Arnold would be handed over in exchange for André, quietly and out of the public view. Such a course would preserve a semblance of British honor, discreetly surrendering the traitor while saving the life of the British major. André's execution was postponed for a day to allow for this resolution. I questioned André for the last time as he awaited word of his fate, but our interview ended with questions he asked of me.

"I understand," he said, "that you held General Arnold in high esteem."

"I did, when I knew him. But that is true no longer."

"So much has changed, has it not?" He turned to look out the window. "I have written to General Washington, asking him to adapt the mode of my death to the feelings of a man of honor."

"There is still hope," I said.

"I foresee my fate," he answered. "I do not pretend to play the hero, or to be indifferent to life, but I am reconciled to whatever may happen. Misfortune, not guilt, has brought it upon me."

"I admire your courage," I said.

André replied without hesitation. "You know the ancient poet, I'm sure, who said it is sweet and proper to die for one's country."

"I do," I responded.

"If the number of my days should fall short, as I suspect they will, they may live on in memory if I make these, my last days, exemplary of honor."

The slightest convulsion gripped his throat and he took a sudden quick breath. For a moment he paused, then continued:

"So I hold on to my honor with every bit of my strength."

We were quiet, and I heard a distant drummer signaling roll call and evening orders.

"It is my wish," I told him, "and the wish of many, that there will be a suitable resolution."

Soon it was dark, and during the night Washington's envoy returned. The British would not exchange Arnold, for they were bound by their agreement with the turncoat general.

André would die at noon.

5

The commerce on the morning of October second was transacted with haste. Soon many more people than lived in town were standing along the half-mile of road between André's prison and the hanging ground. I took a place on the hilltop near the tall wooden scaffold. A baggage wagon which held a casket painted black was centered beneath it. Soon André would stand on the casket with the noose around his neck, helpless in his last moments until the wagon was pulled from under him. A man in working clothes straddled the top beam, setting the noose and adjusting its height at the direction of an officer and two infantrymen, one of whom climbed atop the wagon, stood on the casket and held the noose beside his head, receiving the officer's nod of approval. Across from me a group of ladies somberly observed the preparations when a boy, chasing two brown hens, ran in front of them. The boy grabbed at one hen, but his grasp was tentative, and the hen escaped. He is too gentle, I thought.

The sporadic October wind brought faint notes of the "Dead March," played on fife and drum, and I knew that, far down the hill, the parade had begun. I turned my eyes to look for the boy chasing the hens, but he had disappeared behind the crowd. A memory came vividly to mind, that in my childhood I had been like the boy, chasing hens, a dozen or so, both brown and white. I went out one morning to get the eggs but found the ground strewn with feathers, awash in a bath of bright red blood. All the hens were gone or torn to pieces, victims of weasels or a fox—except one, which was unharmed. I took good care of this hen. It ate the things I offered from my hand: bugs, seeds, grass, and corn. By autumn it seemed to play a game with me, in which I would approach the hen and just short of my grasp it would dodge away. After this game of chase I would give it a few kernels of corn. One winter day I sought after my hen, clutching some corn and eager to play, but it was gone. I found a bucket of hot water, still steaming, and inside by the hearth was my mother, pulling the last small feathers from the hen's meaty carcass. She did not look up at me. "I'm sorry," she said. "We have to eat."

Major Tallmadge was walking toward the gallows, but saw me and stopped. The music of the march was still distant and faint.

"Have you seen the marquis?" Tallmadge asked. I pointed across the road to Lafayette, whose back was turned to us while he spoke with other officers. The Frenchman had sat on the tribunal that judged André a spy. "He is pained over this," Tallmadge said. "He told me that he truly suffered in condemning him."

"I can only believe there was no choice," I said. "Have you seen André?"

"I have. Either he is uncommonly brave, or his dignity has overcome his fear."

Tallmadge joined Lafayette and the officers across the road. The parade turned and climbed the hill and I heard the dire music clearly now. André walked in front of a cavalcade of Continental troops, escorted on either side by two lieutenants. He was faultlessly composed in his polished black shoes and white breeches, and his scarlet coat, trimmed in blue and gold. Townspeople and their country neighbors, two or three deep on either side of the road, fixed their eyes upon him, and his own eyes moved from left to right, looking at the crowd. When he saw Tallmadge, André bowed deeply, sweeping his hat with grace, and the two exchanged respectful words. He politely bowed to Hamilton, who responded in kind, and again when he saw Lafayette, who also returned the courtesy.

André noticed me beside a formation of infantrymen, and we acknowledged each other with generous nods. His placidity, and the cordiality he extended toward onlookers, was an act of bravery like few I have seen. But when his eyes drew upon the gallows he stopped, and I saw fear threaten to break him. He had written eloquently to General Washington, requesting a firing squad as the rightful means of execution for a military gentleman. But there was the scaffold and the noose, befitting a spy and nothing more.

"I am reconciled to my death," André said to his escorts, resuming his march, "but I detest the mode."

André ignored the step placed for him at the tailboard of the wagon and lifted himself up. He stood on top of the casket and gazed out upon the soldiers at attention and the crowd of onlookers. The sunlight illuminated the red, blue, and gold of his uniform. He surveyed farther and deeper into the concourse, and I realized he was searching for General Washington, who was not there.

André let his eyes linger on the far distance.

"It will be but a momentary pang," he said.

He put his hat behind him on the casket and from his coat pulled a white silk handkerchief, which he folded and placed across his eyes, tying it behind his powdered hair. When he sensed the hangman placing the noose, André seized it, and lowered it over his own head, moving the knot alongside his right ear and drawing it tight. He pulled another handkerchief from his pocket and gave it to the hangman, who twirled it into a cord and tied André's hands. The hangman stepped off the wagon and took the reins of the horse, waiting for the provost marshal to extend his sword, then lower it, pointing its tip to the ground.

I glanced downward and noticed a crease in the soft earth of the roadside, made by the wagon on which André stood. My first memory returned to me, yet again. Long ago, on that day when I followed the wheel ruts into the big trees, I fled from the Devil, running the desperate race as only children can. In front of the wooden house was my mother, who held an infant child but knelt down for me, extending a hand and pulling me into her embrace. She calmed my cries and urged me to sit down on her chair and hold the infant firmly in my lap and close to me. Then my mother made haste, away from the house and down the road toward the trees.

The baby, who was my sister, was fretful at first, but I leaned in close so she could see my face, which she had seen hovering over her many times as she lay in the cradle. Her eyes widened and looked into mine. That is how I remember her. From the woods I heard a cry that could have been the bark and wail of a coyote but I knew instead who it was, and the baby heard it, and we sat there, very still, for that was all we could do.

On the hill in Tappan there was silence, and the sword was lowered. The hangman pulled on the reins. The horse pushed against the earth and the wheels turned. I heard the leather soles of shoes dragging against wood, then the stir of air, and the snap of André's neck.

6

"You are wrong," Major Tallmadge said. "There is honor in the service of a spy. It depends, however, on the motive."

I was not inclined to debate the matter, for our nerves were still unsettled.

Tallmadge, though, persisted. It was said among certain officers that he recruited spies and had a network of contacts behind enemy lines. "A scheme for deceiving the enemy in war is regarded as honorable, but it is seldom exercised. It is the motive that gives true character to the deed."

We walked toward the DeWint house. The sun was low and bright in the sky, emblazing the blue and scarlet uniforms of Washington's guard.

"When the motive is purely a mercenary one, the deed is dishonorable. But when it is the desire to serve one's country, unselfishly, the act is certainly honorable."

"That may be so," I said, "but success is met with silence, and failure with an inglorious death. There is little to recommend it."

The guards acknowledged Tallmadge and a sergeant admitted us into a small wooden addition on the side of the brick house. We entered through an outside doorway, through which the evening sun cast vivid amber light into the room until the sergeant closed the door. Against the left wall a fireplace held a cluster of embers, and I noticed to my right that the interior door to the rest of the house was tightly shut. Sitting alone in a wooden chair was General Nathanael Greene, his arms crossed over his chest and his legs stretched out in front of him. The general had presided over the court of inquiry that had recommended death for André, and he had ridden by night to Dobbs Ferry as Washington's high-level envoy, in a futile effort to negotiate a secret exchange of André for Arnold.

Tallmadge introduced me, and the general soon addressed the matter at hand, warning me of the necessary discretion demanded by our conversation.

"I could not persuade the British to give us Arnold. But I am as certain as day turns to night that Arnold will hang for his crime against us."

He paused.

"At General Washington's request, I am assembling a team of two men, who will go behind British lines into New York. Their mission is to capture Arnold, secretly, and deliver him to us, so that he may receive our justice."

He looked at Tallmadge, then back to me, and continued.

"I understand you know Arnold well, in a way that few of us do, and that he would have reason to trust you."

I tried to conceal my discomfort.

"Perhaps, sir."

"I intend to send you on that mission."

Which meant I was to become a spy. I hastened to formulate my reservations, wondering if I could voice an objection. As I tried to gather my thoughts, the heavy click of a metal latch and a firm step on the plank floor drew our attention to the doorframe, where a tall silhouette stood in the glow of the evening sun.

"It is a damned horrible treason," the figure said. I lifted my hand to block the glare, and then I saw clearly the buff and dark blue of his uniform, and the gold epaulettes on his shoulders.

With little formality, General Washington bade me sit down.

"Tell us what you know about Benedict Arnold."

PART 1

Saratoga and Albany

September 1777–January 1778

I write in a very great hurry . . . so will only wish that the acquisition of Boston and Quebec may make the opening of the year '76 an era of Glory to the arms of America, and may hand down the name of Washington and Arnold to the latest posterity, with the laurel on their brow.

MERCY OTIS WARREN to ABIGAIL ADAMS,

February 7, 1776

1

My mother taught me to how to shoot. We had one gun in our house, a musket with a club butt that had three initials and a number carved into it. "This is a gun for a man," she said, "and you are nearly a man now." She showed me how to hold the gun and balance it, stepping back with my right foot and putting the left forward, raising the butt high on my right shoulder and looking along the barrel at a stump in the field. My mother was a lean woman, and when she aimed the gun it looked like an extension of her, taut and strong, browned by the sun. She watched me carefully as I rested the gun at an angle on the ground, poured powder down the barrel, and rammed the wadding and ball to the breech. She showed me how to prime the gun, to half-cock and push the hammer, and place enough powder in the pan to catch a spark.

When she shot the gun her fingers gripped the barrel like a vise and she leaned forward, aggressively, taming the fire that blasted from the muzzle while hardly flinching, spraying splinters from the stump by force of gunpowder and determination. When I pulled the trigger the barrel jumped and knocked my arm, bruising the bone in my shoulder, and the power and blast of flame impressed upon me that this was not a thing of innocence. Black haze and the dry acrid smell of sulfur and wood smoke lingered in the air.

When we finished shooting I hacked at the stump with an axe and we pried out the clusters of lead, to melt and remake into new shot.

"Am I good enough to hunt?" I asked.

"Yes," she said. "Soon."

When that day came we awoke early before the sun rose and walked beyond the field to the woods, to a place where there were many white-tailed deer, where tracks pocked the soil and you would sometimes hear the deer brush against leaves or snap a twig before you saw them. There were short hills with rocky banks and clusters of boulders big enough to form small caves, and there were many long branches of laurel trees, and these were good places to sit quietly and wait for deer to come close.

I carried the gun, which was loaded, and my mother carried the axe and a tin water bottle on a cord across her shoulder. We were downwind of the deer run and our steps were quiet; my mother pointed to a cove of lush laurel branches that would give us cover. As she walked toward them a black mass moved from a bank of stones, slowly and close by, not yet aware of our presence. I lifted the gun and pulled back the cock.

"Mother," I said.

As I stared down the long barrel at my target, I knew she had turned and was looking at the bear.

"*Yes.*"

The gun kicked back as a blast of fire and smoke shot from the muzzle. For a moment I could not see the bear, but I saw my mother holding the axe with both hands, ready to strike if it lunged at us. Then the bear fell on its front legs, its head against the ground. Its thick hind legs tried to push forward, and it rubbed its snout against the dirt while exhaling a wet guttural groan between gasps for breath.

It was the first animal I killed. We stood there, ready with the axe, and then sat down on some rocks. My stomach was unsettled, and I coughed and emptied it behind a tree. My mother gave me water. We watched the bear for a long time; even after it was dead its belly shuddered. Then we dragged it to the field and got a horse and wagon, and brought it home.

Years later, on the nineteenth day of September in '77, at the north edge of an open field called Freeman's farm, I stood partially hidden by a large maple tree adorned with orange and yellow leaves, aiming my musket at a man who crouched behind a tree stump and a pile of stones, whose white breeches were muddied at the knees but whose red coat seemed bright and unblemished. He had fired a shot at a rifleman to my left, before he saw me, and when his eyes met mine he jumped to his feet and leveled his bayonet. I did not hesitate; and through the fire of the muzzle blast I saw him hit, bending in half at the waist for a fleeting instant, his hands flailing outward, as if, in his final moment, he was presenting himself to the king. At the same time a rapid spatter of shots cracked ahead and to my right, where a band of British skirmishers were met by Major Dearborn's light infantry amid the tall oak and white pine at the edge of the woods.

On my left one of Colonel Morgan's riflemen crawled toward me, his brown coat and knee-high green leggings bloodied. Another ran over and stooped beside him. "Pull him back to the log house," I hollered. The riflemen had no bayonets, but their long rifles were far-reaching and accurate. They hid behind the rail fence and among the trees taking careful aim, looking foremost for the shimmer of a silver or brass regimental gorget hanging on a soldier's chest, signifying his officer's rank. Their shots from the fence line cracked loudly, and behind us I heard drum rolls, calling more of our troops to meet the enemy.

Quickly I reloaded and moved forward, passing the British soldier on the ground, certain he was dead and not wanting to see what I had done. At the edge of the clearing British skirmishers emerged from the trees across the field, which was riddled with stumps and fallen timber. They had come up from the river road by climbing the great ravine, lightly equipped but thwarted by the mud on the steep incline and the streams they had crossed. They assembled into their familiar order and moved, seeming ill at ease, toward two farm buildings in front of them. On a signal I did not hear, Morgan's riflemen opened heavy fire and a torrent of shots rattled the air. The skirmishers quickly returned fire but many of them fell in the field. The riflemen saw this and yelled, rising up from their positions to a full-out charge as the British hesitated and then backed away, some turning and running.

The roll of drums grew louder, and Captain Van Swearingen, a Pennsylvanian, drew up on the left, waving his sword in the air and directing the fire as more than two hundred riflemen and light infantry scrambled through the trees to the edge of Freeman's clearing.

I joined with my company from the Third New Hampshire. We quickly formed at the tree line and fired hurried volleys to cover the advance of the riflemen, who were rushing in waves into the field and following the retreat of the British skirmishers. Amid the gunshots there was desperate yelling from some of the fallen redcoats who tried to crawl from the clearing, and much hallooing from the riflemen, all of which was interrupted by the thunderous cough of a British fieldpiece that spit grapeshot into the riflemen's left flank. Morgan's men ran for cover among the stumps and timber and looked for the cannon, which revealed its location with a second blast that hit a cluster of men, felling them like crashing ninepins. Still, Morgan's men fired at the redcoats from positions low and behind cover, but with the third cannon shot came a wave of red uniforms that saturated the woods across the field, revealing Johnny Burgoyne's massed British line.

Across the clearing the whole tree line exploded at once and the air filled with shot. Many of Morgan's men spun and fell, dropping their rifles and clutching their bellies and limbs. Both sides unleashed the fury of their arms, and the rhythm of volleys was lost in the loud and fiery crackle of incessant gunfire. Men in the field, both redcoats and riflemen, shouted for help or screamed in pain, while some tried pulling their bleeding comrades through the grass. From a cluster of trees to my left came a loud turkey call, an excited yelp and cackle that I knew was Colonel Morgan's signal to his riflemen, directing them to fall back.

My light troops continued to fire, giving cover to the scrambling riflemen. British skirmishers also ran to their lines, but on their left a spasm of musket fire commenced, meant for the riflemen but wounding a number of redcoats. Those still standing kept running, but they were unsure where to go. A cannon roared a signal shot, and most of the shooting from the British line stopped. The skirmish had been a full-scale battle for half an hour or longer, but now the cacophony of gunfire gave way to the scuttle of armies regrouping and the moans and cries from the grassy field.

I looked for Captain Van Swearingen. In the clearing ahead of our far left flank he appeared to be wounded, and was being carried to the British line by a cluster of Indians. The several men with him were also taken as prisoners. We reloaded our muskets and exchanged tense shouting among us, but there was nothing we could do. The midday sun parched the field, and we heard the cries of the wounded begging for water and the pleas of the dying to end their suffering. At opposite sides of the clearing both armies hauled their injured soldiers to safety, but those in the middle were out of reach and we left them there. A few men from Putnam's Regiment broke ranks and went into the field, taking what they could from the dead. Walking back toward a log hut behind us, I passed a horse lying on the ground with its front legs broken. Its belly twitched, but I knew there was no life in it.

2

All around the log hut the wounded were lying on the ground. Some were being bandaged and some were loaded into wagons and taken behind the lines to the field hospital. Coming up the road were many hundreds of men: the rest of the New Hampshire regiments, the Second and Fourth New York, two units of Connecticut militiamen, and others behind them. We knew the fight was not over, and there was much clamoring to prepare for what was coming.

A rifleman near me pointed to the road that led east toward the river, and called out, "General Arnold!" Several men quickly stood up from where they rested and looked down the line, shielding their eyes from the bright sunlight with their raised hands, as if saluting. On his chestnut stallion, Major General Benedict Arnold had galloped back from the picket guard of Jackson's Regiment, where he had gone to summon volunteers to join the battle. Now he cantered alongside some three hundred of them while pointing his sword at the British lines and instructing the soldiers on their objectives.

"They are bringing up artillery," he called out to them. "That will be our first target. We will take them from the enemy's hands and make them our own."

His voice was clear and authoritative, and his own excitement palpable.

"This is our battle!" he hollered, "And today we will conquer!"

A chorus of cheers went up from the men. Arnold spurred his horse and rode ahead to where Colonel Morgan was huddled with Colonel Scammel. He spoke briefly with them from his horse, then galloped farther up the line.

A munitions wagon brought musket cartridges, and we hurried to resupply. Goodwin, a private from my company, was hastily surveying the wounded. He looked up and caught my eye.

"Captain Wheatley," he said, making his way toward me. "Have you seen Private Sullivan?"

"I have not," I answered, gazing toward the wounded.

"He's my cousin, my aunt's only son. I'm to look after him."

"When did you see him last?" I asked.

Goodwin was young, and his emotions twisted his face. "Could he be still in the field?"

"Listen to me," I told him. "The best thing you can do right now is prepare for another fight. Sullivan will take care of himself. Get ready."

"Yes, sir," he said, and he walked back toward a wagon that carried the dead.

Men clustered around barrels of water, filling tin bottles and wooden canteens. The air was warm and the wounded had been placed in the shade, and as they were moved back behind the lines, the soldiers who were readying themselves for the next battle took those spots in the shadows. In the two hours since the skirmish at

Freeman's farm our numbers had increased by more than a thousand men, and with this came a notion of strength. We were eager to know if we would attack, or await an attack from the British.

The answer came quickly enough. Across Freeman's clearing, fieldpieces along the British line exploded with a deafening roar. Every man at once took his position. Ahead of us the blasts of artillery shook the earth and clouded the air. Just as we were set to march out from the cover of the trees and return to the field, General Arnold returned, galloping in front of the lines, waving his sword and pointing it toward our foe.

"Providence will give us this day," he shouted, "for our cause is just!"

The men cheered loudly, and the roar of "Huzzah!" nearly matched the noise of the cannons.

With a preacher's conviction, Arnold's voice rose over the soldiers.

"Today we shatter our chains on the anvil of Liberty!"

A volley of musket fire exploded from across the field, but Arnold paid it no heed.

"For this land is ours, men, and no king shall have it!"

Hundreds of troops burst into a cheering frenzy. As his horse pranced anxiously, Arnold pulled the reins and saluted his army, then spurred the stallion and galloped down the line.

Drums rolled and Colonel Scammel gave his command, which ricocheted through the ranks in shouts among captains and sergeants:

"To the front! March!"

The clearing was not large and soon the armies were close enough for the unremitting fire of muskets to reap a crop of men. Officers shouted commands and the men rapidly loaded, fired, and reloaded.

"Front rank! Make ready!"

"Take aim! Fire!"

"Rear rank! Make ready!"

"Take aim! Fire!"

As men in the clearing on both sides fell and officers were cut down, the order of the volleys gave way to an unremitting blanket of fire. The fleeting high-pitched whistle made by every British musket ball delivered a ration of fear, but also rage, and the resolve to strike down the enemy. Leading his soldiers in the field, Lieutenant Colonel Colburn was hit square in the chest below the throat. His men picked him up and ran back to the line, but the blood and the limpness of his body left little hope.

Our advance took us into the clearing where men from the skirmish had died in the sweltering heat of the midday sun, and I was forced to kneel on the field near several who had suffered. Their waistcoats were open, as were their shirts, which were dark red and brown with dried blood, and some had their breeches pulled open. I had seen this in battle, and I knew their last moments had been a desperate search for the spot of their wound. A ball to the leg or the belly will equally knock a man down, but a tourniquet can stanch the bleeding of a limb, and a bone can shatter but need not kill; the surgeons can amputate an arm or leg, and you will be no good to farm or hunt, yet perhaps there will be something for you to do. But a ball in the bowel, or the gut, or the chest: this will be the last thing you know.

A unit from Burgoyne's line lowered bayonets and charged into an outcrop of woods. Some of the Connecticut militiamen ran and opened fire, hitting the redcoats on the right flank before their blades reached the infantrymen in the trees. I aimed my shots at the artillery crews that fired on us from the center of the British line, and at the grenadiers who were coming from the ravine. Far to the left several British cannons were overtaken when Morgan's riflemen expertly targeted the gun captains, but the horses around them were dead on the ground, and our men could not seize the artillery without horses. In the melee I saw General Arnold on the right, charging on his horse, directing the movements of men. I thought he was mad to be in the field, but the men eagerly followed his leadership, and they advanced in waves, in quickstep, gaining on the enemy's right flank.

Beside me, Harris, a sergeant, was shot high in the chest, near his shoulder, which knocked him flat. He rose on one knee and tried to stand, but could not. I stuffed a folded cloth under his waistcoat to stanch the bleeding, which was profuse. He seethed and yelled epithets, damning the enemy, and a private helped me drag him through the grass, running as best we could back to the woods. Harris told me to take his cartridges, and two young drummer boys stood beside him, waiting for others to bring him farther back behind the lines.

Quickly I drank water and looked for a place to reenter the clearing. The tempest of musket fire was as loud as I had ever heard it, and the explosive coughs of artillery changed in tone, for now they fired grapeshot and canister, which buzzed through the air like deadly swarms of unseen locusts. A skittish horse had panicked and pulled a wagon into the field; a cannonball had cut the animal nearly in half and broken the wagon. I ran in that direction, heavy with the extra cartridges I had taken from Harris. Near the wagon a rabbit was running in zigzags with no destination, out of his mind.

Above the rabbit's aimless spinning a flash from a British three-pounder registered in my sight, and everything about the battle suddenly changed. The hellish fire became a dull curtain of chaos, and the horizon slowly descended, until there was only the sky above me. I wondered if I would stay in the air or fall, and then I knew I would fall, and told myself I was falling. My head slammed against the earth, and the sky that had surrounded me transformed into something like ocean water, opaque and rippling. I fought to know who I was. The dull sounds around me blended with a drummer's march, beating directly above my head, which I slowly half-realized was the pounding pulse of my own heart.

I touched my face, and knew the wetness on it was blood. I pulled up my waistcoat and felt a warm pool across my gut, and when I lifted my head I saw my white breeches red with blood.

I heard my own voice, which told me I was going to die here. I wondered, almost pleasantly, if I would see my mother.

"Captain!" someone yelled. Another voice, one I recognized, shouted: "Wheatley! Wheatley! Look at me!"

I thought: I don't want my mother to see me like this.

Then everything went black.

3

A fire smoldered in the hearth, and candles lit the faces of six women in our house; one of them was very old. They had come for my sister. She was still in her first year and had been coughing and crying for two days, but now was quiet. The old woman and another were in the bedroom, and by the candlelight I saw them folding white cloth. The other women sat close beside my mother, whose eyes were closed. One read from a book, and I heard her speak of children, and say, "Forbid them not, to come unto me: for of such is the kingdom of heaven." The old woman came into the room carrying my sister, who was wrapped in the white cloth, and handed her to my mother. The women stayed through the night, and in the morning others came, and I rode in a wagon to the church, and then to the burial ground.

Some time later I found a field mouse near the well. It did not move. From a pile of rocks I took a sharp stone to the edge of the field, and used it to chip at the soil and dig a hole. Mother saw me and asked why I was digging. She fetched the mouse and we put it in the hole and covered it, and I asked her if it was going to the kingdom of heaven. That night I awoke from my sleep and my mother was running her hand across my face and hair. "You must never leave me," she whispered. "You must never leave me."

The soldier next to me in the wagon moaned, and another cried and spoke in broken sentences that only he understood. Overnight, in the hospital tent, my head had been wrapped in linen; now it throbbed as the wagon rolled, and even small bumps worsened the seething pain. My hand touched my gut, which was covered with lint and bandaged with cloth, and the bandages were damp.

The wagon stopped at the bank of the Hudson River. There were dozens of bateaux and several covered sailing barges to take the wounded downriver to the hospital in Albany. The waterway spared us the bumps and jolts of the wagon, although a murmur of anguished moans still testified to the suffering. I was faintly conscious on the river, and while the greatest pain was in my head, I worried most about the belly wound. I asked a soldier attending us if a shot had penetrated my gut.

"I am surprised you can speak," he said. "Lie still—you were shot in the head, and the ball seems to be stuck in your skull."

When the boats docked in Albany there was much calling to and fro, to summon aid and give instructions on moving the wounded. I felt weak. My bandages were stiff and the skin on my belly stung as if cut by knives. My forehead burned; I was afraid to touch the linen wrapped around my head. Still, when two men came to carry me on a blanket stretched over two poles, I enlisted their aid to stand, and walked with them, my arms across their shoulders, onto the dock.

A man from the hospital made a quick examination of my bandages.

"What is your injury, Captain?" he asked.

My teeth were clenched, for the pain was great, but I managed to whisper a brief description: "I am told I have a musket ball in my head."

He looked again at my bandaged head, and then directed the two soldiers to take me to a wagon. I rested on straw, and tried to hold very still. The hospital was not far, but it was on a hill above the city, and we moved very slowly.

In such a place as the Albany hospital, no promises accompany the procedures that are done there: the setting of a broken bone, or the amputation of a destroyed limb; the suturing of lacerations with waxed thread and the bandaging of wounds with lint and linen; the removal of battlefield shot; the trepanning of an undepressed skull fracture. These can mend a body or preserve a life, if no further disturbance interferes and Providence will have it. But nothing is known to relieve suffering, and for this reason the hospital is foremost a place to suffer and to wait—to wait for the body to heal, or to wait for the insidious mortification of the broken body while the mind and spirit look on, helpless. Physical suffering is an equation, a combination of pain plus time. The hospital is an enclave of time, a place to wait, and to wrestle with the torment of hope.

Since I could walk and talk, and death did not seem imminent, I was taken to a bed in the surgical ward, given water, and left to rest. The straw in the mattress was flat and the bed was not tight, and I slept fitfully for a while. Soon, however, I was awakened by the sounds of the surgical procedures going on throughout the ward, which animated me with nervous tension. When a man's wound was probed and cleaned of dirt and shards of metal I could hear him breathe loudly and quickly through his teeth; and when the ligature was stitched into the flesh there was a high-pitched squeal as the needle, dipped in oil, passed through the wound. Elsewhere in the ward, soldiers were having bones set. A surgeon said "*Pull*," which elicited a cry of pain and the sound of a struggle between the surgeon and his assistants as they forced the broken bone to align. I added to the noise with my own low murmur, futilely hoping to obscure the sound of an amputation in the operating chamber beside the ward. Several assistants held the soldier, who had been in the wagon and barge with me. His leg was shattered in many places, and the bone protruded from the flesh. A leather strap between his teeth secured his bite and muffled his screams, but as the surgeon cut through the flesh and the ligaments, the poor man's wail resounded like that of a tethered horse caught in a stable fire. Amid this, the sound of the bone saw drew infinite pity, and the man mercifully lost consciousness as the surgeon drew out and tied the arteries and packed the stump with lint and flour.

I turned my attention to the shard of musket ball in my head. I had heard more than once about trepanning, the procedure to bore a hole into a skull to relieve pressure after a fracture. Surely, I calculated, a bullet in the skull would prompt such a measure. The surgeon, I feared, would cut my scalp and retract it to expose the skull, then press and turn a trephine into and through the bone, as he would a drill, until there was a hole exposing my brain. Briefly I took solace from the notion that the belly wound might kill me before the trepanning began.

The surgeries, but for my own, had passed, and the sounds in the ward were the low moans and quivering cries of men in agonized stupors, and of a man nearby snoring, and a sporadic hum from the hissing and buzzing of flies.

For a while I slept, then awoke to find two men standing at my bedside in the ward. Both wore bloodstained aprons. The white-haired man cut at the bandages on my stomach, while the younger man, who seemed tired but still attentive, looked at the bandages on my head.

"I am told that if I remove these, I will find some piece of a musket ball," the young man said.

He introduced himself as James Thacher, a regimental surgeon. He and his assistant removed the bandages, which by this time were in the early stages of putrefaction from the blood and heat, and the smell from my wounds nearly undid me. My belly was lacerated by splinters of wood, some fairly long, which had cut into me at an angle. I was quite torn apart, which accounted for the copious blood, but there was no puncture into the gut. The doctor and his assistant removed the splinters, needing the regular assistance of a scalpel, which set my teeth deep into a strip of leather. It took some time to cut and pull out the wooden slivers, after which the wound was washed and treated with tincture of myrrh, covered with lint, and re-bandaged. I deduced, from what I could recall of the battle, the likelihood that a cannon shot had smashed the wagon that I had run to, riddling my torso with wooden darts.

Dr. Thacher turned his attention to my head and summoned two other assistants. One held my skull firmly as the surgeon made an incision in my scalp, and the other separated the skin with a retractor. This went quickly, for Dr. Thacher found a flat piece of musket ball or canister shot that he withdrew with a long crooked needle. The discomfort of this procedure was counteracted by my relief that there was no fracture to the skull, and no need for trepanning. With this restoration of hope, I fell into a deep sleep.

The next day Dr. Thacher returned with his assistant to examine my wounds and re-bandage them.

"Word is getting around about the musket ball that stuck in your head," he said. "How did it happen?"

"I was running to a wagon that a panicked horse had pulled onto the battlefield. It was a good place from which to shoot."

"Here, keep this," he said, handing me a flat piece of lead. "It appears the musket ball hit something, perhaps the wagon, before it struck you in the head. Enough power in the ricochet to tear you up a bit, but not enough to break the skull."

"Evidence that Providence was looking out for me, I suppose."

"Providence provided you with a thick skull."

He applied more tincture of myrrh to the laceration on my forehead, and then his assistant re-bandaged it.

"The evidence is irrefutable that you were advancing toward the enemy."

"Well, yes," I agreed.

"There is a soldier in another ward, for whom the same can't be said."

"How so?"

"A musket ball hit him in the bottom of the foot. This has intrigued some of the soldiers, who chide him that he could only have been running *from* the enemy."

"The secret will be hidden in his shoe."

"Yes," Thacher said. "But you will have a scar, my friend, which will attest to your bravery. You are the talk of the wards this morning. Many of the men wish to meet you."

"To see if my head is real?" I asked.

Dr. Thacher dismissed his assistant and sat on a stool. Clearly he was tired. He asked me what I had done before the war. I told him about the year I spent at Yale College, and how I left my studies when my mother took ill. As I told him about my work as a schoolmaster I grew wistful for those days, which seemed long past. I started to recount my year of military service.

His assistant returned, saying Dr. Thacher was needed in another ward.

"We must watch the inflammation and hope against gangrene," he said to me. "Assuming you heal well, you should remain here a week or two before I send you back to your company."

"Has there been word of any fighting?" I asked.

"Nothing has yet taken place, but both armies remain in the field, and I doubt the battle is over."

"I am eager to get back."

"I am sure of it," he said.

He stood to leave. "Perhaps you could be of assistance to your fellow soldiers here."

"Yes, of course—in what capacity?"

"I am obliged to devote the whole of my time to the care of our patients," he said. "There are many here, and more will be coming. We have thirty surgeons, but that is hardly enough."

The soldier in the bed next to me had been delirious since his leg was removed. Now he noticed Thacher and called out, "Doctor—where is my leg?"

Quickly, Thacher finished his thought. "Many of the men would be pleased to talk with you. They need someone to write letters home for them. Some will heal, and need encouragement. Others will not, and need comfort. Let us see how you are tomorrow. Perhaps you could visit a few of the tough cases."

Later in the afternoon I rose from the bed. The lacerations were sore, and I was careful not to disrupt the sutures. I walked to the end of the ward, where my eyes made contact with those of a soldier propped up in his bed. By the sight of it a musket ball had gone through his cheeks, cutting through the teeth on each side, and the substance of his tongue. He motioned toward a stool beside his bed, and I sat down.

We looked at each other. He reached for my hand. I offered it to him and he shook it, as would a gentleman. I pointed above my eyes.

"It seems we were both shot in the head," I said.

With the slightest motion, he nodded.

4

The large General Hospital in Albany was built during the French war and stood on an eminence overlooking the city. It was two stories high with a wing projecting at either end, creating a piazza in front. A large cupola rose from the center of the roof. There were forty wards, and beds for five hundred. Many of the wards were filled with wounded from the battle at Freeman's farm. In the opposite wing, some of the wards contained soldiers who suffered from illness and disease rather than wounds. There were many cases of putrid fever and dysentery, which are especially malignant and baffle the skill of physicians.

The hospital was properly whitewashed inside, and in each ward there was a central corridor between the simple wood and rope bed-steads, lined up in a row on either side, feet toward the middle, heads against the wall. There were large stoves to heat the wards when the chill air returned, and the prevailing whiteness of the walls was re-lieved by some ornaments—stars, circles, and so forth—made of bent twigs and evergreens. Dr. Thacher provided me with a small field desk that I could set on top of my legs, or at the foot of a soldier's bed, if I balanced it smartly. Gently straightening myself to stand, I walked through the wards to see who was anxious to get a message to a wife or family, or who desired the simple comfort of conversa-tion. Many did, and some asked me to read the letters they carried, just to hear them in a voice not their own. I would often turn my attention to those I knew were the worst cases, or walked over to where I heard groans, knowing that comfort was needed there most. There were a few times when I avoided the most desperate cases, but this left me with a sense of shame.

In the second ward was a soldier from Massachusetts whose leg had been amputated. He had another bad wound: a musket ball had gone straight through him and perforated his bowel. When I sat next to him, he asked me to read a passage from the Bible.

"Which one?" I asked him.

"The Resurrection," he said.

I read to him about the last hours of Christ, and of the Crucifixion, and the empty tomb. It pleased him, although there were tears in his eyes. I took his hand in mine.

"I believe I am going to die," he said.

"You don't know that. You must have faith," I told him.

"Are you a religious man?" he asked me.

A patient walked in from the next ward, looking around, confused and frantic. He was naked, and covered his lower parts with his hands. His injury was to his head, and I thought he had been scalped, for I saw a terrible raw redness below the bandaging that was coming undone. Two surgeon's mates rushed in, took him by the arms, and led him back to his ward.

"I should be, I suppose."

"It is my best hope," he said.

He asked me to write a letter to his father and mother; he was a young man, almost still a boy. He spoke with great tenderness about them, and of his siblings, all of whom were younger than he. I held the letter beside him so he could put his own mark. He was very weak.

I resolved to see him again in the morning, but he died during the night.

Another soldier, named Henry Taggart, was eager for me to write a letter for him. He was a sergeant in Major Henry Dearborn's light infantry, with a wife and a son in New Hampshire. As he and his fellow soldiers made their first charge, a cannonball took off his arm. He lay on his back in the middle of the field well into the night, for there was no way for any fellow soldier to recover him without being shot down. He crawled some of the way back toward our line, but the bleeding was profuse, until, with his one remaining hand and his teeth, he tied a tourniquet on his stump. In the dark, coming in and out of consciousness, he emitted birdcalls that were signals to Dearborn's men, and two soldiers made their way, keeping low and quiet, and dragged him to the line. As Taggart instructed, I wrote of his exploits in battle. His son was nearly the age to become a soldier himself, and he wanted his boy to be proud of him.

"I found my arm," he told me, as I finished the letter. "I crawled ten feet toward our line, and there was my arm, right in front of my face. I looked at my fingers: it was as if I was holding my hand before my eyes."

He shook his head with amusement, but it unsettled him, too.

"I tried to bring it with me," he said. "For a little while, I thought I'd try to bring it with me."

He read the letter with satisfaction and put his mark on it, but asked me to add a sentence.

"Tell them this," he insisted: "This letter was written for me by a man who came to the hospital with a musket ball in the top of his forehead, that he got while running toward the enemy."

"And also this," he added: "We are a brave lot, my boy. We are a brave lot."

Some men wrote their own letters. I would put the field desk on their lap, if it was comfortable for them. There were conversations about many things, but the most common, besides family and home, was food. A soldier from the Fourth New York told me about the blackberries he picked in the fields every year, and said he would trade a year's ration of army porridge for a handful of blackberries. There were women and some boys who came to the hospital with cloth, flour, and bread, and other things for the soldiers, which they delivered to the attendants in the front foyer. I asked a kindly woman who walked with a limp, who was there every day with a basket of vegetables and herbs, if she could obtain some dried or preserved blackberries, which she brought for me in a jar with sugar syrup the very next morning. Dr. Thacher told me the New York soldier's leg was becoming putrid, and would be amputated later that day. The soldier had become feverish, and did not know what was in store for him, but when I gave him the blackberries he laughed and cried at once, and savored them.

In a ward in the center of the hospital I found Private Goodwin, from my own company, who had been searching for his cousin. A musket ball had torn through Goodwin's knee; his leg was amputated. He was also sick with dysentery, which caused him great discomfort and impeded his healing. He was bothered by the flies; sometimes he would blow a breath of air to remove them from his lips, or wave a weak hand, but more often he would let them settle, as many patients did, for it was futile to think one could drive them away. I obtained a piece of light cloth, which I designed as a mask for him, but by then he was drifting in and out of the sleep of death, and such a mask did not befit him, because it hid the life that I still saw in his eyes.

I went about the hospital asking if there was a patient named Sullivan, but there was not. I could not find out what happened to Goodwin's cousin, who had been missing since the first fighting at Freeman's farm.

"Maybe he went home," Goodwin whispered.

I asked if I could write a letter for him, but he told me that he had a small diary, and if he should die, I should send it to his family.

It took several days for him to die, and when he did I prepared to send the diary and wrote a letter of my own to accompany it. In his last entry he wrote: *The doctor will not say it, but I fear this day shall be my last.* On another blank leaf he penciled: *Dear brother Jacob. I am gone now. Pray for me.*

No one spoke of burials in the hospital, but I knew that some of the dead were interred in unmarked mass graves. It troubled me that Goodwin would not be buried in a churchyard, or in a plot near his home, to be tended by his family. I feared he would be forgotten, and cringed at the familiar ditty that played in my thoughts:

> Rattle his bones over the stones,
> He's only a pauper who nobody owns.

Dr. Thacher made a request on my behalf; an arrangement was made, and I accompanied Goodwin's body to a burial ground. There were three caskets in the wagon, and within a timber barn I saw a stack of new caskets, and four men sawing pine boards. We waited at the burial ground, for only two graves had been fully dug, and the grave-diggers hurried to finish the third. There was a row of plots where the soil was fresh, marked by barrel staves or broken boards stuck in the dirt. Soon four women appeared, coming up the hill from town. They pulled rakes from a wagon and combed the soil over the graves, and one of the women replaced a barrel stave with a board on which they had painted a soldier's name. In the wagon were other painted boards. When Goodwin was lowered into his grave, the women stood with me and bowed their heads.

I walked alone from the burial ground back to the hospital. Looking to the barn where the caskets were made, I witnessed two surgeon's mates moving toward it, generally out of public sight, except from my peculiar vantage. One held an amputated leg, and the other something smaller: part of an arm, or perhaps a foot. They set their cargo on a pile beneath a vibrantly colored maple tree, and I saw that the pile contained a hodgepodge of pallid limbs.

When I returned to the hospital, Dr. Thacher approached me. He seemed harried.

"Captain Wheatley," he said. "I've received word that another battle has occurred. I'm told that our army was the victor."

My inclination to cheer this development was tempered by what I knew was coming.

"We will soon have more wounded than we can hold," Thacher confirmed. "We are making room in some houses."

Turning his attention back to the wards, he asked me to sit with Private Rogers, a soldier from the Connecticut militia for whom I had earlier written a letter. Rogers had been getting along well until the night before last, when a sudden hemorrhage developed, which continued at intervals.

Before dispatching himself to other business, Dr. Thacher added: "One of the wounded is General Arnold. But I have no details of his condition."

I sat next to Rogers, who struggled painfully for breath, a glaze already upon his eyes. There was a water pail beside his bed, nearly full of blood-soaked strips of cloth. I knew he would die within an hour or two, and there was nothing that could be done.

I read to him from the Bible, and told him the news of the great victory.

5

That evening the stoves were lit, for the air had grown cool, and Taggart came looking for me, waving his one remaining hand.

"You have heard?" he asked.

"About the battle? Yes. A victory, I am told."

"Thank the Lord. Was it decisive? Will Burgoyne surrender?"

"I haven't heard. Dr. Thacher says that many wounded are coming downriver. We'll know more by tomorrow."

"Captain Wheatley, my friend! Imagine the sight of Burgoyne handing over his sword!"

Taggart's excitement was a welcome relief.

"We're well enough to leave here, are we not? We must find two horses and ride north, to Arnold's headquarters—the one-armed rifleman and the shot-in-the-head captain! He will greet us as heroes!

"Yes," I said laughing. "Yes . . . two horses for us." Again, though, the gravity of the war intervened. "But Arnold is gravely wounded."

"General Arnold?"

"Yes."

Taggart's excitement drained away.

"They are bringing him here," I said.

As he stood in front of me, motionless, Taggart's eyes darted about the ward, up and down the long corridor, settling for a few moments on some distance far beyond the hospital walls.

"This arm—the one that is missing," Taggart said, lifting the short stump. "It carried Arnold in Quebec when he was shot in his leg."

"You were with Arnold in Quebec?"

"I carried him; he bled on me," he answered.

The scenes running through Taggart's mind were surely disquieting, for the soldiers who embarked on the Canada expedition had endured great hardship, including disease, starvation, bitter cold, deprivation of supplies, military defeat, and imprisonment. I put my hand on Taggart's shoulder and addressed him with a question, indicating my esteem:

"Sir—You are one of Arnold's 'famine-proof' veterans?"

"I am," he said.

Immediately I desired to finish what small obligations I still had in the wards and learn of Taggart's service under Arnold. I had admired General Arnold, but only from afar, watching him on his horse leading troops at Freeman's farm. I shared the opinion of many, that if victory came to us, great fame would be awarded to both Washington and Arnold. The warrior from Connecticut had mastered the tactics of the battlefield like few others, and he was driven by an impulse to attack, not to wait and react to the enemy's advances—a hesitancy that afflicted many of our generals. The war for independence had barely a sporting chance when General Washington first mustered the Continental Army in Cambridge, as the British army marched in Boston's streets and gripped its harbor in a stranglehold. Meanwhile, Arnold, at the time a colonel, had made his way into the wilderness of Lake Champlain, meeting Ethan Allen—the great instigator from the New Hampshire Grants, with his secret group of rapscallions called the Green Mountain Boys. Early in May of '75, on a morning well before the sun rose, Arnold, Allen, and fewer than a hundred men quietly approached Fort Ticonderoga, passing the charcoal oven, the well, and the Pontleroy redoubt, and skirting the east wall. Despite the dark they could still see the features of the massive fort, constructed in the shape of an oblong square with angular bastions to provide every angle of fire for its cannons. Far below the promenade they could see, too, the dark hue of Lake Champlain, which they had quietly crossed during the night in a long bateau. Dressed in farmers' clothes, they hastened to the center of the fort's south curtain, overpowered the lone British sentry, and stormed through the wicket gate to the rectangular parade ground. The intruders quickly assembled in a hollow square facing all directions, raised their weapons, and shouted three resounding "Huzzahs!" to startle the garrison. A defeated sentry was made to reveal the headquarters; a pounding on the door brought the commander into the night air, and he promptly surrendered.

While Ethan Allen basked in glory, Arnold knew that Ticonderoga was only the first act of a greater conquest. He compiled an accounting of the fort's weapons, knowing—as did the Massachusetts Committee of Safety, and in a short time General Washington, as soon as he arrived in Cambridge to take command of the Continental Army—that there was no better place on earth for cannons than on the eminence of Dorchester Heights, overlooking the city of Boston and its British pestilence. There were more than one hundred big guns at Ticonderoga, more than two thousand cannonballs, and nine tons of musket balls. That November, Washington sent Henry Knox up Champlain to the captured fortress. Knox selected fifty-nine cannons for transport to Dorchester, traveling down Lake George by flat-bottomed gundalows, then overland on forty-two sleds pulled by horses and oxen. At the end of three winter months he delivered the mighty guns to Washington. Soon the British army in Boston looked up at the heights to find a daunting array of artillery. Two weeks later they were in their ships, setting sail, and Boston was free.

As Arnold and Allen seized Ticonderoga, a contingent of Green Mountain Boys took a second fort at Crown Point. Within days, Arnold embarked on a small schooner, outfitted with four carriage guns, up Lake Champlain, and then set off aboard two bateaux with thirty-five men. They traveled down the Richelieu River to Saint-Jean, south of Montreal. Arnold and his men raided the old French military works and captured the redcoats from the Twenty-sixth Regiment who defended it. Then, with prisoners in tow, Arnold attacked his prize: a seventy-ton British sloop, which he handily captured and made ready to sail—along with five more bateaux and two valuable brass six-pounders. The sloop was essential to any hope the British had for recapturing Ticonderoga; now the bold patriot commander had taken it from them and sailed it down Lake Champlain.

The following month the restless warrior returned to the outskirts of British-occupied Boston. Arnold's next play was to make the case for leading an invasion against the city of Quebec, the stronghold of Canada. Soon after the Battle of Bunker Hill, and with General Washington's blessing, Arnold recruited nearly a thousand volunteers from the military units camped outside the besieged city: Taggart was one of them.

I excused myself to go give the soldiers on the wards some sugar candies, which had been delivered to me in the piazza by a group of young ladies. Soon this errand was done and I returned to Taggart, who welcomed my inquisition. We sat near one of the soot-black stoves, where the orange embers glowed through the vent.

"Arnold is a commander of remarkable character," Taggart said. "He is brave—one of the bravest warriors I've ever seen—and he is beloved by the soldiers."

"I have seen him," I said. "He is not a big man."

"No," said Taggart. "Arnold is short, but handsome enough. He is stoutly made, and has a ruddy complexion. I imagine he is in his middle years. I will tell you this: he has great powers of persuasion. Even the fainthearted will heed his command. His manner can be severe, but if you are a soldier who demonstrates spirit and courage, you will have his good will and esteem. This I know."

"Not all generals will charge the field, as I have seen him do."

"How true!" Taggart agreed. "But he reveals his character in small deeds as well."

Taggart looked again at the stump of his missing arm, and emotion seized hold of him, but only for a moment. Gazing at the flickering flames that rose from the embers in the stove, he seemed taken by a trance that returned him to the wilderness.

"We were some thirty miles from Point Levi," he began, "on the southern bank of the Saint Lawrence, nearly opposite Quebec. My God, were we hungry! We marched in straggling parties through a flat country, passing simple whitewashed houses. One of our fellows, ahead of us, reported a slaughterhouse. We approached it, double-quick, nearly running outright, hoping desperately for meat, and there we found a friend who was gladly willing to deal out the sustenance of life to us. He gave us as many pounds of beefsteaks as we chose to carry. When we got to the next house, a mile beyond, one of our men became cook. The good folks who lived there gave us bread and potatoes, and with the accompaniment of the beefsteak, it was the finest meal ever, for it was a meal I had wished for in my dreams. And so I gave thanks and ate, heartily but within reason, mind you—no more nor less than my good wife would feed me. But each of us soon realized our mistake, and me worst of all. My gut had been long deprived of such food, and it must have withered. The march that afternoon was dull and heavy. A fever attacked me. I became the most miserable human being. We did not march far: in this high latitude, a winter's day is very short and fleeting. The evening brought me no comfort, though we slept warmly in a farmhouse."

Taggart paused to look left and right around the ward, gather his recollections, and rub the bandaged stump of his arm.

"In the morning we continued our march, but by noon my disorder had ruined me. I could not put a foot forward. I sat on a log at the wayside, and our troops passed by me. It was the most terrible thing, my friend. Then, bringing up the rear, came Colonel Arnold on horseback. He knew my name and character, and good-naturedly asked after my health. Full of regret, I told him of my disorder, and expected him to ride on; but instead he dismounted, ran down to the riverside, and hailed the owner of the nearest house, one that stood on the opposite bank. The good Frenchman paddled across to us in his canoe. Arnold gave the man two silver dollars, a generous sum, to provide for my care. After I gave my gun to one of our men, Arnold himself helped me into the canoe."

A boy came by with iron tongs to stoke the fire in the stove. We watched him open the door and lay pieces of split wood on top of the embers.

"I slept for two nights in the Frenchman's house, with a high fever and no taste for food. That had been the cause of the disease, and its absence became the cure."

"Did you catch up with your company?"

"In a day, I did. It was a gloomy and solitary march, being without my gun, in an unknown country. My spirits were heavy."

The new wood caught fire and the boy excused himself from our company, bidding us good evening.

"But one thing was clear to me," Taggart said. "It was the thing he did, and how he looked me in the eye, and bade me care for myself. Should I see a redcoat take aim at Arnold, I would sooner stop the musket ball with my own beating heart than let it strike the good general."

6

From the moment I had met Taggart, when he was lying in the hospital bed, still weak from blood loss, he had impressed me with his good spirits. But sitting here, with his eyes fixed on the flames inside the stove, he was serious, even melancholy.

"You returned the good deed," I said. "You fought with him in battle, and carried him from the field."

"Yes," he replied, thinking. "I did. Fair enough."

Taggart described Quebec to me as the stronghold of Canada, built upon a great stone promontory on the north bank of the mighty Saint Lawrence River, where the river bends to the south and east and a much smaller river, the Saint Charles, feeds into it from the northwest. There is an upper and a lower town. The upper town is a strong fortification, a walled city rising more than three hundred feet on steep, rocky cliffs above the lower town, which sits down at the foot of the cliffs, along the bank of the big river. Never, he said, could he imagine a more imposing and advantageous gateway to a country.

"For weeks we encamped on the Plains of Abraham, long flat fields on the west side of the walled city. As we lay siege, we suffered many deprivations; hunger was only one of them. The cold, my friend—the snow and the ice—it conspired to defeat us, with or without any effort from the British. By Christmas we were still waiting to attack, and the snowdrifts were as tall as a man. We dug channels through the snow just to move from place to place."

Taggart bent over to feel the warmth from the stove.

"The British fired shot and shell at us from the city ramparts, day and night, and so we thought that maybe the ice itself could protect us. We struggled to gather large piles of wooden stakes and bundles of sticks. On one bitterly cold night we were ordered out and set to work, erecting the stakes and heaping up straw, while others brought water and threw it on our structure. The water froze, and from this we built a large fortification—a breastwork of ice. Some of the soldiers were badly frostbitten, which was a high price to pay, but just before sunup a fieldpiece brought from Montreal by Montgomery was placed behind it. It was an imposing sight: an ice wall, shimmering in the light of dawn, and a cannon housed within it."

"A fort of ice—a clever idea," I commented.

"Not so clever," he corrected. "Early in the morning cannon fire erupted from the city, and we returned fire from our ice fortress. This kept up until the middle of the day. By that time our heap of nonsense was completely battered to pieces, and our cannon silenced."

He shook his head slowly, as if he were standing in the frozen field, looking anew at the shards of shattered ice.

"And what of Arnold, during this siege?" I asked.

"Arnold was a warhorse champing at the bit," Taggart said. "He had no patience for the hesitation he saw in other officers. A siege made no sense to him—he wanted to attack the city. Our soldiers were worn down, and many of them were anxiously waiting for their enlistment to expire on the first day of January, planning to go home without a moment's delay. If there was to be an attack, it had to happen before the new year. Montgomery and Arnold agreed that we would attack and take the city on the first night that brought the cover of a heavy snowfall.

"Two weeks passed before that night arrived, and then came the worst horrors of war. At five in the morning, amid a fierce and blinding snowstorm, the signal was given and the several divisions, some eleven hundred men all told, moved to the assault. The plan was to threaten every part of the city. General Montgomery, at the head of the New York troops, advanced along the rocky shore road on the bank of the Saint Lawrence to Cape Diamond, which was defended by a few lightly guarded barricades. The first lone sentry they encountered fled when fired on, but the river had heaped enormous masses of ice onto the shore that blocked the road and slowed the attack, and every step was slick as oil from the snow. Several times they had to climb along the edge of the precipice, and Montgomery's progress was not as fast as an attack must be. Still, the general advanced boldly past the barricades, encouraging his soldiers by his brave example, and with two hundred men behind him began to force the next barrier that stood between them and the fortified city. But hiding in a blockhouse were a few British soldiers, who discharged a small fieldpiece loaded with grapeshot, with the Americans only forty paces from it. General Montgomery was killed on the spot. The single cannon blast killed two other valuable officers, as well as Montgomery's orderly sergeant and a private. The horrible loss of their general discouraged the other troops, who did not have the spirit of heroism that animated their commander. The whole division beat a hasty retreat, leaving the British garrison to turn their undivided force against Arnold, coming from the other direction."

Taggart became animated, emphasizing his words with waves of his hand, pointing and moving his finger as if tracing a map, and grasping his forehead when his recollections overwhelmed him. "Captain Wheatley, my friend, I heard the story of Montgomery's charge from every man who lived to tell it." The stump of his lost arm went up and down too, not yet accustomed to being left out. "But all the rest of what I tell you I saw with my own two eyes." Taggart's gaze fixed again on the orange flames that rose and spun within the blackened stove, and he continued.

"Arnold's division moved in from the north side of the city, along the street of Saint Roch, toward the Sault-au-Matelot road. Like Montgomery, Arnold himself led the charge, utterly intrepid. Captain Lamb followed him with his company of artillery, pulling a fieldpiece mounted on a sled. Close behind the artillery was the main body, led by Morgan's company of riflemen. I was with Captain Dearborn's light infantry. We were to join from the right flank, but the snow was so fierce and the morning light so dim, and the route so intricate and unfamiliar, that we had to pause, again and again, to orient ourselves. At first we were glad to see lanterns bobbing in the blizzard, but we couldn't tell if they were friend or foe. I was close by his side when the captain—as he was then—saw a group of men within the pickets, dressed like ours, and made ready to hail them, when one of them hailed Dearborn first. Every soldier strained to hear the calls back and forth:

Who are you? the hidden voice shouted.

A friend, Dearborn answered.

Who are you a friend to?

To liberty!

Goddamn you! came the response.

Then the hostile inquisitor raised himself partly above the pickets. Captain Dearborn leveled his musket, loaded with a ball and ten buckshot, thus certain to give the rascal his due, but to his great mortification the gun did not go off. A cascade of flintlocks snapped, but only one in ten of our guns fired, for they were so exceedingly wet."

The hospital ward was quiet, and as the blue light of early evening came through the windows, all I heard besides his gruff voice was the hollow murmur of the fire burning.

"At last we met Arnold's column, and Morgan's and the others on the Sault-au-Matelot road. The path we had to march was narrowed by blocks of ice thrown up by the Saint Charles River on one side, and a series of obstructions erected by the enemy on the other. They had reinforced their first barrier with a battery of two twelve-pounders. Their two cannons sprayed grapeshot over every inch of the ground we covered, while our right flank was exposed to musket fire from the city walls, and from the pickets of the garrison.

"Against this barrage Arnold advanced. We could see him, and hear him, cheering his men forward—all the men—directing our fire, calling out hazards. I will tell you, my friend: this was the image I held in my mind when the doctor took off my arm with his saw. Arnold was pure courage. In the darkness, harassed by the furious storm, we soldiers fought with all we had, if only to match the example he set. As he gained upon the first battery a ball struck him in the left leg, which knocked him to one knee and turned the fresh snow beneath him bright red. With the force of his one good leg he tried to stand. Two of Morgan's men lifted him. That is when I came up from behind him and went to his aid. He accepted my help, and turning to the soldiers who paused to take his measure, he shouted:

"Rush on, brave boys! Rush on!"

"Did they?" I asked, hoping they were a rebuttal to Montgomery's men, who retreated when their leader was stricken.

"Yes, they surely did," Taggart said. "The snow blew through the streets. Most of the gunlocks were so wet that the guns could not be fired. Our troops marched through the main street of the city and the battle became more and more desperate. The enemy fired from the high walls of the city, from the windows of houses, from every lurking place they could find. Our men were butchered. Captain Hendricks was shot down dead. Captain Hubbard was leaning against a building; I heard a soldier yell to him, 'Are you wounded, Captain?' He answered that he was, but shouted, 'March on! March on!' The orderly sergeant was shot down near me. He fell on his back. He said to a private who knelt beside him: 'I am a dead man. I wish you would turn me over.' The private turned him facedown. We had strict orders, before we marched, not to stop for the wounded or the dying, so we left him in the snow."

Taggart and I sat there quietly. For a few moments he closed his eyes and clenched his jaw as these scenes haunted his mind.

"What did you do with Arnold?" I asked.

"While Morgan's men held him up, I wrapped a cloth tightly around his wound, which caused him great pain, but stanched the bleeding. Then I took his arm and placed it across my shoulder."

"Did he tell you to carry him away?"

"No. Not at all. He insisted we help him march forward to storm the pickets. I looked at Private Sperry next to me; without hesitation we turned him away from the battle. If there were any doubt about it, Captain Lamb ran over and ordered us to remove the colonel."

"Then you weren't captured. You made it out of the city."

"Barely, my friend. The streets were slick with snow and ice, and Arnold had to drag his wounded leg. The morning light was still faint and it was a damn blizzard, and we knew that a wrong turn could mean our end. Within minutes we found Captain Dearborn, and Arnold described the fight. He told Dearborn that our soldiers had possession of a four-gun battery, and our five mortars from

Saint Roch's were heaving shells of all sorts. He told Dearborn to push forward, and carry the town.

"We scrambled to get past the city walls, and found the strangest illumination. Our own troops had created a feint to draw the enemy from our attacks: they set fire to Saint John's Gate with a great quantity of combustibles. Minutes later the enemy, searching for the attackers, lit up the city wall with flares, balls of fire that burned even in the deep snow and gave the advantage to the enemy. Arnold made a noble effort to drag his wounded leg and hobble forward, but soon we lifted him and hastened at double-quick pace, past the light cast by the hellish flares that made the white snow all around us glow red and orange like the embers in this hot stove."

Taggart looked up at me. "The gates of hell could look no worse," he said.

He collected his thoughts, then asked, "Shall I go on?"

"Please, if it does not pain you too much."

"There is no pain, my friend. Only pity is left." He leaned back in his chair.

"For a few minutes we were in a parade of wounded, retreating along the Plains of Abraham as quickly as we could, when I looked back at Saint John's Gate. The enemy rushed out and captured several of the horses and wagons behind us, and all the men with them. Not many of the wounded escaped after that.

"Daylight at last appeared with a break in the storm just as we arrived with Arnold at the hospital quarters. Already it seemed full to its capacity. A surgeon and his mate pulled off Arnold's boot and cut his breeches. They found a piece of musket ball, missing perhaps a third of its lead from hitting a stone wall. The remainder of the twisted shot had ripped into his leg about midway down his shinbone, passing between the long narrow bones and lodging above the tendon Achilles. The surgeon removed the misshapen metal, and the colonel's loud agitation, his curses and condemnations, seemed less from the pain than his concern for the battle and the soldiers fighting it. Word came of retreats, of Montgomery's death, and other sickening losses. We concluded that Arnold's division, put under command of Lieutenant Colonel Christopher Greene, were all killed, wounded, or captured. Major Ogden came in shot through the left shoulder, and gave his opinion that our attack would fail.

"Before we could even digest this news a growing clamor informed us that the enemy was advancing toward the hospital. All the sick and wounded who could stand, and the handful of artillery troops guarding the hospital, were ordered to march immediately into Saint Roch Street behind two fieldpieces. A turn in the street gave us the advantage and the cannons were well directed; their fire put the enemy to flight immediately. We expected them to attack again, so we urged Colonel Arnold for his own safety to be carried back into the country where the enemy would not easily find him. But Arnold refused; he would not be moved, nor permit any man from the hospital to retreat. He ordered his pistols loaded and set a sword on his cot, adding that he was determined to kill as many of the enemy as possible if they burst through the door.

"The second attack never came. In two days our Major Meigs was released out of the city on parole, and gave us a chronicle of the rest of the battle and its aftermath. Our men had got into the city, but their guns were so fouled from the wind and wet weather that scarcely any of them would fire. For a lengthy time they fought almost entirely with their bayonets and gunstocks, and anything else they had, holding the lower town till eleven in the morning, hoping for General Montgomery's assistance. Of course, it never came, so they had no choice but to surrender themselves as prisoners of war.

"All we could do was to watch the walls of the city: behind them were many of our soldiers and officers, and our dead. Colonel Arnold ordered our troops to burn and destroy as many houses as we could obtain, to demoralize the enemy. His wound and a severe case of gout confined him to his bed. For the next ten weeks the winter was the only thing we battled, until troops arrived from Montreal to assist us.

"And then, my friend, I gradually made my way home."

7

In the morning the hospital wards bustled with activity. Many new wounded would soon arrive from the most recent great battle at Saratoga. Patients who were recovering well were moved to local houses. Taggart would be lodging in a house down the long hill and near the river, but said that in two or three days he would begin his journey homeward—and then to a new home altogether. He had received a letter from his wife, who told him that her family's farm, in Connecticut, would welcome them, and would eventually become theirs, through an arrangement with her father.

"I've done well enough in New Hampshire," he told me. "But it seems Providence is looking after this one-armed farmer. A fertile valley, better soil. Fewer stones to haul from the fields with this one hand." He would first return to New Hampshire to load the family's possessions into a wagon, and would then make the trip together with his wife and son. He added, while looking at his only hand, "You don't suppose it will take me twice as long to pack?"

"Where in Connecticut is the farm?" I asked him.

"Near a town called Lebanon."

"Lebanon. Like the Holy Land."

"Aye," he said, "the Promised Land."

We stood near the piazza in front of the hospital, watching the long train of wagons bringing new wounded up the hill, just as we had come weeks earlier.

"I'm the last one to ever ask for help," Taggart said suddenly, looking straight ahead down the hill. "And now I'll be asking someone to lend me a hand damn near every hour."

"Lend me a hand," he repeated. He grinned and shook his head.

I'd seen enough of Taggart to know he was resilient. I could see him working it out in his head, imagining the Connecticut farm and thinking of the kinfolk who would do the things a one-armed farmer could not.

"Ah, well," Taggart said. "My wife will be glad to see me. We will find something for me to do."

"There will be plenty of things for you to do," I said.

"I'm eager to see my boy. I miss him terribly. My son, Robert—he's my boy, but he's eager to be a man. He wants to fight with Washington. I told him, more than a year ago, that when I came back it would be his turn."

Taggart looked at the stump of his left arm, and then at me.

"Do you think this will change his mind?"

"Not if he is like his father," I said.

"Hmm. Now I worry about that."

All of Taggart's things were in his knapsack, which he insisted on carrying himself, hung across his shoulders and secured by the firm grip of his one hand. Several wagons had arrived at the piazza, and the first of the new wounded were being carried into the hospital.

"I pray that General Arnold survives to fight again," Taggart said. "If he dies, I fear some of our courage will die with him."

With his short stump and a turn of his shoulder he pointed toward the wounded. "I would hate for all this to be wasted," he said.

Then, for what seemed several minutes, Taggart looked out over the gabled roofs and the church steeples toward the river and across it to the shadowed hills. I kept still until he spoke again.

"Ah, well," he said, "we try to do the right thing."

"We do," I agreed.

"My father used to tell me," Taggart continued, "and I've told it plenty to Robert, that an honorable man is worth more than a bar of gold. Pa had a voice that could echo in the hills—at least to my young ears—and he could sound like he spoke from the pulpit: 'At the end of the day,' he'd say, 'all a man has is his good name.' I swear I heard him say it again, in the field, as if I were sitting at his feet, the very moment I saw my arm was gone and I was sure that death had come for me. So much noise from the battle, but the only thing I heard was his voice, and for a minute or two I just lay there on my back, bleeding like a barrel that popped its cork, staring at the blue sky and trying to figure out if my honor and good name were intact."

He took a deep breath and looked again toward the hills across the river. I thought to tell him that a soldier fighting valiantly was the epitome of honor, but I hesitated and waited for him to continue.

"I had strong ideas when the war began, and I decided to be a soldier for those ideas. Being away from the farm was a burden on my wife and son, but it gained me good reputation. When my company formed and we drilled on the green we were held in high esteem, and with God as my witness I was a good soldier—I truly believe I was a good soldier."

"A very fine soldier," I said.

"But for an instant," Taggart continued, "as I tried to stanch the bleeding, I felt shame for leaving my wife and son. With my one last hand I was rolling a cloth into a tourniquet, and all the choices I'd ever made about how to live my life—as a boy, as a man, as a husband and father—they paraded through my head, and I wondered if my choices had been right or wrong, and if I could be sure that I was an honorable man. At some point—maybe as a boy following my pa around; maybe as a young man—at some point I decided what kind of person I wanted to be, but at that moment on the battlefield, when I needed to be satisfied with my choices, I was just not sure. And today I am not sure if I should go home a hero of the war, or a one-armed farmer who needs forgiveness. I am simply not sure."

He shrugged one shoulder and made a sort of grunt, as if he were tossing something heavy to the ground.

"To discover what is right, and then to do it," I said, recalling earnest conversations I'd had as a student. "That is the battle we fight the hardest and the longest. And we can hope there is honor in that alone."

"All things considered, I reckon there are worse things than being a one-armed farmer going home to his wife and son."

"And if I may weigh in," I said, "Henry Taggart is a man of the highest honor."

"Gideon Wheatley, you are indeed a friend," he declared.

Then he smiled and grasped my hand, and we said goodbye.

As more wagons arrived, one after another, and the wounded were taken in, I gathered my things and readied myself to return to my company. In the front foyer Dr. Thacher approached me—I presumed to bid me farewell. I was sorry for Thacher, for I knew the kind of work he would be doing for the next several days. It is a great trauma to have a limb amputated, or a hole drilled into one's skull; but it is no small thing to do the cutting, and to do it again and again, day after day.

"Captain Wheatley," he called, as he came near.

Thacher had a nervous energy, like a soldier right before battle.

"I know you are eager to return to your troops; there is speculation that Burgoyne will surrender, and surely you deserve to be present for that. You have healed sufficiently that you can go."

To witness the surrender would be one of the great events of my life.

"But I need you here," he continued, "if you will stay. We will have more wounded than we did from the last battle. You have comforted the men, and the story of how you stopped a musket ball with your head—"

Thacher put his hand on my forehead and inspected the scabbed-over gash.

"—it emboldens the men, and I dare say it encourages them in their healing."

He looked me squarely in the eye, and his request became personal, as if between friends.

"In an hour it will be like hell in here. There is only so much we can do; the wounded need a surgeon, but equally they need a companion. There is so much fear and anguish, for which I can do nothing. But you can—if you will stay and help us."

"Yes," I said. "I will."

I moved my gear to a room in the center of the hospital, on the upper floor, that housed the surgeon's mates. The windows overlooked the piazza, and from there down the hill toward the town, and beyond it the Hudson River. The number of wagons and carts hauling the wounded had multiplied, and filled the road from the piazza as far as I could see to the riverbank, where schooners, barges, and dozens of bateaux crowded the water. At the top of the hill the wagons pulled by horses and oxen were led onto the piazza, where the wounded were quickly inspected again and taken inside on stretchers. From my open window I surveyed the earliest arrivals, who were lying in the wagons on blankets and straw. Amid the groans and weeping, some of the wounded asked worried questions of the doctors and surgeon's mates who met them. A two-wheeled cart pulled by a heavy draft horse drew up to the piazza and turned a sharp angle before stopping. A man walked quickly alongside the cart, and several of the surgeon's mates scrambled to assist him with the three wounded soldiers it carried. One of them was half-sitting in the cart, his leg bound with cloth and thin planks of wood. Another was lying down; he had already lost part of his leg. After these two men were carried on stretchers into the hospital, two surgeon's mates inspected the third soldier, who was lying flat. They touched his head and neck; one leaned in close to his face. He was put on a stretcher; a piece of sackcloth was laid over his face and chest, and he was carried away.

The surgeons attended first to the soldiers with the most dire injuries, and there were many. By evening there was a new bone pile behind the hospital. I did what I could. One soldier seemed to suffer from the noise of war: he had only a mild laceration on his face, but he wept without end and tremors shook his body. I spoke with him, but he responded only in short bursts of incoherent speech, and he did not absorb much of what I said. The soldiers who had sustained lesser injuries—lacerations, mostly—had to wait to be sutured, and I talked with many of these, who mostly desired food and some description of what was to happen to them. From these soldiers I gained a clearer picture of the second great battle of Saratoga, called by some the Battle of Bemis Heights.

Nearly three weeks earlier, on the morning after the battle at Freeman's farm—when I was being taken to Albany—neither the American army nor Burgoyne's redcoats pursued a second day of battle. Had Burgoyne known of the true condition of the Americans, he might have attacked and obtained a victory, for the soldiers composing the left wing, at the heart of the fight, had only a single round of cartridges left. Supplies were down to nothing; there was hardly enough food for a few more meals. Fortunately, provisions arrived quickly from Albany, including a supply of cartridges, powder kegs, and window leads for making musket balls.

Both armies worked diligently to strengthen their positions. Our boys constructed breastworks that began on the hills which rose above the river and stretched nearly a mile westward to Bemis Heights, near the farmhouse of Mr. Neilson. They built strong batteries and deep trenches with pointed palisades, and the magazine was made bomb-proof. The wounded soldiers told me that Burgoyne was equally busy. His camp was pitched within cannon shot of the American lines. He hurried to erect a line of entrenchments, with batteries, across the plain to the hills along the river. The Hessian camp was situated on an eminence about half a mile northwest of Freeman's farm, the site of the first battle nearly three weeks earlier, and was protected by a strong redoubt built of stacked timbers cut from the woods.

While these fortifications were being constructed, there were regular skirmishes between small detachments, sometimes among foraging parties. Not a night passed without the performance of some daring exploit, either for the sake of adventure or to intimidate the enemy. The Americans were constantly gaining new soldiers, and their superior numbers enabled them to launch expeditions to harass the British without weakening their lines or endangering the safety of the camp.

A soldier from Wesson's Regiment whose finger had been shot off told me that the earlier success of the Americans at Freeman's farm, and the rapid reinforcement of the army, had annihilated any loyalist feelings in the vicinity, and made every patriot, whether soldier or citizen, bold and adventurous. At one time twenty young farmers living in the area, intent on having a frolic, decided to capture a picket guard of the enemy stationed near the middle ravine. Each young man was armed with a fowling piece, and plenty of powder and shot. They passed silently through the woods at nightfall, until they got within yards of the picket. The chief of the frolickers gave a tremendous blast on an old horse trumpet, and the noise and shouts of the gang sounded like an entire regiment. The chief cried out, "Ground your arms, or you are all dead men!" Thirty redcoats obeyed, and were promptly marched by the jolly farmers into the American camp like a parade of regular prisoners of war. This, I was told, was one of many similar instances that kept the British camp in a state of constant alarm.

Time rolled on, and the strength of our forces increased daily. At last, Burgoyne's only choice was to fight or flee, and he chose to fight. On the bright and clear morning of October 7, the British commander, at the head of fifteen hundred regular troops, with two twelve-pounders, two howitzers, and a half-dozen six-pounders, moved toward the American left. He was seconded by regiments under the commands of Philips, Reidesel, and Fraser. Small parties of Tories and Mohawk Indians were sent through trails in the woods to harass the American rear and keep them in check.

At the headquarters of General Gates a sergeant arrived with intelligence on the movement of the British army. Now that very same sergeant lay in one of the wards with a musket ball lodged in his thigh. He told me that General Gates heard his report, then sent an aide to discover the exact position and likely intentions of the enemy. The aide found a large contingent of redcoats in the wheat field of Barber's farm, cutting down stalks. He also witnessed several British officers standing on a cabin roof, with a spyglass, looking for the position of the American left.

By early afternoon, both armies jostled for position and summoned their strength for decisive combat. The British line formed on the newly cleared wheat field, preparing to march into action.

The patriots under Generals Poor and Learned were ordered not to fire until after the first discharge from the enemy. When an explosion of musket balls and grapeshot crashed through the trees just barely above their heads, the silence and patience of the American troops ended, and with loud cheers and shouting they sprang forward and returned fire in rapid volleys.

The battle quickly became fierce and destructive. Across the wheat field, as General Poor's brigade engaged the British left, Colonel Morgan's corps rushed down the hills on the enemy's right, hitting the British flanking party led by General Fraser with a such a deadly storm of well-aimed rifle fire that they quickly retreated to their lines. Then, with great speed, Morgan wheeled and attacked the British right flank with so much force that their ranks at once fell into confusion. Before Fraser's redcoats had a chance to regroup, Major Dearborn's fast-moving light infantry leaped the fence between the woods and field and attacked them in front. The British were overrun and fell back, their left and right flanks in disarray.

Our boys rushed to the enemy's cannons, and amid the carriages of the heavy fieldpieces they fought at close range. Five times one of the British cannons was taken and retaken, but at last Colonel Cilley and his men of the First New Hampshire held it and the British fell back. The colonel, who had fought at the head of his troops throughout the contest, jumped upon the carriage of the captured cannon and waved his sword high in the air, while his troops wheeled the muzzle to face the enemy and, with the king's own ammunition, loosed its thunder against them.

As each wounded soldier recalled the battle, there was one constant to every man's memory: General Arnold on his horse, leading the soldiers with uncommon bravery. Arnold, they said, completely engaged the battlefield. The general took command of three regiments; as he rallied them from his steed, his soldiers greeted him with loud "Huzzahs." Without delay he led them to attack the British center with waves of ferocious fire. Every man described some essence of the warrior general: stirred by the din of battle, thirsting for glory, and so burning with a patriotic desire to serve his country that he rushed into the thickest of the fight, brandishing his sword and delivering his orders everywhere in person. The first assault of Arnold's troops was against the Hessians, who held the center of the enemy line: as Arnold dashed furiously among them at the head of his men, the Hessians broke and fled in dismay.

By midafternoon the battle consumed the whole line of both armies. Arnold and Morgan directed the fury of the American storm, while the intrepid British general Fraser whipped up the fighting spirit of his own brigade. Dressed in the full uniform of a field officer and riding up and down the line on an iron-gray horse, Fraser radiated skill and courage in every direction. When the British line gave way, he brought order out of confusion; when regiments began to waver, his confidence and bold example gave them courage. The fate of the battle rested upon him, a fact that Arnold and Morgan clearly perceived. The two patriot commanders spoke; then, as Arnold galloped toward a brigade of newly arriving New York troops, Morgan called his best riflemen around him.

"That officer is General Fraser," he said to them. "I admire and honor him, but he must die, here and now. Victory for the enemy depends on him. Take your stations in that clump of bushes, and do your duty."

Within minutes, the marksmen were ready. A rifle ball ripped the rear of Fraser's saddle; another passed through the horse's mane. One of Morgan's riflemen, aiming from a perch in a tree, fired a third ball that tore into Fraser's gut, lifting him from his saddle for an instant before he fell upon his horse's neck. An aide ran to the general, grabbing him as he slid off his mount, and laying him on the ground as other officers surrounded the mortally wounded commander.

The redcoats saw their valiant general on the ground and the cluster of officers kneeling beside him, and the whole regiment seemed to pause for a moment, waiting for Fraser to climb back onto his horse. When he did not, a panic spread along the British line. It was heightened, at the very same moment, by the sudden appearance of more than a thousand New York troops onto the field. Redcoats began to retreat, first in scattered pockets, then all at once. As the Americans advanced, the entire right of the British line dispersed to a long and winding barricade of timbers stacked between pairs of posts: the newly constructed defensive redoubt held by the British major Lindsay, the Earl of Balcarres. Now the battered British and German soldiers were gone from the wheat field, and a massive cheer went up among the Americans.

At this point the enemy had been driven back to defensive positions, and many generals would have been satisfied and ceased their attack—but not General Arnold, whose warrior heart would not permit the enemy to escape to fight another day. With his sword raised to the sky, leaning forward on his large bay horse, Arnold continued the attack. Rallying both Continentals and militia, he moved rapidly to assault the Balcarres redoubt and the scattered Canadian forces in the field that extended beyond it to the northwest. Across the short rolling hills, anchoring the right flank of the British line, was another long timber breastwork, a redoubt held by the German colonel Heinrich Breyman. If Breyman's redoubt could be taken, the entire British line could be flanked and the whole of Burgoyne's army sent running. The fighting in the field was violent and furious, and the demoralized Canadians withdrew to the cover of a few wooden cabins on the field, leaving Breyman and his Germans completely exposed. At this moment Arnold steered several regiments to the left, leading them to advance and attack Breyman's redoubt. At the same time, Arnold himself galloped around the side of the breastwork, with some two hundred men behind him, and attacked the unprotected rear of the fortification, waving his sword and cheering his men on to conquest.

The outnumbered Germans, who had seen Arnold upon his warhorse in the thickest of the fight, fled for their lives—but not before delivering a volley of grapeshot and musket fire in retreat. One of Morgan's riflemen, named Withers—who lost the toes of his left foot when a cannonball, one of the last fired that day, crashed on the ground in front of him—told me that a cannon shot tore off the head of a New York soldier. A fragment of his shattered skull pierced the head of another soldier, who fell unconscious atop his headless patriot brother.

Within minutes, the Germans would join the British in retreat. But at the moment of this great victory, a musket ball, fired at close range, ripped through Arnold's leg—the same leg that had been injured in Quebec two years before—and tore into the flesh of his gallant steed. The horse instantly fell, its head crashing into the ground and its full weight landing on Arnold's bloodied leg, snapping its bones.

Withers, the rifleman, told me he was among the men who lifted the dying horse off Arnold as the chaotic fighting continued in the redoubt. An infantryman instantly pointed to a particular Hessian, wounded and crawling on hands and knees in retreat, who had shot Arnold. The patriots made ready to run their bayonets through the hapless soldier but Arnold called out, "Don't hurt him! He only did his duty!" and the Hessian was left to drag himself away.

The sun set that night at a quarter to six, an hour and a half after Arnold was wounded. The crescent moon did not rise until three and a half hours later. In that span of darkness both sides took account of the day's battle, and the scope of the American victory became clear.

8

Three weeks had passed since I arrived at the Albany hospital, and my wounds had healed cleanly, without any disease of the flesh. Many of the soldiers who had arrived with me, who had been wounded at Freeman's farm during the first battle of Saratoga, had left the hospital to go home or back to the army, although some were learning how to live with broken bodies, or were still gripped by fever. Others had been taken to the graveyard; I was troubled by how many of the soldiers in the hospital eventually died from their wounds.

For the newly wounded, those who had charged the British from Bemis Heights and fought the second battle of Saratoga, I carried on my work as Dr. Thacher had requested, writing letters to wives and families, and providing company and encouragement. The best of what little remedy I could offer was the story of victory, so I told the men what I had learned of the battle, and how their courage and valor had carried the day. We spoke of the regiments and brigades, and what they had done, and the commanders. The men told me of their fellow soldiers, and sometimes asked if I knew of their fates. Always, too, we talked about General Arnold, his skill and courage on the battlefield, and how he personified the noble virtue of our cause.

The surgeons worked valiantly, and seemed rarely to rest. I saw Dr. Thacher over several days, moving from ward to ward, focused on his work but looking more and more drained of spirit. One could attribute this to a lack of sleep, but most assuredly the mutilated bodies, mangled limbs, and incurable wounds inflicted upon the surgeons their own disease, a melancholia they struggled to overcome.

On the fourth day after the Battle of Bemis Heights, Dr. Thacher approached me as I left the bedside of an Albany County militiaman.

"I have a request to make of you," he said. "I have been attending a patient who is in great pain, but who will not allow the surgeons to undertake the prescribed remedy—which is amputation."

He turned and started toward the center ward of the hospital. "Walk with me," he instructed. We passed through two wards, and by several carts that carried porridge and other food for the soldiers.

"As you can see, I am occupied with a great many patients, but he requires more attention than I can give. Not medical attention—I can provide that—but he is very peevish and impatient under his misfortunes. He is greatly agitated."

We stopped outside the doorway of a small room.

"Your company will be very good for him. We need him to heal."

Thacher stepped into the room, and I followed. The patient was flat on his back, his head turned slightly away from us, toward the room's only window. He wore a loose yellowed linen shirt, his torso beneath a blanket. His hair was disheveled. His left leg, from his foot to his upper thigh, was contained in a stiff wooden box.

He turned his head to look at us, and for the first time my eyes met those of Major General Benedict Arnold.

"General," Thacher pronounced. "This is Captain Gideon Wheatley, of the Third New Hampshire. He is of great help to me, and I have asked him to attend to your needs."

The general took a long, deliberate breath.

"I hear . . .," he began. "I hear you were shot in the head while charging the enemy."

"That is true, sir."

"We should get along fine," he said, closing his eyes.

9

From that moment forward I spent many hours with General Arnold, sitting and talking with him and attending to his needs some part of every day for nearly four months. Here, at the hospital, he was not the genius of war, but rather was a man whose body was broken, afire with seething pain and fever, and whose spirit was rankled by despair.

"There is a fine burial ground in Norwichtown," he began our first conversation, his eyes closed as I wiped sweat from his brow. "See that my body is laid to rest there."

"Be strong, General," I answered. "You are still in this fight."

"My mother is buried there," he said. "I wish to be buried there."

I said nothing.

"My father: he is buried there. His name was Benedict."

He shivered. I pulled a blanket higher on his chest.

"They had a child, before I was born; their first child. They named him Benedict."

He opened his eyes and looked at me.

"An infant. He is buried there."

He closed his eyes.

"And then there was me," he said, making a faint smile. "And after me, my sister Hannah."

He was silent for a few minutes. I pulled a chair closer to the bed and quietly sat down.

"Are you there?" he asked, his eyes still closed.

"Yes, General."

"My brother Absalom was just a child. He is buried there."

The dead were filling the room.

"I was away, sent off to school," he continued, "when my sisters Mary and Elizabeth died."

The general coughed, which caused the slightest vibration in his leg, but it was enough to make him wince.

"Children. Just children. They are buried there," he said, "in the burial ground, in Norwichtown."

He turned his head slightly and opened his eyes, meeting mine.

"See to it, will you, that I am buried there."

10

Eleven days after the battle, a rider passed through Albany on his way to Philadelphia with news that Burgoyne had surrendered his entire army to General Gates. One after another, the regiments of the British line had paraded to a large grassy field on the west bank of the Hudson, marching to the music of fife and drum. They were followed by the Royal Artillery, and then the Hessian regiments. General Burgoyne, in his spotless scarlet regimentals with gold braid and a laced hat, drew his sword and handed it to General Gates, who held it as he accepted the surrender. Then the defeated army marched past the American soldiers, who lined both sides of the road, stretching for two miles or more. The first contingents passed through at midafternoon, and the long march went on until sunset. Quartermasters, chaplains, surgeons, and engineers brought up the rear, followed by an assortment of camp followers and stragglers, some leading deer, raccoons, and other animals from the forest, which they had captured as pets and curiosities.

I wasted no time in telling this news to General Arnold. This was the greatest victory yet of the war for independence—and it was Arnold's victory. After he had taken some broth at midday, I described to him all that the rider had told us about the surrender.

I waited for his reaction; he was quiet for a while, and seemed unmoved.

"Thank you, Captain," he said, and closed his eyes, as if to sleep. I took the empty bowl from the bedside table and made to leave, when I heard the general utter a single comment, spoken only to himself.

"Goddamn it," he murmured, through clenched teeth.

Overhearing this, I did not speak anymore about the surrender. But the next day Arnold raised the topic.

"Do you know what Gates and Burgoyne did after the sword was surrendered?" he asked.

"No, sir."

"I suspect, as would be proper, that Gates invited Burgoyne and his brigadiers and regimental commanders to join him, and his officers, in his marquee tent."

"For what purpose?" I asked.

"To show the honorable intentions of gentlemen," he replied.

I presumed he wanted to talk, so I asked him, "In what manner?"

"A banquet," he answered. "Nothing less than a banquet. There would be boards set across barrels, and on them would be the best meal the army could gather. Imagine: boiled mutton, a goose, ham, beefsteaks."

"To feed them before their next long journey?" I asked, knowing there was more to it.

"To celebrate valor and courage," he said, flat on his back, looking upward at the ceiling. "There would be glasses set out, and liquor, probably rum. Burgoyne would offer a toast, maybe to Gates, maybe to General Washington. Gates would return the honor: I imagine he would toast the king's health. All the officers would commingle: the British and the Germans, talking with the Americans, observing all possible niceties, complimenting the demeanor of their respective armies, outdoing each other in displaying the virtues of gentlemen—gentlemen who go to war, gentlemen who face each other on the battlefield, gentlemen who kill one another—but gentlemen who know that the battlefield is the seedbed of valor, where a man's soul and his character are on display for the world to witness."

He turned his head to face me. "You know this, Captain, as well as any: the battlefield is the theater of courage. As much as we fight to vanquish the enemy, we fight to establish our honor."

Arnold turned his gaze back toward the ceiling. "Mind you, the broth suits me fine. I do not need the fancy meats, nor the pompous conversation."

His eyes shot around the room, looked at me, then rested back on the ceiling.

"But they should know who led the fight. They should know who beat them."

A gust of wind blew against the window.

"You did, sir," I said. But I was only one voice.

11

Later that day Dr. Potts, the surgeon general of the hospital, came with Dr. Thacher to examine Arnold's leg. It was greatly swollen. By pressing the leg, which caused searing pain, they determined that the bones were still crooked and would need to be straightened and reset.

But they had little expectation that an injury of this magnitude could properly heal at all.

Dr. Potts was thirty years old, more or less. He had studied medicine in Edinburgh, and then at the College of Philadelphia. At Fort George, traveling with General Gates, he had done much to combat the outbreaks of smallpox that threatened the army, using techniques of variolation. Dr. Thacher had high praise for his medical skills.

Dr. Potts sat in the chair beside Arnold's bed, while Dr. Thacher stood nearby. I stood well behind them, by the door.

"General," Dr. Potts began, in a sympathetic manner. "Your leg is not healing well. I know it causes you great pain, and this is not likely to stop for weeks or months; it may cause pain throughout your life. The bones, as you know, are shattered, and no matter what we do, the odds that they will return to their same steadiness and utility are very small."

Dr. Potts cleared his throat.

"What I mean to say, General, is that even if the leg is saved, the injury makes it unlikely that you will walk, in the way you have known."

General Arnold, his head propped up on a pillow, looked at Dr. Potts and listened intently as he continued.

"Equally troublesome, if not more so, is the possibility of mortification in the flesh, which could spread quickly. And if that happens, I fear we could lose you."

Dr. Potts gestured to Thacher to come closer to the bedside.

"Dr. Thacher and I agree that the best course of action is to remove your leg by amputation. We can do this surgery quickly, and while it is painful, the pain would subside in a matter of days, and relieve your suffering."

A few silent moments passed before Dr. Thacher spoke. "General," he said, "I know you rejected this remedy when you arrived at the hospital, and we promised to do what we could to save your leg. But the risks of keeping the leg remain grave, the pain will be enduring, and the leg is unlikely to return to a normal condition."

"The decision is yours, General," added Dr. Potts, "but that is our recommendation. I will leave you to consider it, and I'll return in the evening."

Dr. Potts stood and, preparing to take his leave, gazed down at Arnold on the bed.

"I will look forward to your return, Dr. Potts," said Arnold, "for I enjoy your company. But I have made my decision."

"Yes, General?"

"The recent battle is won, but I suspect the war will be long, and I intend to mount a good horse and lead my army. I thank you for your care, but I will not yet abandon my leg. I look to Providence to return me to the field."

"Yes, General," said Dr. Potts. "We will do our very best to save your leg, and to make you strong. But there is still a chance . . ."

"I understand," Arnold said.

Dr. Potts looked at Dr. Thacher, and their eyes met. They bade the general a good afternoon, but Arnold stopped them with a further word as they stepped toward the door.

"I have, you know, been talking with Captain Wheatley," Arnold said.

The general and the two doctors were now looking at me.

"A musket ball crashed into his skull."

"That is correct," Dr. Thacher said.

"But you did not amputate his head."

Thacher and Potts glanced at each other, and the burden they carried momentarily lifted.

"No," Dr. Thacher replied, "he wouldn't allow it either."

As the doctors left the room it occurred to me that perhaps I was becoming more than an aide to the general—that I was his ally, a co-conspirator against fate, a fellow soldier in a battle to defy the odds.

12

After the surgeons again adjusted the bones, probing deep into the inflamed flesh, pulling the bones apart, then pushing them to force the broken tips to meet properly, the searing pain subsided and became instead a throbbing soreness, constant but endurable, which Arnold welcomed as a relief. His leg was again secured in a wooden fracture box, and he was still flat on his back.

"Will you write a letter for me?" he asked. "My sister Hannah will have heard of my injury by now, and I must reassure her."

"I will get my desk," I answered.

Before I could leave, he continued.

"Do you have brothers or sisters, Gideon?"

"A sister, who died a child. No others."

"Hmm," he murmured. "I recall that I burdened you with my catalog of lost siblings."

"It is no burden, General. I know the anguish. I do not regret when circumstance calls on me to remember her."

"Yes. Well, then, please sit, and tell me about your sister."

I set the chair at the foot of the bed, so he could see me without turning his head.

"We did not have much time together. She was not yet a year old when a throat distemper took her."

"The coughing . . ."

"Yes." We both knew the hollow, constricted sound. "I remember her, though not as clearly as I wish. But I can still see her face."

"That is good," he said.

"There was a time," I told him, "in my childhood, when I became timid and fearful. I cried more often than a young boy should. I think there was only one remedy to this affliction: my mother would place my sister in my lap, for me to hold. You would think that my tears would set her to crying, she being just an infant child—but she never did. She looked at me with such curiosity, I guess . . . but it wasn't just that; she seemed to know that our fates were bound together, and from her gentle eyes I understood that I needed to be stronger than I was.

"What was her name?" the general asked.

"Mercy."

He repeated it: "Mercy."

"One day I was holding her. It was winter, and cold, but there was a fire going, and she was all wrapped up. She coughed: it must have been an unusual, deep cough. My mother grabbed her from me, and took her to the other room. She coughed for two days, and that was all."

"In Norwichtown, at the burial ground, there are almost as many children as there are old men and women," the general said.

"Some of them have the name Arnold," I replied.

"Yes," he said. "Yes, they do."

We sat quietly. General Arnold gathered his thoughts.

"Absalom was three and a half when he died; some malady— I don't know what. I was seven. It seems to me that I recall every minute of his life. Before his birth I had two sisters, Hannah and Mary; the arrival of a brother was the gift of a lifetime. I remember first seeing him, and thinking how small and frail he was. I had expected a more capable playmate. When he was taken from us, he was old enough to talk, to really chatter. He called me Benny."

Arnold reached for the water glass on the small table beside his bed, and awkwardly bent his head forward to sip from it.

"My dear mother was a pious woman; she took to prayer. My father . . . he also grieved. As did we all."

He set his glass on the table. I refilled it from a pitcher.

"My father was a merchant; we lived in a fine house. When I was eleven years old, they sent me to school with Dr. Cogswell, in Canterbury—half a day on a good horse. I read Greek and Latin. I read the great work of Cornelius Nepos, *The Lives of Eminent Commanders*."

The general looked at me. "No surprise that it was my favorite, I suppose."

"No, sir," I responded.

"I was a studious boy at Cogswell's school, and well disciplined. I thought I would eventually be a student at Yale College. My father wanted that, I know."

I told him that I was a student at Yale for one year.

"One year?" he asked.

"My mother took ill," I replied.

"Tell me."

"Yes, but another time," I said. "Please continue."

A fly buzzed near the general's face; he waved his hand to brush it away.

"I was saying goodbye, about to begin my second term at Cogswell's. My father carried my trunk of clothing to the carriage. I was twelve, which would make Hannah ten . . ." He thought for a moment: "Mary eight, and Elizabeth about three and a half."

He glanced at the window. There was little to look at in the room, but he moved his eyes about frequently.

"I still see them, Gideon. Hannah was already trying to be a young lady; she had a silk bow in her hair. Mother was reminding me to pay close attention to my studies, and Hannah smiled at me. She handed me a parting gift, a packet with sheets of paper, and said she would like many letters from me. Mary called my name and asked if I would be back home in time for dinner. Mother picked up Elizabeth, and as the carriage pulled away the sweet child waved to me, and then they all waved goodbye to me."

The general rested for a few moments, closing his eyes and letting his head sink against the pillow.

"In the late summer my mother sent me letters. A distemper had come upriver. She said the deaths were multiplied throughout the town, and more were expected daily. She told me that my sisters were still in the land of the living—that Elizabeth was well, that Mary was ill but revived, but Hannah was growing weaker and weaker."

Arnold turned his head and looked at me. "Mother always told me to make the Lord my dwelling place. Now she was emphatic that

I must not neglect my precious soul, for once lost, it cannot be regained; that God was saying to all, even children, be ready."

With his finger he lightly tapped on the wooden box that held his leg firm.

"And even as she admonished me about our uncertain stay in this world, she sent me a pound of chocolate."

"A mother who loved her son," I said.

"Yes, she did, she truly did," said Arnold. "Then came the middle of September; we had ceased our studies for the noontime meal. Dr. Cogswell took me into his study, and held up a letter. Your sister Mary has been taken by the Lord, he told me. But I was not to go home: I was to stay in Canterbury until the distemper passed. Mother wrote to me—I repeated it to myself again and again: *My dear, I should send for you to ye funeral, but ye contagion is such I am afraid. But I must exhort you to prepare for death yourself. Beg of God to sanctify this death to your awakening; how soon sickness and death may meet you, you nor I don't know. Prepare to meet your God before your feet stumble on ye dark mountains.*"

The fly bothered the general about his face again. He closed his eyes patiently; it flew to the windowpane and became silent.

"I did not want to pester Cogswell, but nearly every day I asked him if he had news whether the fever had passed, and if I could go home. No, he told me, and he bade me take solace in my studies. A few weeks after Mary died, he sat me down in his parlor, and told me that Elizabeth had died. That is when grief truly took hold of me, for both of my lost sisters. A grief that made me wail and shiver. Grief, and a new fear of God."

"A new fear of God?"

"That God could not be trusted."

"Did you go home then?"

"No. I stayed with Cogswell for two or three more weeks. Then one afternoon, my father arrived by carriage. He walked up the stone path toward me, but at first I did not recognize him. He had become thin, and tentative, not the steadfast man I knew, and his eyes—eyes that had always been wellsprings of curiosity and wit—they were gray and sunken in his head."

The fly again buzzed over Arnold, but he ignored it.

"That afternoon we went home."

13

I wrote a letter to Arnold's sister Hannah, as Arnold dictated it to me—full of reassurances that his injury, while serious, would heal in good time, and that he would see her again before resuming his part in the war. Then he told me about his "dear innocent prattlers": his three young sons. The oldest, "Little Ben," was nine years old. He requested that I go around town to find candies and small playthings to send to them, with the letter to Hannah.

Hannah was raising his children. Two years earlier, on his return from Ticonderoga and the Champlain region, he had been passing through Albany—the town where he now lay on his back—and was only a few days' travel from home when word came that his wife, not yet thirty years old, was dead. Hastening to New Haven, he arrived to find his father-in-law also dead—shocked, no doubt, by the loss of his daughter. Knowing the grief that consumed his boys, Arnold wrapped them in his embrace, and turned to the warm-hearted aid of his sister Hannah. She was a prayerful woman, who asked the Lord to give her brother the health, strength, fortitude, and valor for whatever task he might undertake. If he were called again to battle, Hannah told him, "may the God of Armies cover your head." With Hannah's blessing, along with her willingness to raise the children in his absence and attend to his mercantile affairs, Arnold had returned once again to Massachusetts, where he met the Continental Army's commander, General Washington.

From there it was to Quebec, then eventually to the battlefields at Saratoga, and now, a sickbed in Albany.

While Arnold slept in the afternoon, I visited the shops down the hill from the hospital, and bought sugar candies for Arnold's children, and three wooden spinning tops that were painted bright colors. When I returned to the wards I found a commotion: a young soldier from Marshall's Regiment, who had lost both a leg and an arm to grapeshot, had obtained a hunting knife from his goatskin knapsack, and with it cut his own throat.

When I entered Arnold's room, he asked about the tumult in the hallways. He grimaced when I told him, and closed his eyes. After a while he asked for water, and again we talked.

"After my sisters Mary and Elizabeth were taken," he told me, "I was an apprentice for an apothecary. One night, my father insisted that I procure for him a vial of arsenic, with which I assumed he was to end his life."

"What possessed him?" I asked.

"Drunkenness," he answered. "I refused him the poison, of course. But I have wondered about the value of a man when he has lost all utility."

I made certain not to look at Arnold's leg.

"But he was a merchant—was he not?—and his business was profitable."

"He was," Arnold said. "But his grief was too much: the loss of his children drove him to the bottle, which, in turn, lost him everything. Business was neglected, and our money dwindled. In time, I could no longer go to Cogswell's school, and became an apprentice. We had gone about our lives proudly, as respectable citizens, in good clothing and shoes; but in time all we had left were threadbare clothes, and we cobbled our own shoes to hold them together."

"Your mother, too, must have been tormented."

"My dear, pious mother." Arnold breathed in deeply, and slowly exhaled. "My poor, prayerful mother. For each year of my life, until my fourteenth year, my father had paid eighteen pounds for us to sit in a box pew at the center of the church; we had to give that up, and sit in the long pews; and when that was too much, we stood in the back of the church, with the poor."

"Were you angry at your father?"

"I pitied him, Gideon. One should not have to pity one's father."

"He was, in his heart, a good man," I offered.

Arnold looked straight up at the ceiling, and considered what I had said.

"He carried with him, always, a small leather pouch. In it was a lock of hair from each of his lost children. There was a fair lock, almost blond, from little Benedict, who had come before me; a light brown lock from Absalom; and darker brown locks from Mary and Elizabeth. On the leather he had inked four words in Latin, from the poet Horace."

Arnold closed his eyes: "Non sum qualis eram."

I thought for a moment. "I am not what I once was," I said, recognizing the phrase.

"One night—one of many nights—he did not come home from the taverns, and Mother sent me to get him. I did not find him at Leffingwell's, so I walked toward Peck's, on the town green. I found him sitting on the roadside, drunk and dirtied. His shirt was torn. A gang of young men had pushed him to the ground and taken turns kicking him. He was sobbing because they had stolen his leather pouch."

Arnold drummed his fingers on the wooden box that held his leg firm.

"They looked for coins in the pouch. They emptied it in front of him, shaking it upside down in the wind. They kept the pouch and left him, and he crawled on the ground, in the darkness, trying to find the locks of hair."

His fingers stopped drumming.

"That was the night he asked for the arsenic."

A moment later I heard, from the hallway, the heavy footsteps of two men walking in unison, and I knew they carried a stretcher that held the body of the soldier from Marshall's Regiment. Then, without aforethought, I ended a lifetime of silence.

"When I was very young," I said, "not yet the age of five, I strayed from the house and walked down a road into the woods. There was a man standing on a wagon, who did not see me, so I walked closer, and saw him put a rope around his neck. Then he noticed me and said—I remember it so clearly—he said something I did not understand at the time, then told me to leave. I started toward home, but I knew—even though I was just a child—I knew he was in despair. So I went back, but it was too late."

Arnold turned his head and looked at me. "What did he say to you?" he asked.

I did not answer.

Arnold broke the silence. "Was he your father?"

"He was."

The general reached from his bedside and gripped my hand. Then he folded both his arms across his chest and turned his wide eyes again toward the ceiling. I sat and looked across the room at the window, through which I saw nothing but gray clouds.

14

For the next several months, as the cold air and long nights of winter came and went; as the bones in his leg gradually, imperfectly fused; as his health wavered, then recovered; as Benedict Arnold slowly overcame despair and grappled with his vexations—he and I left little of life unexamined. The small room with whitewashed walls and a lone window, a chamber meant for the endurance of suffering, became for us a kind of philosopher's parlor.

We spoke at greater length of the sad demise of Arnold's father, the Captain, as he was known. Affronted by their chronically drunk parishioner, members of the First Church had demanded the appearance of Captain Arnold at the meetinghouse, so they could admonish him for his sinful behavior. Defiant, the Captain declined. A committee of church leaders went to his house, but obtained nothing more than the Captain's refusal to ask forgiveness or make a public confession. The full church voted to deny him communion, and fretted about their wayward neighbor until the problem reached a natural solution with the Captain's death a year later.

As much as his father's humiliation scarred Arnold, he held on to a reserve of pride and affection for the Captain, and admiration for his business success before everything had been lost. Arnold told me of his own mercantile pursuits before the war. He told me about his years as an apprentice, and of his first business venture—a shop in New Haven, where he hung a sign that read *B. Arnold, Druggist and Bookseller*, followed by the Latin phrase *Sibi Totique*, which he happily translated for his customers: For Himself and for Everyone. He described how he had wanted to be a merchant-trader, and perhaps someday a sea captain, and told stories of how he courted his wife with letters during the voyages he had taken to the West Indies and along the Canadian coast.

We talked of his mother, and mine. I told him of my mother's indomitable spirit and strength, of how she raised me to honorable manhood, and obtained for me a fine education. Arnold's mother died from disease when he was eighteen. My mother took ill when I was eighteen also; I told him of our last months together, as a cancer in her stomach sapped her strength, but not her spirit.

He talked often of his sister Hannah, and of his three children, Benedict, Richard, and Henry, and I saw how desperate he was to be in their company again. The last time he saw them, they had played a game of tag on the New Haven green that made the boys shout with laughter, even more so when Arnold was on his back in the grass, with his three young boys piled on top of him.

Nearly every day, and on some days for hours, we talked about the war, its challenges, and strategies for defeating the British. He told me about Ticonderoga and Lake Champlain, the long difficult march to Quebec, and the battles at Saratoga. I told him about Henry Taggart, and the story of Taggart's illness in Canada and Arnold's gracious and unexpected assistance, and how Taggart later carried the wounded Arnold in Quebec. I saw how this moved Arnold, and told him of Taggart's devotion, and how he would have given his own life to protect the general. This caused Arnold to become animated, and he asked to see Taggart right away. But then he hesitated, realizing that a soldier who had seen him on the battlefield would hardly recognize him now. I explained that it was moot, that Taggart had gone home.

I asked many questions about General Washington, for whom Arnold had great admiration. He described our commander in chief to me: unusually tall, a full six feet and well proportioned; a straight nose, and eyes inclined to blue. Washington kept his hair in a queue, turned back from his forehead and powdered. His uniform, as Arnold described it, was a blue coat, with two brilliant epaulettes, buff-colored waistcoat and breeches, and a cocked hat with a black cockade. He brimmed with intelligence and dignity, Arnold said, and treated his officers fairly. "He has supported me in military affairs more than any other, and his esteem means much to me," Arnold said. I told him that I hoped to meet General Washington someday.

He was fond of General Schuyler, and still grieved the loss of Montgomery in Quebec. Ethan Allen of the New Hampshire Grants was a capable woodsman, but a "stubborn ass" whose first interest was not the republic. Gates was too hesitant on the battlefield, and played politics "the way a cheat plays whist." Arnold had met Dr. Franklin in Montreal, where Franklin had traveled on a diplomatic mission and to procure food and supplies for the American army. When the Canadians refused to accept American currency, Franklin lent Arnold £346 in gold, from his own pocket, to purchase necessities. "Franklin understands the war better than many of our generals," Arnold told me.

Arnold was a man for whom action was the blood of life. *Post equitem sedet atra cura*, he recalled from the ancient poets—"Behind the horseman sits dark care." Irresolution and passivity, he said, were the breeding ground for anxiety, self-doubt, and failure. During his months in the hospital, with his leg confined in a rigid fracture box, he was immobile. Dark care caught up with him and wore on his spirit like a grindstone. At times he railed against his mother's unforgiving God; he would question her belief and decry an arbitrary Providence, devoid of goodwill. After these tirades he would become sullen and quiet, often for hours, sometimes for days. He quickly grew agitated as he ridiculed the imperial tyranny of the king, and became at those moments keenly aware of the chains of circumstance that bound him to this hospital bed. But of all the torments that besieged him, it surprised me that his doubts about the new republic upset him the most.

"This country," he said, setting up a question. "We are sure to succeed in a cause so manifestly just, if we are virtuous. Do you believe that, Gideon?"

I thought, and answered, "I do."

He countered, bitterly, "I question whether a foundation built of virtue will support the gluttonous weight of the Continental Congress."

Having seen the effect this subject had on Arnold—his quickened breath and gnashing of teeth, followed by hours of agitation and heightened discomfort—I diverted his thoughts to calmer topics. As needful as he was to prove his honor—a practice of mutual benefit, to both him and his country—so, too, was he mindful of offense. He had proved his merit, again and again, but had received little support, and few of the accolades he deserved. Congress had repeatedly scanted his military attainments; its members had humiliated him by denying him due rank and military seniority. The great leaders of Congress who, a year and a half earlier, had debated independence and set the course of a new nation were now engaged elsewhere in war and diplomacy. Without the regular attention of these statesmen, he argued, our democratic chamber was in the hands of inferior men, whose motivations were rooted less in the lofty principles of revolution than in the petty political stratagems that advanced their own self-interests.

"Where is the virtue in this virtuous republic," he would ask, "but on the battlefield, and in these hospital wards?"

In affairs of the heart, too, Arnold was troubled. He told me of a young woman in Boston, named Betsy, whom he had courted to no good effect, and doubted that he would fare any better in the days ahead, deprived of his due fame and crooked in posture, as he now knew that his leg had mended unevenly.

Though he was dispirited more often than not, and could not clearly conceive of how his broken and weakened body could conform to his ambitions, there was some durable force within him that persisted, and against the odds he healed.

15

During the first week of January, three months after his leg was shot and shattered and he was pulled from under his dying horse, Benedict Arnold stood up from his bed for the first time, with Dr. Thacher and me beside him. He had weathered fever and gout, and escaped the mortification of his flesh. In time—a few more months, perhaps—he would walk again, but his leg was bent and shortened by nearly two inches. Dr. Potts assured him that a shoe could be made to make up the difference, but the disfigurement of the bone would likely render his cadence unnatural.

Sitting up, Arnold could write letters on a lap desk, which he did prodigiously. Sensing my own weariness after so long a sojourn in the hospital, Dr. Thacher asked what plans I had for the months ahead.

"Home to New Hampshire," I told him. "Perhaps to rejoin the army. But I will not be a young man forever, and a good wife and family would suit me as well."

"I think you should go home and pursue that end," Thacher said. We had dinner together that night, and a cup of rum.

I told Arnold that I would soon be leaving the hospital to rejoin the militia.

"That is my loss, Gideon," he said. "But I told Dr. Thacher that you should not stay in these wards and wither away on my behalf. I am glad for you."

The general beckoned me to his bedside where he was sitting, his back propped against a stack of pillows, his leg no longer confined by the fracture box.

"You have been a good, kind friend to me," he said, gripping my hand.

When first I saw him, Major General Benedict Arnold was a leader of uncommon bravery, a genius of war, and a paragon of virtue and noble honor. Now, months later, he called me his friend, and I knew him to be an ordinary man, but one with greatness in his heart.

On the day I took my leave, General Arnold looked me in the eye and smiled broadly—a rare thing for him. He bade me farewell with a final thought:

"I will eagerly await the day when our paths shall cross again."

PART 2

New York City

October–December 1780

My instructions are ready, in which you will find my express orders that Arnold is not to be hurt; but that he be permitted to escape if to be prevented only by killing him, as his public punishment is the sole object in view.

GENERAL GEORGE WASHINGTON to MAJOR HENRY LEE,

October 1780

1

Every fighting man sees his reflection in the face of his enemy, in the opposing soldier who takes aim at him, and the closer we are, the more clearly we see it. There are soldiers who load, reload, and re-load again without firing a shot. They are desperate to do their duty, and I have hollered at these boys, and brandished my bayonet as a threat, but they see their own likeness marching toward them, and cannot do the killing. I have fired plenty at the advancing line, but there are many of us shooting and the musket fire comes in bursts from many directions, leaving no certainty that a shot has hit its mark. Still, I know I have done my share of the killing. I saw how they fell, but try not to think of it. The redcoat at Freeman's farm charged with his bayonet, coming fast at my chest. I fired and ran past him, and did not look to see him dead, but I saw his eyes before I killed him, and see them still.

I stood in a dimly lit room. It was nearly midnight on the twenti-eth day of October, and the sentries and pickets were awake, bundled against a cold mist. Major Henry Lee read a folded letter in the light of a single candle, bending the page toward the light and leaning his face close to it.

"Do not assassinate him," he said.

He raised his eyes to meet mine, and I saw in them a reflection of the flame. The third man in the room stood beyond the arc of the light, but I could tell that he was tall and strong, and sensed he would not flinch from this business; and I hoped that I would not flinch.

The letter was Washington's official order: to abduct Arnold and deliver him alive, to be tried by a military court and hanged for treason. But what if all the uncertainty of this mission came down to a single moment of decision, of life or death? By morning I would be a spy, as deep into it as any man could get, pretending to be a defector to the British army. I would be surrounded by those who would have my life, as Arnold would, once he understood that I was his enemy.

A soldier drills in the field, again and again, so the chaos when it comes will not scuttle his actions. If he wants to live, he must also practice alone in the quiet hours, for there will be chaos, too, in this thoughts. Thus, I struggled to see Arnold, in a bright scarlet coat with blue facings and gold buttons; to see him at the moment he recognized I was there to kidnap him, to do him harm, at the moment when decisions would be made. If the moment of surprise was flawed and he drew his sword, I would have the smallest fraction of time to disarm him, or to stab him with a knife. I had to foresee his expression, and how to gauge him; to predict the surge of my step and the force with which I would press the blade into him; to feel the resistance of his waistcoat, and of his flesh and sinew and bone. I had to anticipate the struggle, and to envision how I would push him onto the ground, and that I would see into his eyes. And I had to be confident that I would not hesitate, and with the blade I would finish the work. I rehearsed this on the stage of my mind, but whether or not I could make it real, as I did with the redcoat at Freeman's farm, I could not yet convince myself.

"We will bring him to you alive," I said.

"We will, sir," said the man in the shadow. I turned toward him; his name was John Champe, and we had known each other for less than an hour.

We received the remainder of our instructions: desert to the British, join Arnold's corps, plan and execute his abduction. Major Lee extinguished the candle and we waited for our eyes to adjust to the darkness. Then Champe and I left quietly through a back door into the night and walked to where our horses were tied. Within minutes we would be deserters, riding through the night to the British army in New York, hoping our own brothers-in-arms would not hunt us down.

As we approached our horses, Champe stopped and looked at me.

"Do you think this will work?" he asked, in a near-whisper.

"I don't know," I answered. "Do you think we will even make it to New York?"

"I wouldn't bet on it," he said. "But I'm not a betting man—so what does it matter?"

2

Nearly a month earlier, doubt had surely troubled John André, too, during the two days he made his way on horseback to New York City, traveling south on the roads that paralleled the Hudson River. He had held his secret meeting with Major General Arnold on the west side of the river, near Stony Point, in the home of Mr. Joshua Smith. André had discreetly arrived the previous day on the British ship *Vulture*, but when the sloop received small cannon fire from Teller's Point while anchored downriver and waiting for André's return, it hastily retreated farther south without its most important passenger. Regardless, Arnold insisted that André leave and return to the British in New York by horseback, accompanied by Smith, a local lawyer and mercantile agent who was comfortable working in the shadows. Shedding his uniform and disguised in Smith's clothing, André played the role of a traveling merchant. Arnold gave André a written pass—bearing his signature, that of a major general—to advance him beyond American checkpoints and inquisitors, and trusted Smith to navigate a safe course through the miles of neutral ground between them and the British army, despite knowing the territory was infested with marauding partisans from both sides.

This nearly worked, but for the simplest error. Smith was well known in the neutral ground; his careful knowledge of the roads allowed him to avoid confrontations and his gregarious chatter

won over the few inquisitors who stood in their way. But following a long day of travel and a night spent in a hired room, Smith
rode with André through the early morning mist only a few miles
farther. At Pine's Bridge, over the Croton River, Smith decided to
return home, leaving André to finish the journey to New York City
alone, guided only by a hastily drawn map and an admonition to
avoid the post road. With only two more hours of travel ahead of
him, he would reach the British lines before noon, at which point
he would be safe. But when he slowed his horse to walk across a
small wooden bridge a half-mile north of Tarrytown, André was
stopped at gunpoint by three young militiamen who were absent
without leave from their unit.

Some officers said these fellows who captured André were heroes. Others, Major Tallmadge included, said they were lowbred,
plundering Skinners—marginal patriots who robbed from both
sides in the lawless region between the two armies. For this reason
they were summoned to testify before a board of inquiry not long
after the unfortunate André was hanged. The inquiry took place
when I was still in Tappan, a week before I set off on my feigned desertion with Champe. Tallmadge invited me to hear their testimony,
so I joined him in a pew in the same austere Dutch church where
André's trial had occurred.

Once they were sworn to tell the truth, the judge advocate asked
them to explain how they came upon André.

"We were hidden in the bushes," one of them answered, "very near
the road." While hiding they saw several persons known to them, and
let them pass. Then the tallest of the three men spotted a stranger,
coming toward them on horseback.

"Here comes a gentleman," he said to the others. "Well dressed . . .
Fine boots. Step out and stop him!"

The leader of the group testified that he blocked the horse in the
middle of the road, pointed his musket at the chest of the traveler, and
told him to keep still.

"Which way are you going?" he demanded of the traveler.

"Gentlemen," came the good-natured reply, "I hope you belong to our party."

"What party is that?" he was asked in return.

"The Lower Party," he answered, meaning the British—the army to the south.

The militiaman replied, untruthfully, that he was also of the Lower Party, and the nervous traveler, thus assured, revealed himself.

"I am a British officer out of our territory on particular business, and I hope you will not detain me a minute." He pulled from his pocket his ornate gold watch, of a type often carried by British officers.

The man-at-arms kept his aim on André and told him to get off his horse; that was when André perceived his mistake. He had told Tallmadge he realized, at that moment, that these were Skinners, the rapscallions who sided with the Americans.

With an actor's hearty laugh André corrected himself.

"My God," he said, according to the tall one. "I must do anything to get along." From a pocket he produced the pass from General Arnold, dismounted, and held it out for examination. Only the leader of the three men could read. He took the document and slowly read the order aloud to his fellows: *Permit Mr. John Anderson to pass the guards to the White Plains or below it as he chooses, he being on public business by my direction. B. Arnold, Major General.*

"Gentlemen," the traveler said, "you had best let me go, or you will bring yourselves into trouble, for your stopping me will deter the general's business." He explained that he was going to Dobb's Ferry to gain intelligence for General Arnold.

The militiamen demanded the traveler's name. He said it was John Anderson.

"We would have let him go," the leader explained, "but he had called himself a British officer, so we thought it proper to search him."

André told Tallmadge they had demanded his money, and searched him to look for it. But the militiamen denied this.

"We took him into the bushes," one testified, "and ordered him to pull off his clothes, which he did; but on searching him narrowly we could not find any sort of writings. We told him to pull off his boots, which he seemed indifferent about. We got one boot off and searched in that boot, but it was empty. Then we noticed something in the bottom of his stocking. We found three papers wrapped up next to his foot."

Another continued: "We looked at the papers, and knew he was a spy. We pulled off his other boot, and there we found three more papers at the bottom of his foot."

"We told him dress himself," the leader testified, "and I asked him what he would give us to let him go. He said he would give us money. I asked whether he would give us his horse, saddle, bridle, watch, and one hundred guineas. He told us he would, and he would send them to any spot we chose, even if it was that very spot, so we could get them."

"I asked if he would give us more," added another. "He said he would give us any quantity of dry goods, or any sum of money, and bring it to any place we picked."

But the leader of the trio had his own designs.

"No," he told the traveler. "You may give us ten thousand guineas, but you will not take one step."

The leader smiled at the judge advocate and paused for good effect.

"Then I asked the man, who called himself John Anderson, if he would get away if it was in his power. He said he would, and I told him that I did not intend it."

He surveyed the room for approval. Tallmadge, next to me, broke the silence with a disapproving grunt.

"We reckoned he was a spy," the militiaman continued, explaining that André's countenance changed after they made him prisoner, turning despondent as he walked, leading his horse, for two hours toward a military post. When first stopped he had been uncommonly affable and eager to please, but this diminished as they traveled, and the last words André said to them were these:

"I would to God you had blown my brains out when you stopped me."

3

To get to New York City and feign our desertion, Champe and I would need better luck than André. We would need Arnold's luck, which we learned had been plentiful.

At gunpoint, the militiamen escorted the man called John Anderson to the nearest military post, at North Castle, where Lieutenant Colonel Jameson was stationed with a regiment of dragoons. When Jameson examined the papers found in the prisoner's boot, he recognized the undisguised handwriting of General Arnold. The content of the papers, and the manner in which they were found, should have excited suspicion in even the most obtuse mind. But Jameson resolved—of all things!—to send the prisoner to Arnold. How vigorously the prisoner tried to persuade him cannot be doubted, for surely André wished to make an escape. If he had been turned over to Arnold at West Point before anyone else knew of his capture, they might both have fled down the Hudson to the British lines. Jameson penned a hasty letter to Arnold, saying merely that he was sending under guard a man named John Anderson, who had been taken while going to New York. "He had a pass," Jameson wrote, "signed in your name, and a parcel of papers taken from under his stockings, which seem unusual, if not dangerous." Jameson described the content of the papers to Arnold, adding that he would send them separately to General Washington.

When Major Tallmadge, next in command to Jameson, returned to camp and learned of the matter, he was immediately suspicious of Arnold. Jameson would not listen, refusing to sanction any measures that would imply distrust of the major general. Earnestly pleading for caution, Tallmadge at last persuaded Jameson to recall the prisoner, sending a courier to retrieve André. But Jameson insisted the letter to Arnold must still be delivered to West Point.

At this very moment, while Jameson's letter was being carried to Arnold, General Washington was traveling toward West Point from Hartford, with General Knox, the Marquis de Lafayette, and a small force of one hundred sixty men. Washington and the officers, all on horseback, arrived early in the day on the east bank of the Hudson River, across from West Point. The commander in chief was eager to inspect the garrison and visit with Arnold, hoping to see him regaining his military confidence and ardor.

Two and a half years earlier, in May of '78, less than three months after leaving the Albany hospital and ruefully besieged by his crippled leg, Arnold had traveled by carriage to the Continental Army's encampment at Valley Forge. Four men were needed to carry him into the Dewees house, next to headquarters. The ravages of war that had beset both generals since their last meeting had made the reunion joyful, solemn, and poignant. The commander in chief urged Arnold to postpone his return to the fight until fully healed, but Arnold was eager to return to service.

Finding a way to occupy Arnold until he recovered completely, Washington sent him to Philadelphia as military governor of the capital city, following the withdrawal of the British in June of 1778. Once there, still desiring the good company of a woman, Arnold courted Peggy Shippen, the much-admired daughter of a prominent merchant family, who yielded to his entreaties and became his second wife. He stayed in Philadelphia for two years until politics, financial scandal, and gossip unsettled him. In the midsummer of 1780, Washington planned to put Arnold again on the battlefield, but Arnold instead pressed for the command of West Point. To Washington, this was evidence that the warrior's confidence was broken, and so, with regret, Washington granted the request and sent Arnold up the Hudson River to the garrison at West Point.

Now, on this early morning, as Washington turned down a narrow road toward the waters of the Hudson, Lafayette reminded him that the young Mrs. Arnold expected them for breakfast at Beverly, a fine house across the river from the garrison, which lodged the West Point commander and was not far from the traveling officers.

"I know you young men all wish to be in the company of the delightful Mrs. Arnold as soon as possible," the general chided his officers. "Go and take your breakfast with her, and tell her not to wait for me."

Washington intended first to inspect the redoubts along the river, stating that he would join them at midday. The officers reconsidered, choosing to stay and assist Washington, but two of the aides-de-camp rode on at the general's request to inform the Arnolds of his delay.

The two young officers found breakfast waiting when they arrived at Beverly. Arnold sat down with his guests. As they finished their meal, the lieutenant sent by Colonel Jameson arrived with the letter revealing André's capture. Arnold opened it, undoubtedly expecting intelligence that the British army was moving upriver. The magnitude of his surprise can hardly be imagined. But skilled as he was at duplicity, he concealed his emotion as he explained to his guests that his presence was required at the fort across the river, and that he would soon return.

Knowing that Washington and his contingent of soldiers were nearby, with the damning documents perhaps already in the commander in chief's hands, Arnold hurried up the stairs to bid a hasty farewell to his young wife and infant child, then fled by horse to the dock, where he commanded six boatmen to row him downriver as rapidly as they could. Soon they came within sight of the *Vulture*, which had returned in search of Major André. The British sailors instead found the American major general, standing in a fast-approaching rowboat, waving a white handkerchief: a signal of truce as seen from the *Vulture*; a farewell as viewed from West Point; and in the eyes of Arnold himself, a cloth to wipe his brow, for he had just barely escaped the gallows.

4

Soon after he arrived in New York and was safely behind the British lines, Arnold unwittingly rendered assistance to our plot to capture him. He quickly issued a letter, addressed "To the Inhabitants of America," desperately justifying his betrayal. Then, as a newly minted brigadier general in the British army, Arnold published a "Proclamation to Officers and Soldiers of the Continental Army," calling on soldiers to desert their posts and emulate his treason—imploring them to enlist in a loyalist corps of infantry and cavalry under his leadership.

At the highest level of the American command, and under the firmest secrecy, it was decided that two men would accept that invitation. I was one; the other was John Champe, the sergeant major of Henry Lee's corps of dragoons. Lee, who was encamped in New Jersey some twenty-five miles from Manhattan Island, was brought into Washington's confidence, and Champe was Lee's pick for the mission. Only the few officers who first met in Tappan, in addition to Lee and Champe, knew of our efforts, although a small cabal of Washington's spies in New York would aid us, in ways we did not yet know.

That is how I came to be a spy; with the help of Providence, an abductor as well; and if it came to life or death, an assassin.

Taking leave of General Lee shortly after midnight, I walked with Champe in the dark shadows of the blacksmiths' tents, cautiously eyeing the dim light from the sentries' fires. The ground was wet from the evening's rain, and smoke from the fires drifted through the night air, with the moon, in its last quarter, mostly covered by long sinewy clouds. Tallmadge had made sure I had a strong horse when I left Tappan. Major Lee provided a muscular steed for Champe. Both horses were saddled and tied to a rail. As we approached they shook their heads and snorted, curious at this unusual hour. Whispering to my horse, I checked the girth on the saddle, then rubbed his neck firmly to calm him. Champe, too, was reckoning with his horse's restless curiosity. With a nod to each other we heaved ourselves into our saddles and pointed our horses to a field, away from the sentries, from which we could regain the road farther down. We lowered our reins and let the horses amble, finding their own step and pace. For a moment I trembled as I felt the cool night air wrap around my neck, and realized I was clenching my teeth.

Once on the road, well beyond the sight of the sentries, Champe spurred his steed and we galloped, making haste for several miles, until we saw a farmhouse ahead and a small village beyond it. Champe slowed to a walk and came beside me.

"We shouldn't run through here," he said. "I'd like to hurry, but the sound could excite an alarm."

It would take us the rest of the night and some of the early morning to reach the British garrison at Paulus Hook. We had more than twenty miles still to travel.

"How much of a lead can we count on?" I asked. Suspicion in the camp was palpable as rumors of treason and desertion spread, stirred by Arnold's betrayal and his published missives. It was possible, even likely, that our absence would be discovered before long, and a squad of some fifteen or more dragoons would thunder out of camp to chase us down, convinced that we were deserting to the enemy.

"An hour is my best guess," Champe said. "Major Lee can stall. He'll suggest we're outside the camp for some harmless reason. He'll have them double-check the tents, and dither over who will lead the squad. But he is a good commander, and inefficiencies are not his habit. He can stall, but not for long."

"If they are running and we are not, they will close the gap in no time."

"The village ahead is called Liberty Pole." Champe knew the vicinity well. "Beyond it is seven miles of forest, called the English Neighborhood."

He considered our options.

"Let's pass quietly through the village," he said. "When we get to the woods, we'll make all the thunder we can."

The British garrison we hoped to reach now seemed to be at the other end of the earth.

"Do we need to go as far as Paulus Hook?"

"Maybe not—not if we're in trouble," he assured me. "There are two roads leading there. At the far end of the English Neighborhood there is a hill. By the time we reach it the sun will be rising. We can look to see if we are followed."

"And if we are?"

"The road splits at the Three Pigeons Tavern. We'll call it then: one road or the other. If all hell is breaking loose we can go south toward Bergen, and see if we can find some damn British somewhere."

"Right. Find some British."

"Yes," he said. "Christ help us."

I trusted Major Lee to select a good companion for me, but now I was beginning to see for myself the virtues that Champe brought to this mission. Like Lee, Champe was a young man, and a Virginian. He was above the common size, all bone and muscle. Lee had told me his sergeant major possessed abundant courage and perseverance. Most importantly, he assured me, Champe was a man he would trust with his own life. In the shadow of Arnold's betrayal, when suspicion became the common currency, I knew trust of that kind was worth more than the king's silver.

It was not long before Champe and I rode into the village called Liberty Pole, a crossroads with a dozen buildings, all of them dark and silent. We trotted side by side past the buildings, eager to reach the cover of the woods. There was no more talking. Curtains of clouds made the night sky even darker as the moon set in the west. I felt a mist and drops of light rain.

As we passed through the crossroads Champe extended his arm, pointing his finger to direct my attention to the northern road at his left. The silhouettes of three horsemen occupied the road. They were far enough away that we could slip by; we'd be gone from their sight in a moment. As we passed, however, I turned my head to see one of the horsemen break from the others and ride toward us. Ahead were two more stone houses with fields beyond them, but in the distance I could see a dark mass that I knew was the forest.

"Halt!" the horseman shouted, his call muffled slightly by the distance and the rain. "Advance and be recognized!"

"Are you ready?" Champe asked, no longer concerned with being quiet.

No answer was necessary. Instantly we dug our spurs into the flanks of our steeds. I bridged the reins and arched forward, tight to the horse and following his reach, focusing intently on the road. Champe ran just ahead of me, to my left. After several minutes I looked quickly over my shoulder and saw one rider still pursuing us, but he was losing ground.

We galloped hard for nearly two miles, then slowed to let the horses rest. There was a stream not far off the road. We stopped among the trees so the horses could drink.

"Militiamen," Champe said. "Our pickets."

"I suspect they went to the camp for fresh horses, and to rally a squad of our dragoons," I said.

Champe agreed. "I am sure of it."

Our rest was brief. We let the horses trot, taking advantage of the forest and knowing that once through it, we would be among villages and towns, more mounted patrols, and militiamen who would issue an alarm and pursue us—two disheveled galloping soldiers racing toward the British.

We rode to the south and east, and saw the first rays of light as we emerged from the forest. There was candlelight in the kitchen of the Three Pigeons Tavern, and a man collecting firewood in the dim light of early morning.

"Good day, sir," Champe called to him. "Is one of these roads ahead a quick way to Paulus Hook?"

The man took two steps toward us, then stopped.

"Go to the right. That road goes around the west side of Bergen village to the bridge at Prior's Mill, then on to Paulus Hook.

"I'm told there is a shortcut to the bridge. Do you know it?"

He thought for a moment, then nodded.

"There is one. Take the left fork toward Bergen," he said, pointing. "But a mile up, look for a sandy road on the left that skirts the salt marshes. It loops around the east side of the village. It will take you to the bridge, and from there to Paulus Hook. Not much of a road, but two men on horseback—it might save you some time."

We made haste along the road to the left, which would take us toward Bergen, and the shortcut to Paulus Hook. The road was flanked by salt marshes on both sides for nearly a mile. The sun was up, casting long shadows, and the smell of tidal salt and mud was strong.

"Keep a keen eye out for the shortcut road," I called to Champe.

"Don't worry," he answered. "I know it well."

Champe led us directly to it, hardly more than a path, easily overlooked amid tall marsh grasses and clumps of brush. Before turning we looked to the hills behind us. On a rise above the Three Pigeons Tavern, at the edge of the woods, were a dozen or more mounted dragoons. The silvery hilts of their swords, sheathed in scabbards alongside their saddles, and the buckles and buttons of their blue and white uniforms reflected the rising sun and infused them with a visible energy that I felt waning in myself. They were surveying the plain. One broke from the pack and led the others toward the Three Pigeons.

"They'll ask at the tavern about two early morning travelers," I said.

"If they talk with the woodcutter," Champe said, "they'll chase us on the shortcut."

"If not, they'll take the road to Paulus Hook."

"Or split up."

"Then we need to follow the only road left. To Bergen?" I asked.

"To Bergen," Champe said. I realized then that he knew the dragoons would ask questions at the tavern, and that our best chance was to ride straight through the village. By asking the woodcutter for directions, he had planted the seeds of deception.

We pushed our horses hard again, galloping on the sandy clay road, for now it was an all-out race.

As we neared Bergen, Champe pulled up on his reins and stopped in front of a barn, hiding himself in a long shadow.

"Look," he said. "Up over the marsh. They split up, just as we thought, and converged at the bridge."

"Do you think we're done with them?" I asked.

"Not at all," Champe said. "They know we're on the Bergen road now."

"Is there another way to Paulus Hook?"

He shook his head.

"Listen," Champe said. "Those dragoons will get close, and when they do they'll track my horse."

"How?" I asked.

"Our farrier uses a common mark, with a notch."

I looked on the road at the tracks made by our horses. They were well defined in the damp, sandy clay.

"They'll follow my tracks. Yours will blend in with others. If we need to, we'll split up."

We spurred the horses. Champe looked over his shoulder as his mount surged forward.

"Can you capture Arnold on your own?" he called to me, not expecting an answer.

We could dodge our pursuers for a few minutes in the grid of the village roads, which were pocked with enough hoofprints to make it difficult to track Champe's particular mark. But once through Bergen there were only two roads that went south toward the British garrison at Paulus Hook.

Champe knew the roads. We cantered past an oxcart loaded with barrels and followed a long stone wall to a row of wooden houses and storefronts. Casting my eyes left and right for militiamen and mounted patrols, I observed the morning habits of the village: storekeepers opening shops, a blacksmith stoking his fire, and somewhere the faint smell of bread baking.

"This way!" Champe called, cutting left into an alleyway between a tailor's shop and a stately white inn, where a group of men standing on the porch turned their heads toward us. We trotted through the alley, past the back doorways of houses and stores, then turned a sharp right into another narrow passage and past a brick wall. Across a grassy field and behind a fence was a stone building with barred windows, which I quickly surmised was a jail, to which I might soon be delivered, in shackles.

The horses were tired: foam sprayed from their mouths. Champe spurred his mount quickly past a burial ground and a simple white wooden church. Ahead were several carts and wagons that were stopped while their drivers conversed. We turned right to avoid them but Champe pulled up short: ahead of us several townspeople were talking with a mounted dragoon.

We spun around and went back toward the jail, then turned right down a muddy road past chicken coops and a pig barn. My horse shook his head in annoyance, demanding water, but I spurred him and insisted he run. I looked behind for the mounted dragoon and listened for the sounds of pursuit. Champe, twisting his head to peer in all directions, turned left again and spurred his horse to gallop for a hundred yards, then reined him to a sudden halt and shot to the right, past a house where a woman carrying a bucket stepped back quickly from the street.

"Up ahead," Champe called. "The southern pike." The way looked clear, and we gambled on a quick count that all the dragoons had followed us onto the streets of Bergen. We spurred the horses hard. The road became sandy as we passed between marshes and then up a crest.

Champe hauled on his reins; his horse kicked up muddy sand. I pulled low and hard to stop my horse, and saw the cause of Champe's skidding halt: ahead, hardly a quarter-mile, were eight dragoons at a standstill, waiting for us.

"Goddam it!" Champe hollered. He wheeled his horse around. I yanked the reins, pulling to one side; the horse sensed danger and kicked his hind legs hard into the dirt.

"I'd be proud of the sons of bitches," Champe said as he leaned forward and spurred his horse, "but today they want to kill *me*."

There was one other route to Paulus Hook. A road ran two miles south to Communipaw, a small hamlet on the upper bay. From there, a cart path followed the shoreline and the salt marshes north and east for a mile or two to Paulus Hook. We charged back toward Bergen and barely slowed to round the corner toward the bay. We galloped past farm wagons and riders who, seeing the state of our horses, surely recognized our desperation, even if they could not guess the cause. In the near distance we sighted the king's colors flying from the mast of a British frigate, patrolling the bay at the mouth of the Hudson.

Within minutes we reached Communipaw, riding past the row of houses that made up the hamlet. Champe pointed to the path that led up the shoreline to the British garrison. We looked back toward Bergen: three dragoons were closing in.

"We need to split up," Champe called out, nearly breathless. "You ride to Paulus Hook. You can make it. They'll follow me. I'm going to swim for the frigate."

"I'll see you in New York," I shouted.

I spurred my horse onto the shoreline path. Looking back for an instant I saw Champe leaning forward in his saddle, his legs pulled up tightly, pumping the reins and charging toward the water's edge.

I had a mile or two to go. My horse had little left to give. I drove my heels into his flank and shouted a sharp command. The four-beat gallop would need to last a few more minutes and I could present myself to the British garrison.

I called out as I neared a fisherman, speeding past him only to pull to a sudden halt, spin around, and reverse course, shouting commands at my bedeviled horse. Three more mounted dragoons were blocking this path, and snapped into action when they spotted the whirlwind of my retreat.

The dragoons following Champe would already be at the shore, chasing him into the water if they hadn't already captured him. Moments earlier I had noted a pathway through the tall reedy grass of the salt marshes that led toward the water. I searched keenly for it, found it, and turned to the sea, hoping the path would take me to the shoreline somewhere near the frigate. The horse persevered through the soft sand but violently shook its head, exhausted. I spurred it through a marsh and a foot of water, which it fought to drink, but I shouted, insisting we charge. Suddenly we were upon a narrow stretch of beach, smooth and wet at low tide. Farther down the shore I saw Champe running in the shallow water, stepping high and splashing, running toward the frigate in the mouth of the Hudson. The dragoons were riding onto the beach, slowed by the salt marshes but still charging toward him.

I could go no farther. I pulled to a halt within feet of the water's edge and jumped from the saddle. I tore off my coat and undid the buttons of my waistcoat with a vicious tug. Hopping on one foot, then the other, I pulled off my boots, all at once speaking the Lord's name in vain while beseeching Him to help me.

My dragoons came over the crest, spotted me, and charged onto the beach. I managed to say "good horse" and slapped him on the haunch. I bolted into the shallow surf, smacking the frigid water with my quick, high steps.

I trembled upon hearing a cascading blast of musket fire, and tensed with fearful expectation. Then, ahead of me and slightly downriver, a cloud of gray smoke hovered and dispersed off the rail of the frigate. The British had fired at the dragoons on the beach behind Champe, halting their chase and giving Champe cover. His arms flailed as he swam, and he was nearly to the ship.

Knee-deep and still running, I yelled as loudly as I could: "Over here!" As I dove into the bay I could see an officer on the ship pointing at me, and three of His Majesty's marines aiming their muskets toward the shore behind me.

5

I swam hard toward the frigate, but the current was strong and my shirttails and breeches were heavy in the water. It was three weeks into October, and the river was cold. I swam with urgency, recognizing that it might be impossible to get to the British ship, which was sailing upriver and passing me. The marines fired a volley over my head at the dragoons, and I assumed that finally put an end to their pursuit. But my muscles were cramping from the shock of the cold water, and the ship was moving faster than I could swim.

I lifted my head above the chop to check my direction and saw that a jolly boat, lowered from the frigate and propelled by four oarsmen, had reached Champe. Two British seamen pulled him over the gunwales. I forced my arms to draw me forward with a dozen strokes, then looked to the frigate: the officer was pointing at me—not as a target for his marines, but to direct the rowboat that now carried Champe. When the boat reached me, the two oarsmen on the starboard side raised their oars and I lifted my arms into the air. The clutch of a sailor brought a visceral relief, for I was a minute or two away from losing myself to the Hudson.

The recognition that I was sitting in a boat belonging to the Royal Navy quickly dispelled my relief. I shivered violently and was barely able to speak, which bought me some time to consider the position that Champe and I were in. The petty officer surprised me with a woolen blanket. Befitting a great navy, I thought.

"Are you a deserter from the Continental Army?" he asked me.

I nodded that I was.

"Can you climb a ladder?" he asked us both at once. We were coming in close to the frigate. "If not, we will haul you up in the boat."

"I can climb the ladder," Champe said.

"Yes, ladder, thank you," I added.

As the crew secured the boat to the hoist, an officer in a blue coat and several marines in familiar red and white uniforms looked down upon us. From the boat, the petty officer called up, "Deserters, sir."

I climbed first up the rope ladder, followed by Champe.

"We've been expecting you," the officer said. "I hope there will be more to come. Your General Arnold says there will be many."

My teeth resumed chattering, sounding in my head like a drumroll.

"These men will take you to warm up and change into dry clothing. Then we'll have some questions to ask."

"Thank you for getting us out of the water, sir," Champe said, as would a proper deserter. "I am much obliged."

Draped in wool blankets, our clothing dripping wet, we passed a cluster of marines and curious seamen who stared as we entered the forecastle of the ship, where a cast-iron stove warmed the crew quarters. Champe and I were directed to sit on the low benches near the stove, while the petty officer went to find us dry clothing. Two armed marines stood near the door.

For the first time since climbing onto the jolly boat I communicated with Champe, silently meeting his eyes with mine, and detecting a faint but assured nod of his head.

We changed into washed-out blue breeches, wool stockings, and checkered shirts like those worn by the seamen, as well as somewhat tattered blue woolen jackets and simple shoes, a sort of black leather slipper. A couple of seamen took away our waterlogged clothing. Soon a lieutenant entered the forecastle, gave us a self-important admonition about behavior and etiquette aboard a Royal Navy vessel, then took us, followed by the two marines, across the main deck to the captain's quarters. The captain greeted us hospitably and bade us sit down at a small table laden with documents and the remains of his meal. The lieutenant stood in the corner, while the two marines waited outside the door.

I shot Champe a look of relief; I was glad we were together for our first interview. "Tell me, gentlemen," the captain said. "What is the reason for your desertion?"

I spoke first. "The war has been caused by agitators and malcontents who fail to see the advantages—and honor—of our association with Great Britain and His Majesty the king."

Champe glanced at the scraps of food on the captain's plate. I continued.

"I wish to add that I fought with General Arnold at Saratoga, and I attended him after he was shot in the leg, during the months he was in the Albany hospital. Where he leads, I wish to follow."

The captain nodded, and looked to Champe.

"I know General Arnold only by reputation," Champe said. "But I am also disheartened by this war. I know Captain Wheatley as a friend, and I know his many virtues. I am willing to follow his lead."

The captain turned to me. "You are an officer?"

"Yes," I answered, "in the Third New Hampshire."

"And you, sir?" he said to Champe.

"Sergeant major, Fifth Regiment, First Continental Light Dragoons." I noticed Champe swallow, and I knew his discomfort was real, as was mine.

The captain paused for a moment, then asked, "Major Lee's command?"

The specificity of the captain's knowledge startled me. There was no room for error in our deception.

"Yes, sir," Champe replied.

"Major Lee and his cavalry gave us a great deal of trouble at Paulus Hook."

Champe's face was set in stone. Over a year ago, Lee had led his dragoons in a bold nighttime raid on the fort at Paulus Hook, taking more than one hundred fifty prisoners and disrupting British control of New Jersey. Champe was among the soldiers commended for valor in the battle.

"Regretfully, sir," Champe said.

"Regretfully," the captain repeated, drumming his fingers on the table. "Truly?" he asked, taking our measure.

"I brought with me my company orderly book," Champe informed the captain. "In the haversack." It was a testament to Champe's strength that he hadn't discarded it on the beach.

The captain looked at his lieutenant, who nodded. "Bring it to me," he told him. The lieutenant stepped outside the quarters and returned within a minute, holding a square book that was swollen with saturated pages.

"Yes, that is my company orderly book," Champe repeated. "It proves the failing morale of the Continental Army."

It was Lee's idea for the sergeant major to take the book as a prize for the British, to make his desertion more convincing. How it would demonstrate low spirits among the soldiers was unclear to me, although the waterlogged book was swollen and the pages would tear if pealed apart, which meant only Champe could say what it proved.

"See if the steward can dry that," the captain told the lieutenant. He returned his attention to Champe. "The morale of the troops is low?"

"Yes, sir," Champe answered.

"How so?"

"The winter encampment will take its toll. They fear another hard winter."

I weighed in. "Most say the war has gone on too long, with nothing to show for it."

The captain nodded his head.

"They want to get back to their families," Champe said.

"Should I expect more deserters?" the captain asked.

Champe and I exchanged glances.

"I am confident that more men would answer Arnold's call," I said, "but the commanders have doubled the sentries and pickets."

"It has nearly become a prison camp," Champe added.

I told the captain how we had left at midnight, evading the sentries, and set out for the British garrison at Paulus Hook; and how the dogged pursuit of the dragoons had cut us off and forced us to separate, and to swim for our lives.

"If we hadn't been patrolling the river, you would have been captured," the captain stated.

"Yes," Champe said. "We were outnumbered, and they were coming for us from every direction."

"What would they have done with you?"

"They would have hanged us," I answered. Champed nodded.

The captain explained that he would be docking in New York at day's end, and that we'd be held for questioning and given the opportunity to make a formal request for British protection. He instructed the lieutenant to take us to the galley and give us a meal.

"You are dismissed, gentlemen," he said. As we stood up and turned to leave the captain's quarters, I realized how tired I was, and how eager I was for the food.

"Wait."

Champe and I both turned to the captain, standing straight.

"You say you know Arnold well?"

I hesitated, feeling an onrush of fatigue and apprehension, not knowing what to say, not wanting to say anything.

"Do you? Isn't that what you told me?"

"I believe I know him as well as any man does," I answered.

"Why do you trust him?" the captain asked. "Why should *we* trust him?"

"I have seen General Arnold command an army like Caesar," I told the captain, "and charge across a battlefield like Hannibal."

"I grant you that," the captain said.

He waited for me to say more, and when I did not, he asked again:

"But why do you trust him now?"

"I trust General Arnold—"

The captain interrupted. "I knew Major André," he said. "I knew him well." For a moment he was silent. "Why should anyone trust a traitor, no matter whom he has betrayed?" A long silence followed his query.

"I am told it is hardest to navigate in a storm, sir," I answered, finding the words. "This war is a tempest. General Arnold has struggled to right his course."

"To right his course, you say . . . I am sure he is being generously compensated by the king."

"He left everything behind, and sacrificed his fortune."

"Then, you are telling me, Arnold acted out of virtue?"

"The war has turned things upside down," I replied. To some extent he was taunting me, but clearly the British, too, were trying to make sense of Arnold. "We are schooled to live by God's commandment not to kill," I said, "but the war comes, and we are admonished to kill in large numbers. There are perhaps two sides to virtue."

"As there are two faces to Arnold," the captain asserted. He looked knowingly at the lieutenant, and I suspected they would have saved André, and let the Americans take their revenge on Arnold.

"I cannot yet attest to his virtue," he said, "but I am convinced of yours. When we dock later today I will turn you over to the adjutant general. But for now, go and eat, gentlemen."

Crossing the deck, I saw, off the starboard side, a large ship in poor repair. Its rigging was disordered, and its braces, bowlines, and halyards had been removed. No cannons extended from the gunports; I squinted and saw that the ports were crosshatched by black iron bars, with the faces of men pressed against them. It was a prison ship. Golden sunlight from the east illuminated the captives, a light for which they seemed hungry. Upright in the glare, the masts from dozens of ships crowding the harbor cast long shadows on the water, crossing one another, climbing and arcing up the sides of other vessels, mimicking the web of black iron that imprisoned the men in the hold of the frigate.

Back in the forecastle, the steward gave us each a plate of food: a piece of pork, two biscuits, and a sweet boiled pudding he called dandyfunk. Champe and I sat near the warmth of the stove. Two marines still watched over us. We looked at each other a few times as we ate, but said nothing. There was little we could do but pray to God Almighty, and wait.

6

In the midafternoon the frigate crossed the brackish river and docked in New York. Word spread quickly that it brought ashore two defectors who had been chased by their own dragoons and had desperately swum toward the British vessel. We were treated respectfully and with more hospitality than I expected. Still, on our first night we were given bunks in a jail; we were not behind bars, but in a holding room of some kind. The British army oversaw the jail, and most of the personnel were redcoats, although some civilians came and went. If Champe or I crossed the threshold we could expect a bayonet at the chest.

Champe and I had occasion for some whispered colloquy. To assure ourselves, we reviewed the fictitious details of our friendship, and confirmed how we would communicate with each other, and our rebel contact in New York. In the dim unlit cell, the sound of the guards' footsteps on the wooden floorboards seemed to come from several directions. Champe was the first to sleep, and his deep rhythmic breathing at last lulled me to a fitful rest.

Sometime at night I awoke in the darkness; the faintest light from a lantern seeped beneath the closed door. Champe's breath had a hollow sound; from elsewhere I heard gurgling, snoring, and whistling, testifying to the population in other rooms. Down the hallway a chair slid along the floorboards and I heard steps, and waited for them to come toward our chamber, but they did not, and I could not tell their direction or destination. My own breathing was quick and quiet. I strained to hear every sound, and to clarify my identity, both fictitious and real. I reminded myself that worry was my enemy right now; I needed rest, so I turned my thoughts to home, and the young woman who waited for me, Catherine, whose mere existence, though faraway, often comforted me to sleep. The sounds seeping into the room diminished, and I relaxed my stare at the shadowy outline of the doorway. Then, in my half-sleep, I saw her, and heard her voice.

"Yes," Cate said, "I will."

I soothed my doubts and fears with a memory: I was home, after Saratoga and my long stay at the Albany hospital. I would return to the war in a month, but in that short time a long-simmering desire between us ignited into a flame. I had known Catherine since my youth, and now we wanted to spend all of our years together. We stood on the bank of the Nashua River, where a large pool of water lay calm and flat like mirrored glass. It was evening and fish were rising, and we watched for them, spotting their quick gulps and the gentle ripples that radiated outward across the surface.

I asked her if she would wait for me, until the war was done and I returned, and she said yes.

"How long do you think it will be?" she asked.

"I don't know."

She asked me to promise that I would do everything in my power to come home. She knew, she told me, that I was a dutiful man, and she believed I was a courageous man, and that I would shoulder my share of the burden. But when it was done, she said, I must hasten home. Gladly I made that promise, for there was nothing I desired more. Left unsaid was that some soldiers would never come home, yet we both knew that this one thing, this nearly unthinkable thing, could not be bargained away in even the most sincere commitment.

"Yes, I will," I said. I told her that every morning when I arose and first set eyes on the rising sun, I would fix my compass toward home and to her, and that all my days' efforts would be expended to bring that moment closer.

Often I thought of the future, of the triumph of return and the happy, respectable life that awaited us. I had not finished at Yale, for circumstance did not allow it, but I was a teacher. After the war I would run a school and, having fought nobly in the war, I would return to become an honorable husband.

In the dark chamber I heard a man cough, or so I thought. I raised my head quickly, alarmed, but heard again only the scattered commotion of snoring and wheezing from the other rooms. Champe slept silently now. I rolled in my bunk and turned toward the wall.

Eventually I slept, and my mind found comfort again in a familiar place. I was standing outside a house I knew. It was spring, and

I smelled the boxwood bushes and honeysuckle in the air. There was a young woman in the garden, kneeling as she tended the soil and planted seedlings. I waited for her, and when at last she came over I realized I was lying on the ground, on my back, craning my neck to look up at her.

"I have come home," I said to her, "but I have lost my legs."

I raised my two stumps inches off the ground to show her. They were wrapped in linen and the ends were encrusted in dried blood, which made them look like hoofs.

But then I stood up; my legs had returned. I felt a wave of relief and good feeling, and I reached for Cate's arm, for she had turned away toward the garden and could not see me. I made sounds, a few partly formed words that I struggled to emit, and when she turned and saw me she drew up her hands and pressed her palms to her eyes. I hurried and spoke more incomplete words, straining to tell her how a shard of canister shot had torn through my cheeks, tearing off my tongue and breaking apart my jaw. Soon the word noises became sobbing sounds, and they grew louder as I stood beside the garden, beseeching Cate to look at me, and they rang in my ears as if coming from someplace else.

I had awakened myself in the dark bunk, groaning as in my dream. I compelled myself to lie still and silent, and perceived that Champe was likely awake.

"I'm sorry," I whispered, not sure if he would hear me.

"I know," he whispered back. "We're in a strange place."

There were no signs of light anywhere. "Try to sleep again," Champe added.

I shivered and pulled my blanket around my neck, which exposed my feet to the cold; I drew my knees close and tried to sleep again, but sleep did not come. Eventually the sun rose and the guards came and gave us freedom in the yard, telling us there would be flour cakes and milk porridge. In the clarity of the morning light I focused my thoughts, resolving with all my strength of will to capture Benedict Arnold.

7

Later that morning a grenadier sergeant and two privates escorted Champe and me for several blocks to the British headquarters at number 1 Broad Way, which faced the Bowling Green. Some knew it as the Kennedy Mansion, which had housed General Washington and his staff early in the war, before the Battle of New York. Surely it was one of the finest houses in the city. Its grand entryway was topped by an elegant fanlight, above which, on the second floor, a large Palladian window adorned the façade like a monarch's crown. A rooftop platform and cupola capped the peak, from which the city and its surroundings must have been visible for miles in every direction.

We were taken inside to the long center hall and directed past British officers who spoke among themselves as they moved back and forth between rooms. I gave a sideways glance to the left and saw a large parlor, which contained a long table covered in maps, and perceived it to be the commander in chief's office. At the end of the center hall, past a grand staircase, a corridor led to the back of the house and several smaller rooms where we would be interrogated. Champe was escorted to one and I to another littered with mismatched chairs—an improvised meeting room. There I was introduced to Major Beckwith, the assistant adjutant general, whose knowledge of the American forces quickly revealed his mastery of British intelligence. If pressed on our acquaintance, I knew there were gaps in the story Champe and I would tell, since we had had little time to contrive anything more than generalities. But the major did not inquire beyond some perfunctory questions, and my account seemed to withstand his examination.

Instead, what most interested him was the morale of the Continental soldiers and their disposition toward the newly announced alliance with the French. His questions revealed that the naval captain's assessment of our honor was shared and accepted by the military staff onshore. I told him that the soldiers feared another brutal winter, and that already, with winter still a month or two away, rations were being given out irregularly. On some days, I told him, there were no rations at all. As for the French, I said, the soldiers were at best uninspired by these new allies, and at worst dissatisfied, even angry. Many of the older troops had learned the ways of war while fighting against the French, I told him, and that animus had not faded. I did not tell him, of course, how I had witnessed regimental commanders announcing the French alliance to their units, and heard the men raise cheers of "Huzzah!" for Washington and Lafayette.

"I would like to recommend to General Clinton," the major said, "that you be welcomed into the king's army. He cannot give you an officer's rank," he continued, "but I am certain he would grant you a respectable enlistment."

I was grateful for his consideration, I told him, but the risk of being captured and hanged by my former brothers-in-arms was substantial, and gave me pause. I would seek the counsel of General Arnold, I told him.

"Understood," he said. "But I am sure Arnold will want you for his legion; he will convince you."

The major excused himself and left me seated alone in the room. When he returned he stood with the grenadier sergeant who had been our escort to the British headquarters.

"General Clinton wishes to speak with you," he announced with fitting formality. As he spoke I heard footsteps coming down the corridor, and saw the sergeant straighten. I stood, not knowing what to expect, just as General Sir Henry Clinton, commander in chief of the British forces in America, came through the doorway.

General Washington's counterpart was not his equal in appearance. Sir Henry was the height of an average man, perhaps a bit shorter, and nothing about him was physically imposing. His uniform, not his presence, conveyed his command: his bright scarlet coat was adorned with chevrons and epaulettes, and blue facings turned back with gold embroidery and buttons. A red sash embellished his white waistcoat and breeches, and his shoes and their buckles were finely polished. Without formal introduction he looked me up and down, and with rapid diction made his inquiries.

"You are an officer?"

"Yes, sir, the Third New Hampshire."

"Where have you seen battle?"

"At Saratoga, Monmouth, and Newtown."

"Saratoga?"

"Yes. I was wounded there."

"How so?"

I pointed to the scar on my forehead.

"You have not been in the South?"

"No, sir."

"Only in the North?"

"Yes."

"In New York? Along the Hudson?"

"Yes, sir."

Sir Henry, I assessed, looked and spoke like a barrister, or a member of parliament.

"Please be seated," he said, extending his hand toward one of the chairs. He also sat down, as did Major Beckwith.

"Tell me," the general said, "did you witness . . ."

He paused.

"Did you come across Major André?"

"I did, sir. Once."

"His execution, I presume."

"Yes."

"You saw it?"

"I did, sir."

Beckwith looked at the general, but the general's eyes were fixed on me.

"Please tell me, how did he fare?"

"I was only one among some thousand or more, but I believe Major André left an impression on every person who set eyes on him."

"And what was that impression?"

"Of uncommon bravery, sir. If he knew fear, he did not show it."

"But how so? Why do you say this?"

I told him how André had walked to the gallows with dignity, cordially acknowledging the very men who had sealed his fate, as if wanting to assuage their fears for him. The general pressed me further, and I recounted how André tied the handkerchief across his own eyes and placed the noose around his own neck.

"Did he say anything?" the general asked.

"He reassured himself that the moment of dying would be only a momentary pang."

"Was Washington present?"

"I did not see him."

Sir Henry turned his eyes to the window, and for a moment it was quiet in the small room. Beckwith looked downward at the floor. I heard the mumble of conversation and activity that carried down the corridor from the busy center hall.

"It was a tragedy, sir," I said.

The general nodded.

"I understand you are acquainted with General Arnold?"

I told him how I had tended to Arnold at the Albany hospital.

"He will be glad to see you," he muttered, seeming distracted by other thoughts.

The general rose from his seat, and I immediately rose also.

"Shall we expect more deserters?" he asked.

"I believe so," I said.

At that, General Sir Henry Clinton took two steps to the doorway and left the room, Major Beckwith behind him. In a few moments the major returned.

"You are free to go about your business," he told me. "The sergeant will accompany you out. Speak with . . ." He hesitated, betraying a muted distaste. ". . . General Arnold. Speak with him, and should you wish to enlist in the British cause, he will arrange it." He handed me two guineas to help me get settled, for which I thanked him.

Seated on a bench in the center hall was Champe, who rose and walked with us out the main door. We descended the few steps to the walkway and onto the cobblestone street.

The sergeant handed Champe a sack that contained the clothes we were wearing during our swim in the Hudson. "Good luck, lads," he said as he turned toward the Bowling Green and walked briskly away from us in our handed-down naval outfits.

Tied to a buttonhole on my damp breeches was a small pouch—happily, not lost to the Hudson or a sailor's sticky fingers—which held three guineas given to me by Major Lee. He had thought to give us more but did not want plentiful coins to raise suspicions. Champe and I had two guineas each from Major Beckwith; together we now had seven. It was a start.

"Let's walk," I said, both of us knowing where we had to go next.

8

Heading north from the Bowling Green up Broad Way, I was surprised at how many soldiers we passed. The Foot Guards and Royal Regiments near the headquarters were expected, but we also passed grenadiers in tall bearskin caps, Highlanders in Scottish bonnets, and mustachioed Hessians. New York was fully garrisoned. Saying nothing as we walked, I knew Champe shared my discomfort at passing within inches of those we knew from fields of battle.

The population of soldiers thinned as we approached the burned-out shell of Trinity Church, one of many scorched ruins left from the fire that raced through the western quarter of the city four years earlier, soon after Washington abandoned New York in retreat. The character of the city had changed dramatically since my brief sojourn here before the war. From behind the church a stench—of garbage, fish guts, and smoke—rose from the wharfs, a stone's throw to the west.

At the edge of the churchyard, from a cavernous sugarhouse that now appeared to imprison men, I saw a dead cart rumble away, heavy with the bodies of those who had succumbed overnight. With a nod of my head I pointed us to the east, down King Street, but when we saw the French Church had been commandeered as a barracks, and near it the Provost's Prison, I turned us away from the gathered redcoats and turned again northward, up Nassau Street, where we passed a group of free black tradesmen carrying timbers and tools. At John Street we headed up Golden Hill, a neighborhood without prisons or barracks; here instead were the shops of milliners, dressmakers, wigmakers, and coach makers, scattered among the tidy houses of artisans and the Methodist Meeting House at the top of the modest rise. Some redcoats came and went as they did business, but they were few—and there was no outward reason to fear them, I reminded myself. The grassy green at the center of the neighborhood offered us a respite, and we sat, our backs against a large stone, as there were few trees to lean against.

We had much to talk about, yet we were mostly silent. After a few minutes' rest, I said to Champe:

"I am acquainted with Mrs. Latrobe, who sends you her compliments for the dress you made of Spitalfields silk."

He considered my words carefully, and said, "Yes, that's right."

We stood and walked down Golden Hill toward Beekman's Slip on the East River, and noted a dramatic change in the character of the city. Here were elegant mansions, painted in welcoming yellows, reds, blues, and greens, with long balconies overlooking the river, and abundant shade trees lining the street. Merchants of wealth and position lived here. Within eyesight were the many ships that accounted for some of their wealth, and the shops interspersed among the grand houses were the most fashionable in the city.

Once more we looked over our shoulders to make sure no loyalist escort was keeping an eye on us. Then Champe walked toward the waterfront, to wait for me near Beekman's Slip. I proceeded alone along a walk of cobblestones and crushed oyster shells, past a fine mansion and several well-appointed shops, to the address 23 Queen Street, a wide building of two stories, painted dark green, with a gracefully lettered sign beside the door that read *Hercules Mulligan, Tailor.*

Affixed to the glass of a window was a printed promotion of his stock, which included fine clothes of the most fashionable colors; gold and silver lace, with some half-laces for hats; gold and silver spangled buttons and loops; gold and silver treble French chain, tassels, vellum, and thread; rich gold and silver Brandenburgs; epaulettes for gentlemen of the army and militia; Irish linens; and silk breeches of every color. At the end of this detailed list was Mr. Mulligan's promise to outfit his patrons in a most elegant style. Through the window I saw two men working at a table, surrounded by bolts of cloth and stacks of folded fabric.

On entry, I was met by a boy who carefully held a yard of red silk. I asked him for the proprietor. Within a minute I was greeted by a sturdy Irishman of ruddy complexion and a wrinkled brow, whose eyes were fixed in a squint. He was well dressed, in a green-striped waistcoat, appearing to be more artisan than workman, befitting the elegance that was his trade.

"I am newly arrived in the city," I told him, "and have come without a wardrobe."

"I can help you there," he agreeably answered.

Then I repeated the sentence I was told by General Lee: "I am acquainted with Mrs. Latrobe, who sends you her compliments for the dress you made of Spitalfields silk."

Mulligan looked me over, and the furrows beside his eyes deepened.

"Was that the red dress?" he asked.

"No. I believe it was the blue and gold dress," I answered.

His eyes met mine. "Well, I am glad to hear it," he said. With a swoop of his hand he directed me to a room down the hallway where, he said, he might have some ready-made clothes for my physique. Once there, he closed the door behind us.

"I fear I may be arrested any moment," he began, quickly and in a low voice. "Arnold must know something of this operation, and surely he spoke of it with Clinton."

"Can you leave?" I asked him. "Cross the river, or ride north?"

Mulligan shrugged. "I know many in the British officer corps; that I have dressed them so well may be my salvation. Is there a chance you were followed?"

"No," I said. "I took precautions."

"Are you in this city alone, or with others?"

I told him about Champe, and briefly described our exploits as deserters.

"There is a man—we'll call him Mr. Baldwin—who will provide a rowboat for you to dispatch Arnold across the river to the New Jersey shore. I will see that he knows you are here. We were not confident that your . . ." He paused, searching; ". . . your *journey* would be successful."

Mr. Baldwin, he said, would get instructions to us.

"How?" I asked, eager to put pieces together.

"We'll find a way," he assured me, resting his hand on my shoulder. "It is like mending an old coat: there is always a way."

He stopped and listened. Several horses seemed to have halted in the street outside. When they resumed, and Mulligan heard the clatter of iron-shod hoofs trotting up Queen Street, he relaxed.

"Go to Mary Underhill's boardinghouse. Not far—just up Queen Street. She and her husband, Amos, are with us. They will give you lodging. Tell them I sent you, but tell them nothing else."

He opened a drawer and pushed aside spools of thread to seize a small leather packet of coins.

"This should replenish your empty pockets," he said, handing it to me.

He opened the door and we stepped into the hallway.

"Wait, wait," he said. "Stay right here."

Mulligan darted into a room across the hall. When he returned, he reached for my hand and placed in my palm a small sheathed dagger, not much longer than a man's finger.

"To hold in reserve," he gruffly whispered. "If things don't go right, cut the wicked bastard's throat."

Then Hercules Mulligan put his hand on my back and escorted me up the hallway to the door, saying loudly, and accentuating his Irish lilt, "Soon you'll be one of the best-dressed men in this fine city. I will see you again soon, my friend."

As I took my first step out the door, he leaned forward with a final word.

"Godspeed," he said.

Then, glancing up and down the street, he added, "Do not come back here."

9

Mary Underhill fed us bread and stew. Her husband, Amos, looked us over and offered any information about the city we might need. He strained to suppress his curiosity, and we offered little beyond small talk. That night I succumbed to a deep and dreamless sleep that even thoughts of Catherine could not pierce.

In the morning I determined to find Arnold, to pay him my respects, assess his circumstances, and devise a plan to abduct him with all due haste. I wanted to be done with this. Shortly after a quick breakfast of bread and cider I left Champe, who would reconnoiter the landing sites near the wharfs on the Hudson shoreline, and walked down Queen Street on my way to British headquarters by the Bowling Green. During our interrogation, Major Beckwith had told me that I would find Arnold at number 5 Broad Way, one of the elegant townhouses adjacent to Clinton's headquarters.

The early morning autumn sun spread shadows among the houses and shops. I heard the work at the nearby docks and thought of briefly turning left off Queen Street and down a narrow lane to

Rodman's Slip, one of the small rectangular inlets where ships tied up on the East River, where I could warm myself in the sun and watch the activity there. But when I spied a patrol of British regulars with two mounted officers of high rank turning onto Queen from Crown Street, I hastened a few steps to a big tree beside the lane. The redcoats marched in my direction, passing several houses until they reached the home and workplace of Hercules Mulligan, where they presented themselves with a loud knocking on the door. Keeping my distance, I tarried by the tree long enough to see a figure—Mulligan, I'm sure—taken into custody by a sergeant and presented to the mounted officers. A wagon drove up from Rodman's Slip, and as it crossed Queen Street I pressed myself beside it and blended into the traffic of seamen and merchants.

Mulligan was surely bound for the horrors of the Provost's Prison, or one of the decrepit sugarhouses crowded with captives, or the worst possibility, a wretched, fetid prison ship. I paced among the commerce at the docks and worked my way north to the old palisade, then circled back to the Underhills' boardinghouse and entered hurriedly. From the windowsill in the upstairs room, where I had left it, I pocketed the sheathed dagger Mulligan had given me, and resumed my mission anew.

There was a lingering chill to the air, but I thought little of it as I trekked across the city to the Bowling Green, where I paced back and forth across from the building that housed Arnold. It was natural, given our past acquaintance, that I would climb the steps and request to see him. I hesitated for some time, inhabiting my role as a deserter, observing the green, the buildings, all the comings and goings, and hearing a drummer beat the Adjutant's Call. The time kept by the drummer, swift and sharp, matched the percussion I felt beating in my neck. My hand touched the dagger in my pocket. It had been a mistake to bring it, I thought. I tried to quiet myself.

Across the green a door opened, and a general—a brigadier—stepped forward at the top of the steps, alone, in a fine scarlet coat, his cocked hat in one hand and a cane in the other. The gold buttons on the coat's dark blue facings reflected the morning sunlight, which illuminated them, and his epaulettes shimmered. He took a moment to survey the activity on Broad Way, and set his hat upon his head. With his free hand he gripped the balustrade, then tilted his body and lowered his other hand to set his cane firmly against the step below him. His torso twisted as he stepped down. He slid his hand an increment along the balustrade, pressed his cane against the next step below him, and descended another step. He winced as he repeated this movement, but hurried through it, until he stood at the bottom of the steps, where he straightened himself, his eyes again scanning the street, making a quick study of the people who passed near him.

He saw me approach, and I spoke as I drew near.

"General Arnold."

"Wheatley!" His face brightened.

"Sir, I . . ."

"I was told," he interjected, "last night, that you were here, that you arrived after a harrowing escape."

"Yes," I said. "Yes, well yes, I did."

"I am so glad to see you here," he said. "Will you join my American Legion? No—never mind that for now. Join me for dinner. Tonight. Join me for dinner tonight."

"Gladly, sir," I answered. "Many things have happened since we were last together."

"Many things, indeed," he said. "There is much to talk about."

He brushed his hand against the tangled tassels of the epaulette on his shoulder. He told me what hour to return, and excused himself for some business regarding his anticipated legion of American deserters.

"I am so very glad to see you, Wheatley."

Arnold walked away, toward British headquarters at the Kennedy Mansion. There was an unnatural twist in his left leg. He was trying not to hobble. When he stopped, as if he might turn around, I hurried in the other direction.

10

Arnold the warrior general, who had made his name on battlefields, I had seen only at a distance, sitting upright on his steed, inspiring the troops with optimistic passion and resolute courage, and surging forward toward the enemy with sword in hand. The Arnold I had known in the hospital was an invalid. He had spent every hour of three months lying on his back, his shattered leg in a fracture box. In the week before I left the wards he could sit up and carefully stand beside his bed, but the effort to lift himself revealed how emaciated his body had become: even his gaunt frame was too much for his weakened muscles to support. Now the man I spoke with beside the Bowling Green, who fussed with his new uniform, whose mincing steps betrayed his deformity, whom passers-by seemed to avoid—this was a different Arnold still, familiar but unknown to me.

Shortly before the dinner hour, I again approached Arnold's townhouse and made a quick study of it. It was a handsome house of three stories, with a three-bay façade and an imposing staircase leading to the door, adorned by an ornate fanlight. I climbed the steps and knocked. Presently, Benedict Arnold himself met me at the door, not in his uniform but dressed in blue breeches, a buff waistcoat, and a crimson coat. The warmth of his greeting was genuine. Walking with a silver-tipped cane, he directed me to the parlor, where a young woman in a yellow and green petticoat stood beside the bay window.

"Mr. Wheatley," Arnold said, avoiding any allusion to military status. "It is my pleasure to introduce you to Mrs. Arnold."

I suspect he was watching me to gauge my surprise, although I suppressed it as best I could. I bowed, and the fair young woman extended her hand. She was indeed young—perhaps twenty years of age—and any man would instantly acknowledge her feminine beauty. But when I met her eyes, face-to-face, I detected her fatigue. She seemed to harbor no suspicion, and appeared happy to accept me as a friend. Arnold quickly recounted their courtship and marriage in Philadelphia.

"I have heard about you, Mr. Wheatley," she said. "Without your kindness, Benedict might not have survived."

"True," Arnold said, looking at me. "You see I'm getting along, but I could be better still." He glanced at his cane. "Perhaps your good company will again have a curative effect."

Arnold nodded at his wife, and she excused herself momentarily.

"Peggy arrived here only a week ago," he told me. "It has not been easy for her, as you can imagine. I have been working ceaselessly on raising my regiment, and the officers' wives here—I will confide in you, Wheatley—have not given her the welcome I expected. Perhaps that will change. It has been hard on her."

Mrs. Arnold reentered the parlor, holding in her arms an infant, dressed in bright white linen and delicate lace. I suppressed neither my surprise nor my delight.

"This is Neddy," Arnold said. "Edward Shippen Arnold—who is not yet ten months old."

Mrs. Arnold's smile overwhelmed the fatigue that had furrowed her brow. She tickled her baby's chin. The child's blue eyes scouted the room, looking at the evening light passing through the window, at the brass chandelier that hung from the ceiling, at the stranger admiring him, and at last settling on his father, who brushed his cheek with a finger and passed his hand over the lace bonnet atop his head. Glancing sideways at this, I saw another facet of Arnold I had not known.

Mrs. Arnold excused herself, having already dined, to leave us to our conversation. Arnold poured two glasses of Madeira and we sat at a table in the adjoining room, where a servant brought a loaf of bread, a bowl of oysters, and baked cod.

Now it was time for business, and Arnold's first priority was justification. The wine loosened both his tongue and his temper. He spoke rapidly of the indignities he'd suffered in Philadelphia as the city's military governor, and of how he was tormented, and his reputation besmirched, by Joseph Reed, the scoundrel who lorded over the Pennsylvania Council. He'd been persecuted, he told me, because he expected efficiency from his soldiers; because he used public wagons to transport private business goods, for which he duly reimbursed the city, he insisted; because he wrote passes—a meager handful—for suspected loyalists, purely out of compassion, he said. Indeed I was astonished to hear that the council had filed charges of corruption against him, alleging financial misconduct and abuse of power. Arnold had demanded of Washington an immediate court-martial to clear his name. His face reddened as he rapidly recited his defense.

"I have made every sacrifice of fortune and blood," he continued, rising to his closing argument, his hand trembling and his face taut. "I spent years away from my family," he said, leaning toward me across the table, tapping his finger on the wooden surface to emphasize each word. "At any point I could have walked away, gone back to Connecticut to raise my three boys to honorable manhood. I could have cared for their mother. I could have tended to my business and given my family the benefits of prosperity."

He extended an arm, fist clenched and angled, as if pointing his sword and leading the charge.

"Instead, I heeded the call to war—as you did, Wheatley—and left my family behind. I sacrificed my personal fortune. I fought on the battlefield as courageously as any man for this cause. And for what?"

With his fingertips he wiped a corner of his eye.

"I have become a cripple in the service of my country." He glanced down at his misshapen leg, which extended outward from his seat, oddly twisted and unusually bent at the knee. "I am a goddamn cripple!"

I thought to say something, but did not know what. It seemed that his audience was not just me, or hardly me at all. He was speaking to himself, and to the world.

"These small men, these puny tyrants, they tore at me, at my honor, my reputation, my good name—because of what was carried in a public wagon? They would deprive me of every shilling and insist on my financial ruin. And then they torment me for riding through the city in a carriage—like royalty, they say. But would they wish a cripple to mount a horse!"

He emptied his glass. The servant entered the room and poured more wine.

"There is no virtue in this revolution, Wheatley. It is chaos, from which only the licentious will truly benefit. We are trading one kind of tyranny for another."

For a moment he was silent. Above me I faintly heard an infant crying, and his young mother singing a lullaby that passed to us through the ceiling like a whisper.

"Posterity will judge us, Wheatley. Good men, bad men—they all die. But posterity will see the rectitude of what I've done."

Arnold paused, awaiting my affirmation.

"That is why I am here," I said.

We spoke deep into the evening, emptying a second bottle of Madeira, and perhaps a third. He inquired about André, and though I told him the only thing I knew was the scene at the gallows, that alone caused him anguish. He blamed Washington for André's death, castigating him as a scoundrel who flouts the conventions of warfare.

"He will probably lose the war," I suggested.

"Probably?" Arnold countered. "I am certain of it."

I anticipated that Arnold would inquire about Champe—his history, military service, and character—and that he would desire to recruit us both into his American Legion. He asked many questions about our daring desertion—our escape, he called it—and was both entertained and impressed by how we outran the company of dragoons. Like Sir Henry and the officers who interrogated us, Arnold, too, wanted to know about the morale of the soldiers, and whether they would heed his call to desert from the Continental Army to join his regiment. I fed his fantasy, telling him how hungry and ill-equipped the men were, how disillusioned by the new alliance with France, and that he should expect some of Washington's best men to join his band of loyalist Americans.

"I pray that you and Champe will be among the first to join my ranks," he said.

"That is our intention," I told him, grateful that I had rehearsed these words.

He explained—apologized—that he could not acquire for me an officer's commission, but that I would have the rank of sergeant, a noncommissioned officer in the British army. As a brigadier general, Arnold had plenty of British officers around him to assist with military planning and procedures, but he recalled the letters I'd written for him at the hospital in Albany, and insisted that I serve as his personal assistant charged with attending to his non-military letters and other communications.

With this settled—I would bring Champe to meet him the next day—I was eager to end our conversation and report to my brother-in-arms the magnificent trouble I had gotten us into. But Arnold became wistful, recounting scenes from the Albany hospital, especially those feverish discussions with Dr. Thacher in which he refused consent to amputate his leg. He confessed to me that he had doubted his decision at times, mostly at night, when the pain and fever and the inability to move seemed to suffocate him, as if he were on his back in a pond or a puddle, merely a foot deep, but deep enough for him to drown.

He tapped his shoe heel several times upon the floor. "It is not perfect, but at least it's still there," he said.

"It should go without saying that you are the most courageous man I have ever known," I replied.

As I emptied my wineglass, the general reconfirmed our planned meeting with Champe and the adjutant general, who would enlist us into Arnold's regiment. With that, we ended our long supper. When I opened the door to leave, Arnold said calmly, as if speaking to a confidant, "Trust me, Wheatley: we will be the victors, and there will be no stain upon our honor."

I walked down the steps and across the street, passing the redcoats of the night guard who surrounded the Bowling Green. Once in the shadows I hurried through the dark alleyways and avenues back to the Underhills' boardinghouse on Queen Street, where Champe was waiting for me. I repeated to myself, over and again, "There will be no stain upon our honor."

11

There were four components to our mission. The first—get to New York and convince the British that we were defectors—was done. Next, Champe and I had to observe Arnold, learn his habits, and assess the regular movements and activities of the soldiers around him. Once confident in this intelligence, and more familiar with the city itself, we would plan the moment to apprehend him. When we settled on our plan, we would need to communicate quickly to a third man called Baldwin, yet unknown to us, who would supply an ample rowboat and oarsmen. We would then abduct Arnold and speed across the Hudson to the New Jersey shore, where Major Lee's dragoons would meet us—with a friendlier disposition, I presumed—and spirit Arnold to Washington's headquarters, to be tried and hanged.

At sunrise Champe and I went downstairs for breakfast. I did not know if there were other boarders in the house, but we sat alone at the table. Mary Underhill served us queen's cake and cider. As we made small talk about the weather and the sounds from the docks, her husband, Amos, came in from outdoors. He moved a chair to join us at the table. Mary poured cider for him in a pewter mug, and left the room.

Amos made no small talk. "Mulligan is in the Bridewell prison," he said, quiet but firm, his eyes fixed on his silver-gray mug. "Major General Jones arrested him in person, took him from his house."

It was the scene I had witnessed the previous morning.

"Why?" I asked. "Why now?"

Amos leaned back in his chair and looked past us.

"Yea, mine own familiar friend, in whom I trusted, which did eat of my bread, hath lifted up his heel against me."

"Arnold," I said, recognizing the passage from the book of Psalms.

"Yes," Amos said. "Our Judas."

"Arnold knows names?" Champe asked.

"We are certain of it," Amos said.

I wanted desperately to know who, and how many, were included in this "we."

Mary came back into the room. Amos looked at her. She nodded at him, as if to say "go ahead," then walked down the hall and stepped outside, pulling the door tightly shut behind her.

"I have instructions for you," he said.

Champe raised an eyebrow. We hadn't known if Amos and Mary were informed of our specific purpose. Until this moment we thought Amos would give us no more instruction than on where to buy bread and milk.

"As soon as you develop a plan to seize your prey, you must get a message to Mr. Baldwin, who will arrange for a boat and oarsmen to take you and your prey to New Jersey."

"You know the identity of our prey, I assume?" Champe asked him.

"I do not. But I have a guess, and if my guess is correct, I will forever hold you in the highest esteem."

"Mr. Baldwin, you said?"

"Yes. A boat and two oarsmen will await you at the time and place you designate."

"Can we trust Mr. Baldwin?"

"I believe you can. Tell him the day and time when you want the boat, and the place, and he will see to it."

"How do we get that message to him?" I asked.

Amos reached into his pocket and produced a glass vial the size of a man's thumb, tightly stoppered by a cork, containing a pale yellow-tinged liquid. Then he gave us instructions on how to get a message to Mr. Baldwin—instructions that were at once both simple and complex.

"How will we know the message has been received?" Champe asked.

"Our laundry line beside the house," Amos said, leaning to one side and pointing toward a window. "If Mr. Baldwin has your message, and all is well, a red towel will hang among the laundry, at the end of the line."

I looked at Champe, who nodded.

"Take your things, boys, and do not come back here. I fear that Arnold knows many names. There will be others like Mulligan."

"Is there a chance he knows your name?" I asked.

Amos shrugged. "I say my prayers in the morning and at night," he answered. "We'll see." He looked toward the window.

"I wish I could see what ships were coming in," he said, "but Mary has the laundry up, so all I can see is sheets and breeches." He took a piece of queen's cake and washed it down with the last of his cider.

"Well, boys, I've got some wood to chop." He stood, and left through the back door.

12

We took our few possessions with us that morning when we left the Underhills' boardinghouse to join the British army in the service of Arnold's legion, and made our way across the city with little distraction. A company of redcoats drilled on the Bowling Green, while soldiers and civilians came and went up and down the streets, attending to business. New York was at war, and war was evidently good for commerce.

As we approached Arnold's building, at the end of a row of townhouses all housing various commands, a private carrying copies of *Rivington's Gazette* scurried up the steps and let himself in the door. We followed, and once inside were greeted by a meticulously dressed sergeant, who seemed to be expecting us. Within a minute Arnold himself appeared in his crisp uniform, cordial but businesslike, every bit the general I remembered from the battlefield but for the silver-tipped cane in his left hand, which he pressed against the floor. He directed us to the room at the end of the hall, a long chamber serving as his office, with a large table covered in dark green baize and a handful of maps and lists drawn up on paper. The walls were the color of light bluestone and the curtains the green of summer grass. An imposing secretary desk occupied the far wall, its bookcase and ornamental pediments reaching nearly to the ceiling. We were alone in the room with the general, while several redcoats attended to duties across the hall.

As the three of us sat at the table, Arnold conducted a thorough interview of Champe, already convinced of his allegiance but curious about the man and eager for information. He asked detailed questions about Champe's military service, the battles he had fought, and his conduct in them. He asked about Major Lee and the morale of the Continental soldiers, to which Champe convincingly recited our crafted responses. It would not take a seasoned general long to determine that Champe was indeed a soldier's soldier, and I could see that Arnold was pleased. He expressed his gratitude to Champe for defecting, acknowledging the great personal risk, and reiterated to us both that he would value our service in his American Legion. It was his intention, he said, to make Champe his recruiting sergeant, charged with supervising the enlistment of new recruits—which was to say, new deserters. Champe dutifully accepted the assignment. Then Arnold informed us that we would be housed on the upper floor of the townhouse, in a large room with a fireplace and several campaign beds—small folding cots canopied for warmth. As I thanked the general for the opportunity to work at his side, and the generous quarters that would allow us to be ever ready, I saw Champe crack the slightest smile: we were in.

First, however, was the necessity of enlisting in the British army. Arnold dispatched an aide from across the hall to summon an officer from Sir Henry Clinton's headquarters, several houses down from us. As we waited, the duty of making small talk was taxing. Champe began to compliment Arnold on his great success at Saratoga, but realized the awkwardness of this, and skillfully evaded any mention of the place and proffered a blanket admiration. Arnold then described his efforts at recruiting American deserters, chiefly through newspaper reprints of his "Proclamation to Officers and Soldiers of the Continental Army." He again pressed us—Champe in particular—for opinions of this effort and the likelihood of success. "How many can we expect?" he asked several times. Champe suggested that mass desertions would be triggered by the hardships of winter, which was perhaps still a month or two away—long after our mission would be completed, which made this an easy prediction to toss off.

Something more discomforting came next. The aide who had been dispatched returned with a major who carried a regimental book and a muster roll. The major seemed in a hurry, and was polite but avoided looking Arnold in the eye. He asked our names and their spelling, which he wrote in both books. Then he instructed us to raise our right hand, and we repeated, after him, oaths of fidelity and allegiance to our Sovereign Lord King George, to serve him honestly and faithfully, in defense of his person, crown, and dignity, and against all his enemies or opposers whatsoever; and to observe and obey His Majesty's orders, and the orders of the generals and officers set over us by His Majesty. Then, taking quills from the inkwell at the center of the table, we signed our names in the larger of the books. The major then excused himself to General Arnold, who tapped his cane on the floor and instructed his aide to escort us to a storehouse a few blocks away on Murray's Wharf to be properly provisioned, and once done, to take us back to our quarters in the house.

By late afternoon we had all the provisions and the full uniforms of proper British soldiers. We returned to the townhouse and were shown to our quarters on the upper floor. Against the white walls were three canopied cots, each with a small trunk, and a table covered in green baize near the fireplace. Champe and I made a quick survey of the cots and set our new knapsacks at the foot of our chosen bunk. Champe sat in one of the caned chairs beside the table. I stood in front of the window, looking west at the modest untended garden and narrow courtyard that led to Greenwich Street. There was a path of stone and crushed oyster shell crossing to the far side of the garden, where stood two privies: white wooden structures, each with a single door, set atop brick-lined privy pits. Twenty feet to the north of the privies was a decorative fence of brick posts and whitewashed wooden rails. The fence separated the yard from a narrow alley that ran between the townhouses—an alley that was our quickest route from Broad Way to Greenwich Street. Across Greenwich Street was the rocky bank of the Hudson River.

Adjusting my eyes to the changing light, I noticed my own reflection in the glass and focused on it: there was the red of my new coat, faced in blue with descending rows of pewter buttons, a white waistcoat with a sergeant's crimson sash, white breeches, and polished black shoes. I turned to look at Champe, who looked at me and then at himself, and who began to laugh—not a jovial laugh, but a laugh that came in fits and spasms, from an untangling of wrought muscles, which he struggled to suppress. The same affliction immediately overcame me, sparked by the sight of us dressed impeccably as redcoats, lobsterbacks, loyal soldiers of the king—an inflamed hysteria born of days we believed could be our last. Soon enough this nervous fit was exhausted, and I searched for a cloth to wipe the tears from my face.

We heard someone on the stairs and recomposed ourselves. The footsteps—of one man alone—reached the landing at the top of the stairs and came toward our room. In stepped another loyalist soldier of the British army, dressed nearly identically to us.

"Gentlemen," he said, "I am Nathan Frink. I understand we will be working together, and that I am to take the remaining bed."

Within minutes he revealed that he had been a cavalry captain under Arnold in the Continental Army, and had ridden through Westchester alone without resistance until he met British soldiers in Kingsbridge, just north of Spuyten Duyvil Creek, and gave over his allegiance to serve again with Arnold.

As he spoke I looked repeatedly out the window at the yard, the fence, and the Hudson. Champe and Frink were telling stories of combat; Champe was gregarious, and was winning over our traitorous companion, who was clearly relieved to have the danger of his desertion behind him, and to be in the company of those he thought were kindred souls. For the first time I wondered, how many troops would desert to join Arnold's legion? Frink caught my eye as he proclaimed that we were now on the winning side, and smiled at me. I smiled back so he would not know that I despised him.

As if making room for our bunkmate, I pulled my cot a few feet along the wall to the window. Again I studied the yard, the fence, the street, and the river, mapping them in my mind. There would be nothing easy about this, but the message I would send to Mr. Baldwin was beginning to take shape.

13

More deserters came than I expected, among them a Connecticut Yankee who had served with Arnold at Saratoga, but whom I did not recognize, and a young man from the prominent Livingston family. Scores of enlisted men came, and several sergeants. Still, this was fewer than Arnold's mighty self-regard had anticipated. This befuddled and angered our general, who declared that Washington himself must be intercepting the reprints of Arnold's proclamation announcing his American Legion. Champe and I reassured him that more deserters would come as the privations of winter demoralized the soldiers. In the meantime, Champe and Frink prepared regimental rolls and books for the legion. While British officers handled Arnold's military communications, I drafted mostly personal correspondence for Arnold, transcribing letters that justified his actions to relations and former business associates. Often, seated at a small writing desk with a sharpened quill in hand, I thought back to the days in the hospital when I wrote letters to his sister and his children in Connecticut. I buried these thoughts as best I could.

We knew from the first day we arrived in New York that our abduction had to be done at night. The Bowling Green was thoroughly trafficked from daybreak to sundown with soldiers who fought for the king. Each day, as dusk ebbed into darkness, we looked for the moments of least attention, when the city half-closed its eyes. In the night hours any passerby would pay little notice to an unruly lout being helped along by two others at a rapid pace. A single firm assertion—"He's sick with drink"—would buy the time we needed to get our captive into a rowboat and across the river to the New Jersey shore, where a squadron of American dragoons would be waiting to take Arnold into custody.

It was difficult to observe Arnold's habits in the evening, after he retired from the public spaces of his headquarters. He took dinner only with his wife, but on one occasion had me join him for Madeira. I asked him how, when a battle was pending the next day, he had lulled himself to sleep at night. By clever diversion, I directed our conversation to nightly rituals of rest, of slowing the pace of the mind and easing it to slumber. He allowed that he often spent his final waking hour of the day in a parlor by his map room, so as not to disturb—or be disturbed by—his infant child. The parlor was visible from the central stairs. Peering down from the landing, Champe and I had seen Arnold at the table there, studying papers by the light of a few candles. But his attendance in that evening spot was not constant, and our plot to seize him required that we find some habit of his we could depend on.

On most nights in our quarters, Frink produced a deck of cards and entreated us to play All Fours. I played against him once, because I sympathized with his loneliness, but found his company unpleasant; a genuine deserter, he possessed the defect with which I was temporarily branded, and did not like to look upon in another. Champe was better at games and agreeably entertained Frink, who sipped brandy

with enthusiasm while he played. Sometimes it made Frink boister-
ous, and other times it quieted him so much that he ended the gam-
ing and took to his bunk, lying quietly awake, facing the wall.

A full month had passed since we'd arrived in New York and
claimed our places in Arnold's legion. The general, we had discovered, was almost never alone, and the idea of abducting him amid all
the commotion of this city—of seizing and dragging him to a rowboat on the riverbank—seemed ever more a fool's errand. I sat on
my bed by the window, feeling ill at ease. I watched Champe—my
steely compatriot, my fellow spy—deal cards to Frink, the traitor in
our midst, and wondered how we would put this nuisance out of our
way when the time came—if it came at all—for us to act. They played
quietly, given the hour, and Frink had his share of brandy. In due time
both men bade me good night and Champe extinguished the light,
but sleep did not come quickly to me. Through the window I could
make out in the moonlight the docks and wharfs and the vast array of
ships, and in the distance some faint lights on the New Jersey shore. It
was that space, the distance between me and the far flickering lights,
that I had to travel: to get the man with the crooked leg into a boat
and to those lights. But how to cross that gap eluded me.

Then I saw it: below the window, shimmering through the windowpane, a pale glimmer of moving light appeared, traveling the path
through the yard to the privy. I lowered my head to conceal my profile
and put my eyes near the glass. It was a man with a lantern, in a loose
greatcoat or cloak that obscured the telltale limp. I waited, and hid my
eyes still further in the lower corner of the window. On his return I saw
his shoulder lift and drop as he hurried, and any doubt disappeared.
I made a quick calculation of the late hour, and resolved to be again at
this station the next night, hoping I might seize upon a habit to exploit.

I stood this watch for two weeks, more or less, sitting or lying on
my bunk, my face turned to the window. Every night, without excep-
tion, Arnold—with a young wife in his bed and a vain reluctance to
soil a chamber pot—made his very last deed a night visit to the old
thunderbox.

When the first rays of sunlight awakened us each morning, Champe shot me a look across the room and waited for my nod, acknowledging to him the unbroken consistency of Arnold's late night sojourns. Having endured a thousand moments of doubt, we knew this was our chance. We knew Arnold would hang for his treachery. We knew we would go home.

14

We began to prepare. It was the first week of December; the sun set early now, and the air grew colder in its absence. Champe and I walked north up Broad Way toward King's College. It was evening, and we were not dressed for cold, each of us having only one set of clothes other than our British uniforms. I did not want to be in New York long enough to need a woolen coat. Besides, my tailor was in the Bridewell prison.

"We wait in the garden," I said to Champe, "behind the trees, in the shadows for as long as we can."

"Will we see him when he goes to shit?"

"Yes—he always takes a lantern."

"We should pull him out with his breeches down."

"There's a latch," I instructed.

"We could kick his bare ass down the street."

Champe was excited; I was nervous.

"There's a latch. Once he goes in, we should approach very quietly, so he can't raise an alarm."

"An alarm?" Champe repeated, amused. "*Help me! I'm having difficulty in the shithouse!*"

King's College Hall was a four-story sandstone building in the English style, with several entrances, and a rooftop cupola at the center. Lanterns flickered through the windows and I could imagine the interior from my schooldays at Yale: a library, recitation rooms, accommodations for students, and perhaps a central prayer hall. But no students were within, as the building had been requisitioned for use as a military hospital. A few people walked here and there, but the yard in front was empty.

"Really," Champe continued, "if someone called for help from the shithouse, who would come running to assist? I wouldn't."

We walked the perimeter of the college, mostly to stay warm.

"I've looked at the fence," I said. "We can easily fix a few rails so we can push them aside."

"I'll take care of that," Champe said.

"Good," I said. "The boat can wait for us across from Morris Street. The riverbank is clear there, and any spot closer to the headquarters might raise suspicion. We'll run him down the alley, up Greenwich Street to our waiting boatmen, and we'll row like hell for New Jersey."

"Our dragoons will be glad to see us this time," Champe said. I imagined the sight of them, a line of mounted infantry waiting on the New Jersey shore with Major Lee.

We were both quietly running through the details as we returned to the front of the college yard.

"It should be quiet on the streets," Champe said, "but if we run into someone?"

"Just another drunk being carried to the barracks."

"Plenty of those," Champe said.

"But what about Frink?" I asked. Our late night absence would alarm him. He had few acquaintances among the troops as yet, except for us, and he was an unhappy fellow. If we told him we were going out, he'd ask to come along, and he'd pepper us with questions. If we were not in our bunks at night, he would likely watch for us out the window, and perhaps even go looking for us.

"I've thought about that," Champe said. "Let's go this way." A block later, as we crossed Barclay Street, the character of our surroundings changed from the gentility and decorum of the college grounds to a rundown degeneracy. Disagreeable shouting startled me from within the dirty windows of an unnamed tavern, where a boister-ous crowd was fueled by tankards of rotgut. A red sign speckled with yellow stars advertised the skills of an astrologist; high above it I made out the not distant steeple of Saint Paul's Chapel, and between streets caught a glimpse of its burial ground. I suspected every soul we passed was an inebriate, a swindler, or a whore, or all three rolled into one. This was the Holy Ground, a slum where forlorn soldiers and idle men found sinful, intimate connections with jades and hags. The boldest of these catcalled to us with foul invitations. A tart boy dressed almost like a clown beckoned us into a molly-house, while drunks from the shipyards were gathered in rowdy gangs on street corners. Champe walked purposefully and I followed, past more taverns, pawn and tallyman shops, fortune tellers and spiritualists, and slovenly leering hawkers insisting we enter this brothel or that. We stepped past a sad wench seated on the ground, her eyes cast downward, who said nothing, but lifted a sacking-swaddled infant in an act of supplication. All the soldiers and sailors had things to say about the Holy Ground, bawdy stories at first, followed by cautionary tales, of men barbarously castrated, or an old whore long dead, found rotting in an outhouse.

"You have been this way before?" I asked Champe.

"Only out of curiosity," he answered. "There are things here that might help us be on our way."

We stopped beside a pawnshop, at an arched wooden door pinched between two buildings. A small barred window was cen-tered at eye level; beneath it, in weathered gray paint, was written *Midwife*. Champe knocked loudly. A midwife in the Holy Ground performed only one service: dispensing a harsh physick to empty the womb. Behind the bars a pair of eyes appeared; in a moment the door opened only enough for words to be exchanged, the links of a chain restricting any breach.

"I am told you will sell me laudanum," Champe said.

A woman we could not see answered, "None for sale."

"I will pay a half-guinea," Champe replied.

There was a pause, and then the woman's open palm appeared below the chain. Champe pulled a gold half-guinea coin from his waist-coat pocket and put it in her hand. The door closed, and we waited. When it opened again, the hand reached out with a blue glass vial. Champe took it, and the door closed. A heavy metal latch clanked shut. We walked quickly to Greenwich Street, which followed the riverbank, and headed back toward the Bowling Green.

"Frink?" I asked. "Poison?"

"Not poison—just something to put him out," Champe explained. It wasn't meant, at first, for Frink.

"It was to be a contingency plan for Arnold," Champe said. "If all else failed, I thought we might slip some into the general's Madeira glass." A group of young men, probably soldiers, hurried by, and Champe paused until they passed us.

"At Morristown," he continued as we walked, "our colonel's wife and young son made a visit to see him at headquarters. A high fever gripped the boy, which did not pass and greatly alarmed the colonel and his wife. At first they gave him cold baths, dipping him quickly into the water, then rubbing him dry with towels, wrapping him in flannel, and bracing him with two teaspoons of brandy. But no cure came of it. So they summoned the surgeon, who gave the boy lime water and laudanum, which put the boy into a deep sleep."

"Did it cure the child?"

"I suppose it did. We were all anxious, but the child recovered."

We would use the laudanum not to subdue Arnold, but to silence Frink on the night of the abduction; his insistent meddling and loyalist devotion were the first obstacles we had to overcome. We discussed how to mix the laudanum into Frink's brandy following dinner, with an early invitation to play a game of All Fours with Champe. If Frink wasn't unconscious in his bunk by the hour of our departure, Champe assured me that he would be too groggy to cause any nuisance.

With this amendment added to our plot, we reviewed all of our steps, and appraised every pitfall that revealed itself to our imaginations. Our plan was a good one. The only question left was, when? We considered the various comings and goings that would fill the week's schedule, and decided to move as quickly as we could: we would abduct Arnold on Monday night, December 11. The moon would be full but we hoped that Providence would obscure its light with an overcast sky. There was no cause to wait, and many reasons to hurry. I would deliver a message for Baldwin tomorrow, and he would have two days to make his preparations. Then Frink would take his nap, while Champe and I hid in the shadows, waiting for Arnold to go shit.

15

I made sure to adhere carefully to the instructions Amos Underhill had given us. Reprinted broadsides of Arnold's "Proclamation to Officers and Soldiers of the Continental Army," ordered from Rivington's press, were plentiful in the downstairs headquarters. I removed a copy from the trunk at the foot of my bed, and took hold of the small vial tucked beneath the folded breeches I had worn the day I fled the dragoons. On the table I lit a candle beside the inkwell and readied myself to write, sharpening two quills with a penknife.

On the back of the proclamation I wrote a list of dry goods and foods that a soldier, such as myself, would desire to purchase: red linen cloth, thread, two buttons, sugar, molasses, mustard, Madeira, pepper, tobacco, plums, salt pork, smoked hock, Indian meal, butter. The list signified nothing, but the last two items were of utmost importance:

Apples
Walnuts

These revealed the design of my cipher. Baldwin knew that my message would be in code; this was the simple key to unlock it. I composed my message on a small piece of scrap newsprint I removed from my pocket. Above each word I transposed the letter, until my encrypted message was complete:

ikjzwu zayaixan aharaj xapsaaj jeja kyhkyg wjz iezjmcdp
wp neranxwjg sdana cnaajseyd iaapo iknneo opnaap

It was a simple one-letter transposition cipher. The final items on my list, apples and walnuts, signified that A was written as W—and following that, B was written as X, C was written as Y, D as Z, then E began the alphabet anew as A, then F as B, and so on. A British officer familiar with ciphers could decode it fairly quickly, but it was an obstacle to the untrained eye. Still, a visible coded message would create immediate suspicion, so a second level of obfuscation was necessary. I extracted the cork from the small vial Amos Underhill had given me and dipped the second quill. On the back of Arnold's proclamation, below the list of goods, I carefully penned the two lines of my encrypted message with the milky yellowed liquor. When I finished the second line I saw that the first line was gone from sight. I watched as the last words seemed to evaporate, then held up the paper to examine it. There was no trace of my message. I had to trust that Baldwin had the revealing liquor that would bring my mishmash of letters to light:

monday december eleven between nine oclock and midnight
at riverbank where greenwich meets morris street

I put the merchandise list into my trunk and pulled my chair toward the window to gaze out at the dark empty courtyard and the shadowy gray shapes of the privies. Tomorrow I would deliver the message; then I would find a strip of cloth for a gag, and a piece of wood to make a cudgel.

I recognized Frink's footsteps coming up the stairs. I slipped the proclamation into my trunk and greeted him.

"Good evening, Wheatley," he replied. Then, extending a pointed finger toward the table, he asked, "So what's in this tiny vial?"

I grabbed it, enclosing it in my palm. "A tincture," I said, "of mercury, for sores."

"Sores?" Frink said. "Have you been visiting the madams in the Holy Ground?"

"No," I answered, with a feigned laugh. "There is nothing there that interests me."

The next morning, Arnold was called to a meeting with Sir Henry at number 1 Broad Way, leaving me to my own purposes. I retrieved my message from the trunk and made for Hanover Square. The usual activity at the Bowling Green moved at a somewhat quickened pace, as both soldiers and merchants felt the blast of cold air that had arrived overnight, presaging the arrival of winter. Passing the commotion, I turned onto Beaver Street and down Broad to Mill Street, taking a slight indirection to my destination, a nod to doing the true work of a spy. Once I was past the small Jewish synagogue and its carefully tended grounds, the mercantile character of Hanover Square came into full view. There was more than one coffeehouse, and several printers and bookshops. Walking briskly along Smith Street I passed a watchmaker, glover, furniture maker, wigmaker, milliner, and silversmith before I came to the shop I sought. A sign above the door featured a twist of ribbon, a saltcellar, a bottle of wine, and the name *Oakham & Townsend*. I entered, feeling some trepidation. The capture of Benedict Arnold depended on my simple cipher, invisible ink, and whatever cryptic conversation I was about to engage in.

The shop was empty but for two ladies who appeared to be together, completing their transaction with the shopkeeper, who stood behind the long counter. I busied myself looking at cutlery and cloth, and bottles of wine, until the women stepped out, bidding the shopkeeper goodbye. Then he addressed me:

"May I assist you, sir?"

"Is this the establishment of Oakham and Townsend?" I asked, as if I hadn't seen the sign.

"Yes," he answered. "I am Mr. Townsend."

"Very good," I said. "I have a list of items that Mr. Baldwin would like delivered."

I looked at him inquisitively, perhaps pleadingly, for I needed this to work.

Mr. Townsend glanced at the door, then looked at me.

"You've come to the right place," he said quietly, with a nod of his head. "Give me your list and I will deliver these items right away."

I handed him the list. He skimmed it, then looked briefly at Arnold's printed proclamation on the reverse.

He nodded again. "Be assured I'll take care of this. You may go about the rest of your business."

"Thank you." I hesitated, then said, "Good day, Mr. Townsend."

"Good day," he replied, and walked toward the back of his store.

I went quickly up Smith Street, but then allowed myself to wander about Hanover Square. I had delivered the message; whether we had a boat was now in the hands of Mr. Townsend and the mysterious Mr. Baldwin—and perhaps in the hands of Providence. I paused to look at the hats in the milliner's window, and to admire the silversmith's elegant creamers, cups, porringers, and salt spoons. In the window of the glover's shop my eyes were drawn to a pair of lady's gloves made of light green silk. Embroidered on the back of the hand was an arrangement of three colorful flowers with dark green leaves that emerged from a delicate basket stitched in light brown thread. I went into the shop, feeling free to spend some guineas, since I would be gone from here within days. The gloves were light as a feather. I could secure them in my clothing, in a pocket, and they would hinder me not at all. I bought them for Catherine. The glover put them in a blue linen envelope, tied with a yellow ribbon.

Late in the afternoon, I took leave again from Arnold's townhouse for a brisk walk across the city to Queen Street, then turned in the direction of Peck's Market. Passing Beekman's Slip, I looked toward the house of Amos and Mary Underhill. Hanging on the laundry line was a single red towel.

16

As the sky brightened at dawn the next day, I peered out the window to gaze at the way home—across the Hudson to New Jersey—which was illuminated by sunbeams and shadows pointing westward. There, on that far shore, the veil soon would be removed from my feigned transgression. Those who cursed Champe and me—and surely there were many, beginning with the dragoons—would hold us blameless, and recognize our courage. While I strained not to lose humility, I foresaw recognition for the risks we took, and for the reason we took them: the virtue of duty to country, and the necessary deeds it demanded. I hoped to meet Washington again, together with Champe, in the company of our brothers-in-arms, and to have a brief moment on the pedestal that would ensure my reputation.

I held on to those thoughts as a man overboard would cling to a rope, for the current of anxiety that pulled me downward was overbearing. With every impatient tap of my foot, and each rapid pulse of my heart, I considered the missteps, known and unknown, that could mean my death. A misstep, or a break in the chain, and I would be hanged as a failed spy by one side in the war, and reviled by the other as a deserter, a traitor, and a minion to Arnold.

Before beginning our usual clerical work, Champe and I entered the barren garden behind the residence and examined the fence along the alleyway with deliberate attention, appearing to make quick repairs with an iron crowbar while detaching several planks and resecuring them lightly, to fall away when pushed. There was not much to it, and we were done within minutes. Surveying the Bowling Green we noticed an unusual movement of the Queen's Rangers, bearing knapsacks and blanket rolls, marching up Broad Way toward the wharfs. We went about our business, and counseled ourselves on the virtue of patience. After the midday meal I wrapped and tied a piece of cloth around the top half of a short wooden club, to inflict upon Arnold a bloodless silence and induce his addled, drunk-seeming condition. Against an imagined head I swung the cudgel, driving it quick and hard, to practice and regulate the blow. In two nights, in the garden, I would hit Arnold from behind as he left the privy. Champe would grab him and I would force a gag into his mouth and tie it behind his head. With his arms slung across our shoulders we would pass through the breached fence and down the dark alley, then up Greenwich Street to an unknown man who would direct us to the waiting boat and oarsmen. For Champe and me, it would be the apex of our Revolution, and it would take less than ten minutes.

Footsteps sounded on the stairs. I put the cudgel into my trunk. It was Frink, who entered the room flushed with some excitement.

"We're shipping out," he declared.

"Who? What do you mean?"

"We are. We're loading up and leaving New York. General Arnold's entire command—his American Legion, the Bucks County Volunteers, and others. We'll be a fleet of more than twenty ships."

"Where are we going?"

"We have not been told yet—not till we're at sea."

There had been no hint of this in the correspondence I wrote for Arnold, but military affairs had not been within my purview. I strained to conceal my enveloping panic and asked the life-and-death question.

"*When?*"

"General Arnold is preparing the fleet. Some regiments have already boarded. We board later today. We sail in a few days."

Frink opened his trunk and put clothes onto his bed. He collected things into his knapsack.

Could we take Arnold tonight? Could I get a message to Baldwin? How? There was hardly time for a coded message. If a message got to Baldwin, how would I know? What if we grabbed Arnold and there was no boat? To be reckless would be to sign our own death warrants.

Still, I would try. I had to try. In my trunk there was another reprint of Arnold's proclamation and the small vial of invisible ink. I looked at Frink, who was pondering his possessions as he sorted them. He wasn't leaving. There was no time for a coded message. I hastened down the stairs and hurried outdoors. A unit of Hessian grenadiers had mustered on the Bowling Green, and began marching to a drummer's roll. I passed them, walked quickly by Sir Henry's headquarters at number 1 Broad Way, and skirted the edge of Fort George, where the Eightieth Regiment of Foot was assembled for inspection as quartermasters arranged supplies in military wagons. I ducked onto Bridge Street and across to Dock Street, past the large fire shed filled with leather buckets and a London engine for pumping water, and onto Hanover Square. I paused to catch my breath, and looked to see if I'd been followed. Then, going quickly up the steps, I entered the store.

Several ladies and one gentleman were examining merchandise while the clerk, an older man who wore a wool cap, exchanged money with a boy who had been sent on an errand. I waited, impatiently.

"May I see Mr. Townsend?" I asked.

"He is not here today, sir."

"Do you know where I might find him?"

"He was to go to Peck's Slip this morning, but other than that . . . Perhaps I can help you?"

"No," I said.

I thought of walking to Peck's Slip and looking for Townsend; then I realized that I had set eyes on him only once, for a few moments behind the counter, and I would barely know him if he presented himself. The Underhills had some connection to Baldwin; someone had told them to signal me. I took several uneasy steps toward Queen Street as I reviewed my past conversations with Amos, and then I stopped. I stood in the midst of Hanover Square, shivering and confused, sickened with despair. We would leave New York as members of Arnold's Loyalist Legion. Two nights from now, Baldwin and his men would wait for us in the shadows of Greenwich Street, but we would not come. On the Jersey shore, Major Lee and the dragoons would stare into the dark mist that hovers above the river, waiting throughout the night until the sun rose up, but we would not come.

In his camp, inside his tent, Washington would wait, and wonder, but there would be nothing to report. Arnold would be gone. Champe and I would be lost.

At the townhouse I found Champe, who, for the first time, looked washed out and pale.

"We'll go," he said. "What else can we do? The game is not over. We'll ship out, hope for another chance, and fight another day."

17

Nathan Frink was gone before evening, already settled on one of the frigates and brigantines crowding the harbor. The recruiting sergeants had been summoned to the ships for some new duty, so Champe hoisted his knapsack and blanket roll onto his back and headed for the wharfs. I was to board in the morning with Arnold—on what ship I didn't know—after assisting him again with correspondence.

When night fell, the townhouse was nearly empty of its former inhabitants, and the silence within its walls was stark. Outside the window I could see the faint shadows of the garden and the ghostly gray of the whitewashed privy. There were more ship lanterns than usual swaying on masts in the harbor. Sailors and soldiers could be seen scuttling about the decks amid shadows and flickering lights. Again, as I did so often, I looked past the ships to New Jersey, hoping to see distant lights, or even nothing more than the long, thin silhouette of its shore. Its proximity, I realized, was the dearest thing I possessed. I feared leaving sight of it.

Sleep would numb my discontent, but my mind would not rest. My possessions, what little I had, rested on the table: a tin cup, a knife and fork, a pewter spoon, a candleholder, flint and steel, quills, a tin canteen, a comb and polished mirror, a linen haversack to carry rations, and the blue linen envelope with the green silk gloves. Also on the table was Mulligan's dagger in its leather sheath, and the cudgel I'd made, which might be a welcome helpmate in a scuffle, but now I had no plan for such a thing. It was perhaps best not to bring it, but I could decide in the morning.

My first tepid breath failed to blow out the candle. I sat for another minute, then blew it out and sat unmoving in the wooden chair. My eyes adjusted to the dark. My feet, in thin woolen stockings, were cool against the floorboards. I heard a faint repetition of bells from the chiming clock on the first floor, marking ten o'clock.

Willing to end the day, I went to close the door to the room, but reaching for the latch, I stopped and held still. Spread across the landing at the bottom of the stairs was a dim fluttering light that mimicked the rectangular shape of the door through which it came. I heard my breath quicken, and quietly stepped back to the table, where I reached for Mulligan's dagger. As quietly as a whisper I descended several stairs and pressed myself against the staircase wall, where I could see, but not be seen. In the room below, three small flames reaching upward from a candelabra illuminated a man in a shirt and waistcoat, with a knit cap atop his head for warmth. He sat at the table, writing, but not in the usual hurried hand that I was accustomed to seeing from him. Rather, he wrote slowly, in deliberate script, a result of the late hour, perhaps, or the care accorded to reflective thought.

I could end his life in seconds. With quick and quiet steps I could be upon him like a cat. If he turned his head to see me he would be surprised but not alarmed, and his eyes might welcome me at the same time that I thrust the dagger into his neck; or coming upon him undetected, I would pull back his head and draw the blade across his throat. There would be no cry for help, but his body would buck and shudder and his breath would hiss, and I would hold him in his chair, pressing downward on his shoulders, until his lifeblood ran out. Mrs. Arnold was surely asleep, and the residence was all but empty. In minutes I could gather my things and be in the streets. There was no Mr. Baldwin, no boat and oarsmen ready to aid my escape, but I could be lost and gone from the city before anyone found the general dead. I would scramble through the Holy Ground with my head down, in the manner of countless men who traveled there, and hurry past the foundries to the farmland, where I would solicit a journeyman with the two guineas I still had to row me across the river, or commandeer a rowboat or sailing skiff, and then this wretched episode would be done. It would all be done and over.

Major Lee's admonition resounded in my head: *Do not assassinate him*. This, he told us, came from Washington himself. Assassination was dishonorable; the British would howl that it was vulgar for the American commander to send ruffians to assassinate Arnold. But what refuge would honor have if Arnold lived to fight another day, and drew the blood of a hundred Continental soldiers? Honor came at a price, against which it should be measured on a scale. Justice for the arch traitor, rightly done, would come from the edict of judges and the work of the hangman. But no man was better suited to judge than I, who had heard his confession and witnessed the scorn he held for his countrymen; who had taken testimony of his intent to spill the blood of my brothers-in-arms; and who knew his capacity to fulfill his designs. The odds that Arnold would yet be captured and abducted were nothing a gamester would wager on; there was little hope left for that. At this moment there was only acquittal, begotten by his escape, or the rough justice of my judgment and Mulligan's razor-sharp blade.

It would be a few quick actions: Walk. Grab. Stab. Hold.

Then it would be done.

Then I could make my way home.

And yet, as I readied the dagger, I hesitated.

In the dusky candlelight I could not blind myself to the man who had given two silver dollars to a Frenchman to care for Taggart on the road to Quebec; or the man who confided in me as he struggled to beat back fever, death, and the loss of hope; who had befriended me as we told stories of our youth; or the man who had defied a thousand British muskets and a hundred cannons aimed at him, to the cheers of his men.

Still, I steeled myself for the attack; but this dark stairwell was not the battlefield, on which the moral order was unruly and the targets of our violence remote and returning fire. As he wrote in the candle-light I would grab his hair, bend back his neck, and cut his throat. My hands would do this work, and my will, alone, would direct them. His eyes would question and plead, and he would know the intimacy of betrayal. Neither of us would have time for regret, and there would be no chance for redemption.

Images arose from the shadows. In the flickering glow I conjured the boy sent to the taverns to fetch his father, who found him besotted and gone to waste, and carried him home.

Non sum qualis eram, I thought, remembering. *I am not what I once was.*

I told myself, insisting: Walk. Grab. Stab. Hold.

It will be but a momentary pang, André had said.

Then, from the darkest shadow the vision came, and I saw the man—my own father—collared by a knotted rope, standing on a wagon beneath an oak tree.

What are you doing? I called to him, in a child's voice.

Then, before the mind's eye, as he always did, he propelled himself forward. The rope jerked tight and kept him from hitting the ground, and I heard a child crying.

Arnold stopped writing and tilted his head, almost imperceptibly. I listened, and from somewhere in the residence the faint nighttime cry of his infant child touched my ear. It continued for only a moment. Then everything was silent, and Arnold again took up his quill.

My grip on the dagger loosened. For some time I must have stared at the faint light that came from the parlor, and the shadows it made. Quietly, I retreated up the stairs, walked into my room, and closed the door.

In the morning I boarded a forty-four-gun fifth rate, the HMS *Charon*, the commodore's flagship in a fleet of twenty-three vessels, to be joined at sea by seven more. It did not escape me that our ship was named for the ferryman of Hades who took the newly dead across the river Styx.

As I stood on deck, gazing at the far shore, a squall stirred up the harbor. When the sickness came to my stomach, I said it was from the sea.

PART 3

New York City, Richmond, Virginia & New London, Connecticut

1780–81

There was One man Drest in Red Stud up in the Starn of

One of the botes, with his Sword Drawn & Brandishing itt

Over his head, & Said Pull a way, God Dam you, Pull away,

which I thaught was Arnald.

NARRATIVE OF JOHN HEMPSTEAD

ON THE BATTLE OF GROTON HEIGHTS

1

The plan to send their new brigadier general on an expeditionary raid was made in secret by the British high command, who were eager to cement Arnold's loyalty and utilize his knowledge of American forces. When a sudden influx of new deserters arrived in the first week of December, bringing the total to over two hundred men for Arnold's legion, it was decided by Sir Henry Clinton to board the ships immediately, well ahead of departure, in part for lack of ready quarters in the city. It was anticipated that the fleet would set sail within four or five days of loading soldiers, but bouts of foul December weather and bothersome delays securing provisions stalled us, and we spent all of nine days in New York's harbor. General Arnold remained for two nights at the townhouse with just his wife and child and two servants, and once onboard the *Charon* he shuttled to and from the headquarters at number 1 Broad Way only when necessary to see Sir Henry; his twisted and foreshortened leg made it difficult to pass from the warship to the dispatch boats. Others who needed to speak with Arnold were required to come to him, which caused some visible annoyance in the British officers climbing the rope ladders that were lowered over the side for them. The orderly books revealed that Champe was aboard the twenty-gun sloop-of-war *Bonetta*. A midshipman answered my inquiry and pointed to the ship, but it was too far away to identify anyone on its deck.

At Arnold's direction, I penned some of the dispatches that he sent from his quarters on the upper deck of the *Charon*, and learned through piecemeal disclosures that the mission of Arnold's fleet was to sail to Virginia, to assault fortifications on the banks of the James River, and destroy the arms depots and shipbuilding warehouses in Richmond. When I was confident of this information, I requested a few hours of shore leave to obtain additional paper, ink, quills, sealing wax, and various personal necessities. From my knapsack I retrieved my only remaining copy from Rivington's press of Arnold's proclamation, and a handful of small items, and sank them deep into the pocket of my scarlet coat. I climbed into one of the dispatch boats that ferried soldiers and sailors to shore and back with regular frequency.

As the oarsmen rowed toward the dock, I fretted over my duty in this war, and the likelihood of my survival. Once ashore I could leave the war for good. I could discard this detestable uniform, obtain clothing from Mulligan's tailor shop, and make my way quickly up the Bowery Lane past the farms and fields to Kings Bridge, then cross Harlem Creek into the neutral ground. Or better still, I could find passage across the East River to Brooklyn and journey eastward on Long Island to the villages on the north shore, then seek out an uncurious fisherman to ferry me across the sound to Connecticut. Neither route was a certain bet; both promised a thousand unforeseen hazards. Suspicion is the thing most abundant in a country at war, and I—a lone stranger—would sooner or later be questioned. Answering any inquisitor would be a walk on a knife's edge, since both the British and Americans had reason to hang me.

There was another choice. It was repellent for a hundred good reasons, but possessed some utility: I could remain at Arnold's side, passing secret information to my countrymen, and hoping for some providential escape, however long it might take for that moment to occur.

Either way, it seemed, was a roll of the dice—and a bad roll would get me killed.

At King's Wharf, I climbed out of the boat behind a half-dozen sailors whose lecherous talk revealed they were headed for the flesh-driven comforts of the Holy Ground. I hurried down Partition Street to Saint Paul's Chapel, one of the few churches that the British hadn't converted to a prison or sick ward. Inside the sanctuary, rays of sunlight entered through the clear glass of the arched windows on the east wall, which, passing through invisible airborne particles of ash and dust, became radiant, illuminating the holy place as if

God himself were looking in. I was alone, except for an old woman bundled in a cloak who sat upright with her eyes closed, and a sexton who was polishing a chalice on the altar.

Chairs were arranged in blocks on either side of a long center aisle. I took a seat midway down the sanctuary, near the wall, away from the light. I looked to see if the sexton was watching me, or if anyone else had entered. Nearly alone and unnoticed, I leaned forward, bowing my head. Then, from a pocket, I removed my tools: two quills and two small vials of ink—one black and one clear, the latter only half-full—and a note I had scratched on a slip of paper. These items I placed on the chair next to me. I unfolded Arnold's proclamation and spread it open on my knee. Dipping a quill into the black ink, I wrote at the top margin, above Arnold's rousing call to treason:

Forced to leave early. Could not deliver apples and candles.

The recipient would suspect the identity of the sender, and he would know that the words "apples" and "candles" provided his instruction for a cipher. Seeing no additional writing, he would apply the liquor that would reveal the hidden message.

I corked the black ink and returned it to my pocket. Then, carefully holding the vial of invisible ink in my left hand, I picked up the second quill. Glancing repeatedly at the small note lying on the chair in front of me, I drew damp letters between the lines of the proclamation, watching them disappear as the quill moved across the page:

Ngvvgtu yknn eqog
vq Jcppcj Fgnn kp aqwt ectg
Uvwfa vjg kphqtocvkqp
—Hnggv ucknu vq tkejoqpf—

With my feigned prayers finished, I raised my head. The sexton was still polishing and the old lady appeared to be asleep. I gathered my supplies and walked out. The small vial of clear ink had only a drop left, not enough for another word.

There was no time for me to find Amos Underhill, and a lone redcoat walking at a quickened pace the distance to his boarding-house was likely to attract suspicion. I hurried instead toward Hanover Square, where I knew I could find the writing supplies I'd promised to return with, and went directly to the shop of Oakham & Townsend, hoping this time that Mr. Townsend would be attending to his customers. I saw the now familiar wooden sign with its ribbon, salt, and wine, and bounded up the steps. The latch did not open the door. Then I saw a posted notice: *Gone to Dinner*. I did not know *who* had tended the shop on this day and gone for his midday meal—was it Townsend or his clerk? I thought to search through Rivington's Coffee House and other nearby establishments. But looking for Townsend held no promise, and waiting for him was futile.

Frustrated, I walked over to the center of Hanover Square, where my eyes searched among the merchants, laborers, servants, bankers, and well-dressed ladies. On the grassy square a young boy was waving a stick, playing a game by himself, lost in his own thoughts. I approached him.

"Hello," I said. "How old are you?"

My abrupt query startled him. *Calm down*, I instructed myself.

"Ten years, sir."

"I would like to hire your services, young man, for an errand."

"Yes, sir."

"You do not bear ill will to a British soldier, do you?" It seemed a necessary question, although I did not like the sound of it.

"No, sir."

"Would you carry a letter for me?"

"Yes, sir. Where to, sir?"

"You seem to be a fine young man. Can I trust you to take it up Queen Street?"

"I know Queen Street, sir."

"Good," I said. "I have picked the right young man." At this the boy smiled. "Do you know the Underhills' boardinghouse, near the corner of Beekman Street, before you get to Peck's Market?"

He thought for a moment. "Why, I do, sir!" he said, pleased to pass the test. "It's a yellow house."

"Very good!" I said. I had not run out of luck completely. "Here is a shilling for your excellent service." It was the smallest coin I had, and his eyes widened at his good fortune. "Take this to Amos Underhill, at the boardinghouse. If he is not there, you can give it to his wife, Mary Underhill."

"I will, sir," he declared. "I will do it right now."

"To whom will you give it?"

"Amos Underhill. Or his wife."

"Mary."

"Or his wife, Mary Underhill."

"Amos Underhill or Mary Underhill. Nobody else. Do you understand?"

"I *do* understand."

"Very good. You are an exceptionally bright young man."

He held the coin tightly in one hand, the folded proclamation in the other, and started uptown at a quick step.

With some luck, or the favor of Providence, Amos would receive the folded paper, recognize the cipher, reveal the invisible message, and look for my occasional missives. If so, I could be of service. I would take it on faith that my words would reach him:

Letters will come
to Hannah Dell in your care
Study the information
—Fleet sails to Richmond⁻

Included with the mail that would return to New York on dispatch ships, I planned to send Amos occasional letters for a fictitious boarder, the fair Hannah. These would come from a lovelorn soldier, whose courtly musings would contain snippets of intelligence, revealing naval activity and troop movements, which a knowing eye could piece together.

With this message, carried by the boy, I wanted to let Washington know that the fleet being assembled was headed south and his position upriver on the Hudson was in no danger from it. With very good fortune a warning might also reach Richmond. So much would depend on luck.

I watched the boy hurry past the square toward Queen Street, intermittently walking, skipping, and running. He had no idea he was doing the work of a spy.

2

For several more days, as the weather allowed, the ships continued to be loaded with supplies. Barrels of water were hoisted aboard the *Charon* with block and tackle, followed by casks of salted meat and fish, oatmeal, cheeses, dried peas and the like; smaller barrels of butter; cases of eggs, biscuits, and tobacco; and lastly, butts and hogsheads of beer and rum. Stores of musket balls, round shot, grapeshot, and chain and bar shot—to tear apart the rigging on an enemy ship—were resupplied, and great care was taken with the many barrels of gunpowder that were brought aboard and stored in the powder magazine deep belowdecks. Several of the ships were pulled to the wharfs, where horses were lifted by slings and halyards into the hold, then put in stalls and secured against the rolling sea with wide canvas slings that passed under their bellies from a ceiling beam.

Midmorning on Thursday, the twenty-first of December, our departure having been stalled for days by ill winds and postponements, signal shots were fired at last. Cheers went up from each ship as sails were raised and the sea breeze pulled them taut. Approaching Sandy

Hook, the fleet was joined by an armed three-master, two sloops, and four brigantines; I was told these were vessels of the army, not the admiralty. Passing into the ocean waters, I looked upon thirty warships of various design, all under full sail, and I understood in magnificent detail that I was at war with a great power.

We sailed south for Virginia and the Chesapeake in late December's cold wind and water. The fleet was large and I could see billowing sails ahead and behind, and to either side of the *Charon*. The gales of winter whistled through the rigging, and ominous churning swells lifted up from the depths, building hills and gullies of water that sometimes hid the smaller vessels from sight. Sudden and unpredictable waves sprayed the frigates and brigs, and spilled over the smaller sloops and schooners. On the decks below, where I spent most of my hours, each footstep to move about the ship was an act of anticipation, a guess as to the next tilt or roll. Only the hammocks offered reprieve, and I craved my allotment of time in one so I could sleep, dream, and so allay my troubles.

Conditions grew worse. We had been six days at sea when the winds began to howl and scream and became unremitting, spraying rain and ice from all angles and roiling the seas such that the *Charon*, a heavy frigate, rose and fell in the great waves with a shocking, unsettling crash. On the gun deck, the gunner of the watch ordered all guns secured, and gun mates and sailors attended to this work with urgency, passing a heavy rope through the eyebolts on either side of the gunport, and through large ringbolts on the sides of each gun carriage. Wedges were hammered beneath the cascabels. On deck the guns were secured in the run-out position, their barrels extending out from the gunport, while belowdecks they were pulled back and tied in the housed position so the gunports could be closed and sealed from the weather. The sound of men and metal on the decks above us made a great commotion, and the soldiers below barked their words so as to be heard. But when a warrant officer urgently shouted down the ladder for hammocks, all of us pricked up our ears for trouble above, knowing that it was a call not to air the bedding but rather to capture a loose gun.

A cannon ahead of the fore hatchway had pulled from both breeching bolts and broken away from the tackles. As the ship rolled, the heavy gun skidded from one side of the deck to the other, crashing into the coaming of the hatchway. The ship's second master directed that several hammocks be extended as a web, with four men pulling on each side, and when a heavy lurch propelled the gun back into its proper port, the web caught the cannon and the second master chocked the after-trucks at the same time the ship was brought to the wind, which caused a swirl in the bellies of the soldiers but made the gun deck a stable platform. We waited to hear if any men had been crushed by the wayward cannon, and were relieved that none were.

The storm continued for hours. Like me, most of the Tories and redcoats did not possess sea legs, and many of the men retched into buckets set by the hatches for that purpose. I had skipped any food at daybreak, and though my head and gut were ill at ease, I had no need for the bucket. But the sight and smell of it threatened my disposition, so when I sensed the storm had surrendered some ferocity, I climbed the hatchways to the top deck to brave the foul weather for the reward of unsickened air.

On deck lifelines were rigged and a tarpaulin was spread in the mizzen rigging to shelter the sailors. The wheel of the ship was double-manned, and a handful of soldiers stood at the middle of the deck, steadying themselves against the ship's boat ahead of the mainmast, getting fresh air as I intended. The rain was middling now, but came hard at an angle and hit the skin like needles. The soldiers focused their attention to starboard, and there was a good bit of cussing and swearing—not at their discomfort, but at the sight of three masts a half-mile away and a hull nearly hidden by the waves, heavy with water and in danger of sinking. A tall redcoat, a lieutenant who squinted into a spyglass, exclaimed, "God help them all!" Shaking his head, he took the glass from his eye and passed it to one of Arnold's legionnaires, who leaned back against the ship's boat while he held the glass with both hands.

"They're pitching things overboard!" he called out.

"What things?" shouted another over the noise of the storm.

"Trunks and barrels."

"What about the guns?" called another.

"Who the hell can lift a cannon?" the lieutenant called back.

Squinting at the swamped vessel, the legionnaire shouted, "Good Christ, they're pushing horses overboard!" Grimacing, and wanting to see no more, he handed me the spyglass. I focused quickly on the distressed ship, first noting how low the hull sat in the water, with waves breaking over it, and the wet and torn foresail half-ripped from its rigging and flailing in the wind. Then I scanned the deck till I saw six or eight men pushing a horse against the gunwale, heaving against the animal as it shook its head with desperate agitation and tumbled overboard. Scanning farther aft, I saw this urgently repeated several times in different positions on the deck as more horses, slipping on the wet decks and throwing their heads, consumed by panic and desperately fighting their bridles, were pulled to the gunwales and mercilessly pushed by men into the sea. My eye followed one light chestnut horse over the gunwale and into a ring of spray and foam where it entered the dark green churning water. I saw its neck and head strain in horror, reaching skyward to find air as it bobbed and swam before a wave took it down. Near it, another hit the side of the ship, pushed into it by a crashing breaker, and then slipped into the deep. Another fell into my view, tossed from the desperate sinking ship onto a floating cluster of castaway wooden trunks and cases, which caught its hind legs and propelled the horse forward into a wave. Before I could turn my eye away, a gray horse followed it, hitting the water nearly upside down. I could not bear to see any more, and handed the spyglass to the lieutenant. Without the glass the chaos was barely visible, but having seen it, I knew that each flicker of movement signified a sickening horror. The distressed ship seemed hardly to move, like a boulder that barely shows itself above the surface, while in the sky behind it great cracks sheared the heavy clouds of the storm, revealing for a moment the huge fire of the sun, and casting vibrant sheets of orange, red, and yellow light into the turbulent sky.

By nightfall the storm's fury had abated. Word passed among us that several ships in the fleet could not be spotted; it was hoped that they had been pushed off course by the storm and would rejoin us, although, on hearing this, every man gave a knowing look acknowledging that the ships may have gone under. The vessel that had dumped cargo and horses was afloat but still listing; two sloops attended to it. I found myself uncertain about my wishes: whether to hope that these ships of the Royal Navy might be spared, or lost to the sea. I wondered about the ship carrying Champe, and how he had fared.

Appetites returned. Tables were lowered between the guns, and the cook and his mates served pease pudding and biscuits, promising a proper dinner the next day when the seas calmed and the galley and stores were set aright. A lieutenant declared that the captain had authorized a ration of rum for each man, meeting with cheers of approval as jugs were passed to the tables. From across the deck I heard a commotion as sailors beseeched one of their mates to play his fiddle, which he soon produced and agreeably played "Drops of Brandy" and other jigs and reels to the great satisfaction of all aboard. When the music stopped, a deep, coarse baritone started a song:

God rest you merry gentlemen

The sailors and soldiers quickly joined in, relieved by the return of fair winds and thankful for this light-hearted respite, filling the air with a chorus of voices:

Let nothing you dismay

I remembered: it was Christmas Eve. I cast a weary eye across the deck at the British soldiers and sailors, and the American loyalists who were betraying their own people. These men would soon invade the new capital city of Virginia, sacking stores and burning buildings, killing those who resisted, sending mothers to hurry away with fearful children. They sang loudly and robustly, raising their cups of rum.

To save poor souls from Satan's power
Which long time had gone astray

The man beside me was a redcoat named Davies. He slapped his hand onto my shoulder, and the row of men on the bench swayed left and right to the rhythm of the song. Across from me a corporal, who had stood nearby as I watched the horses fall into the sea, lifted his rum cup to his lips and smiled broadly, meeting my eyes with his.

I cleared my throat. Hesitantly, I began to sing.

3

Six days later the fleet anchored in the Chesapeake Bay off the coast of Newport News. Although the wind was strong again and the small boats that ferried between ships could hardly hold their course, a signal was given of hoisted flags and gunshots, calling for the commanding officers of the various regiments, corps, and brigades to report to General Arnold onboard the *Charon*. I was hoping to see Champe, who sailed on the *Bonetta*. I spotted the ship and, leaning over the bulwark, watched as each jolly boat pulled alongside the dangling rope ladders, but he was not among the soldiers who accompanied officers to the *Charon*. As the boats arrived, oarsmen maneuvered to hold a steady position as the waves lifted them unevenly beside the ship. Some officers exhibited skill and grace climbing the ropes, while others leaped precariously or bumped hard into the hull. Arnold instructed the officers to supply their men with five days of beef, biscuit, and rum, and to have their men ready to disembark at his command. His intention was to proceed up the James River to Richmond, to burn the military stores and powder magazines, and to chase the rebels out of the city.

Earlier in the day, during the several hours when we had sailed from Hampton Roads at the mouth of the James River to Newport

News, Arnold had hailed me on the deck and huddled near me to conceal our conversation. He extended his arm against the mizzen-mast, holding tight to a lanyard to balance his uneven legs against the rolling seas.

"How are you getting along, Sergeant Wheatley?"

"As well as anyone. And you, sir?"

"I'm at home on the sea," Arnold said. "I sailed these waters before the war. I must have told you"—here he cocked his head and feigned a conspiratorial whisper—"I ran molasses from the West Indies more than a few times."

"Aye-aye, sir."

"What is your sense of the men?"

"They are seasoned soldiers, but eager to get their feet on land." Then I realized what information Arnold was looking for.

"I have heard them call you the American Hannibal."

"Truly?" It pleased him to hear this. He stood a bit straighter, and smiled, satisfied. "Then I shall not let them down."

At this, we both looked out at the sea, and at the sails that were filled with a brisk wind. As he swung around to turn his back against the breeze, his movement revealed a small pistol in the inner pocket on the skirt of his scarlet coat. He noticed my glance and lowered his free hand to rest over the brass butt cap.

"If I am captured," he said somberly, "I will be hanged within hours. You might be afforded a few days, but in the end our fates will be the same."

The captain of the *Charon* stood several yards ahead of us at the edge of the quarterdeck. Beside him a lieutenant called out: "Top-Gallant and Royal Yardmen in the tops! Stand by to take in all the studding sails and royals!" The ship was preparing to anchor.

Arnold looked me in the eye. "Be careful, Wheatley," he said. "We all want to go home someday."

The next morning, the thirty-first of December, all the troops of the Queen's Rangers, the Eightieth Regiment, Robinson's Corps, the Hessian and Anspach foot Jägers, the English grenadiers, the

Althouse sharpshooters, and the one hundred or so men of Arnold's legion boarded smaller boats and open sloops to ascend the James River toward Richmond. Gunships carefully watched the shoreline and the big vessels came behind slowly at a fair distance, bringing the artillery and the horses of the mounted rangers, as well as provisions. I kept a keen eye out for Champe, but it was hard to distinguish one man from another on the crowded decks.

As evening approached, a band of Americans was spotted on the left bank. Arnold ordered a squad of Jägers and the Althouse sharpshooters to disembark and pursue them, with rangers close behind, instructing the Hessians to take prisoners who could tell him the strength of American forces and their locations. There was a brief skirmish, but the Americans fled inland and no prisoners were taken. Arnold went ashore and praised the bravery of the men now under his command. The captain of the Hessian Jägers noted that the Americans had bayonets and could have defended the steep bank, but fortunately did not. He was agitated and spoke in broken English, explaining that his riflemen would have been defenseless against a bayonet charge. Arnold nodded silently, as though unsure how to take the Hessian's reprimand, and ordered the troops to spend the night on land.

With methodical haste the tents were brought from the provision boats and a few small fires were lit for boiling water, although they were not much needed for warmth since now the air, inland from the ocean, seemed oddly untouched by winter. The Jägers arranged themselves for a night watch to defend the camp, expecting some harassment from local militias. I sat against a tree with a cup of hot water and morsels of dried beef. A man came from around the tree and also sat against it, facing west while I faced south. It was Champe.

"I am going to run," he said.

"When? How?" I asked.

"I don't know—but when a fair opportunity is presented."

"Either side could hang us a traitors," I said. "We are in an unforgiving position."

"I know. I have family in Virginia. It is my only hope. I'll travel at night and avoid every living soul."

I reached into my haversack and passed him half my provisions. "Take this."

"You should come with me," Champe said, not taking the food.

"I would never get home," I replied. "I have a woman who is waiting for me. I have to get home."

"Then you will stay with Arnold until he returns to New York?"

"That may be. I have sent coded messages to Amos."

"Will harm come to you if it's known that I've deserted?"

"No," I answered. "You should go. But I beseech you—go with all caution, and find your family and your freedom." I reached beside me and grabbed his arm. "Live a long and good life, my friend."

I pushed the rations closer to him. He put them in his haversack.

For a moment we were quiet, watching the small conversations and habits of the British army, soldiers who would soon wreak death and destruction on Richmond.

Champe stood up, lifting his gear.

"Trust in this," he said. "I will not forget you." Then he walked toward the tents and among the soldiers, and I lost sight of him.

The camp arose in the morning, greeting the first day of the new year. Fresh provisions were bought or pilfered from a nearby village. The troops boarded the vessels and the fleet continued upriver. When Arnold discovered a fortified position on the heights of Hood's Point, he ordered the warships *Hope*, with twenty-four guns, and *Cornwallis*, with twelve guns, to bombard it. This was met by twenty cannon shots fired by an American detachment elsewhere in the heights, killing one sailor. A squad of Jägers and sharpshooters landed on shore and attacked the detachment from behind, chasing the Americans into retreat and seizing three twenty-four-pounders and two howitzers.

The next morning the fleet anchored near Westover, alongside Colonel Byrd's plantation on the northern bank of the river, a thousand acres of tobacco crop with several dozen fine buildings and a large population of slaves. Arnold told me that Byrd had played his hand cleverly in the war, giving one son to the British and one to the American forces. He extended welcome hospitality to the invaders, and many of the troops were assigned to quarter in his buildings. In a cellar attached to a long narrow warehouse made of Virginia red brick and whitewashed timber was a large store of wine and beer. Whether the consumption of this treasure was part of the colonel's hospitality was unresolved, but in the evening it was consumed nonetheless. A group of Jägers set their blankets at one end of the long open room, and soldiers from Robinson's Corps and Arnold's legionnaires spread out from the other end toward the center. The sweet earthy smell of cured tobacco infused the floorboards. Barrels were moved to the center to make tables and stools, and soon the corridor resembled a beer hall. By nightfall, two-thirds of the men were drunk, barking at one another, laughing and singing.

I did not produce my tin cup, fearing that I would follow the first drink with a torrent of wine to dull my soul. I sat on the floor against the wall, in the shadows. The Jägers and the redcoats knew different songs; one group generally deferred to the other as each robustly sang. The British sang "Some Say Women Are Like the Seas" and "Heart of Oak." The Hessians sang their drinking songs in German, but gave a sporting try to some English lyrics. When they knew the words in common, an aura of good feeling seized the room. Some of the Hessians knew "We Be Soldiers Three" and sang it loudly with the British:

> *Here, good fellow, I drink to thee*
> *Pardona moy, je vous en pree;*
> *To all good fellows, wherever they be,*
> *With never a penny of money.*

A handful of redcoats followed that with a song I recognized. They were good singers who know more music than the common growl of a boozy round. Still, they kept to the theme:

Of all the Friends in time of Grief,
When threatning Death looks grimmer,
Not one so sure can bring Relief,
As this best Friend, a Brimmer.

But Valour the stronger grows,
The stronger Liquor we'er drinking;
And how can we feel our Woes,
When we've lost the Trouble of Thinking?

I recognized it from the *The Beggar's Opera*. Years ago I had seen the play done to great comic effect at Yale. The villain, Macheath, the leader of a gang, escapes from his captors again and again to return to his beloved. As the soldiers sang, bottles were passed and cups were refilled. There was clapping and a round of "Huzzahs!" when they finished, and they sang it again with most of the redcoats and some of the Hessians joining in on the verses they remembered.

It was getting late; no light passed through the windows and only a handful of lanterns illuminated the revelry indoors. I listened and sang quietly to myself, trying to settle my mind on a happier time. Then, as if from nowhere, I saw a figure across the room from me, in the shadows opposite. He stood with his back flat against the wall, both arms extended straight downward, one hand holding his knapsack low to the ground, pressing himself against the boards. Illuminated in a flicker of light he nodded to me, then he walked through the shadow, opened the door, and went outside. Only the knapsack gave away that he wasn't simply a soldier going to piss.

That was the last I ever saw of Champe.

The next morning, at the first light of day, I awoke in a large room full of snoring soldiers, many of whom were rolling about, trying to find elusive comfort on the wooden floor for the last minutes of rest. As consciousness seeped in, I recognized that now I was brutally alone. More troops came ashore in the morning, along with horses, artillery, and provisions for the attack. During the day Arnold collected favorable information and the assistance of reliable guides who knew the tidewater. Beyond Westover the James River narrowed dramatically, so the corps broke camp and marched northwest on the roads to Richmond. Squads of Jägers marched along the fences, on the lookout for an ambush, while thirty mounted Queen's Rangers followed behind them. Six platoons composed of more Jägers, the Althouse sharpshooters, and the light infantry came next, followed by four light six-pounders and the grenadiers, the Eightieth Regiment, and Robinson's Corps. At Bailey's Creek the Virginians had demolished the narrow bridge, but the men of the Eightieth Regiment rebuilt it within half an hour.

Brigadier General Arnold arrived in Richmond at midmorning the next day, with an army that vastly outnumbered the two hundred Virginia militiamen who briefly tried to defend the city. My coded message had been meant to assure General Washington that his position was not the target of this fleet, but I had hoped a warning would also reach Virginia's new capital in time. It had not. The city was ill-prepared to defend itself, and the governor, Thomas Jefferson, was said to have fled to the countryside when the militiamen were overtaken. Meeting little resistance, the king's newest general issued commands for every kind of destruction. He sent a detachment to wreck the cannon foundry, where the redcoats destroyed the tools and machinery of the furnace and blew up the powder magazine. The magazine held seven hundred barrels of powder, and the explosion sent thunder through the ground and lightning into the sky. Arnold's own legion of turncoats set fire to all the magazines and workshops for shipbuilding. They carried barrels of powder to the unfinished hulls that still sat in the blocks and blew them up, spreading the fire till there was nothing left but ash. By afternoon it appeared that half of everything in sight was engulfed in flame. Boats that weren't burned were loaded with prizes for the corps and sailed down the James River.

The men who'd been singing comic opera two nights earlier laid waste to every trace of civilization. Stores and warehouses were sacked and burned, homes were plundered for prizes, and even churches and holy places were ravaged. But this would not be the worst of the savagery. Arnold's next attack, on his own homeland, was still eight months away, and would reveal to me the depths of the Devil's own wickedness.

For the rest of the winter and through the spring, Arnold and his corps remained in Virginia, building fortifications in Portsmouth on the Elizabeth River, raiding American militia posts, and compelling Virginians to take oaths of allegiance to the king. I spent many hours at Arnold's side, and the orders I discerned through overheard conversations and written correspondence called for him to return to New York with his legionnaires while most of the British and Hessian regiments joined Lord Cornwallis as his corps arrived in Virginia. I buried this information in another installment of the delirious, lovelorn drippings sent to Hannah Dell. This was the third letter I'd sent her, care of Amos Underhill, from her sad beloved soldier—whose name I had decided, and affixed to the letters, was that of my shipmate, the deserter Nathan Frink. Should his indiscretion result in his bare back being flogged with a cat-o'-nine-tails, I would take it as a sign that my letters had been intercepted, and perhaps hasten a desperate getaway. But no consequence came of it. I did not know if my dispatches succeeded, but I had written them as an act of defiance and hope.

The months in Virginia were the loneliest of my life. The only respite from my discontent came with sleep, which was rationed on a British naval vessel like everything else. When my time came to swing in a hammock, I primed my mind to dream pleasantly of the things I desired; but such dreams seemed rationed too. Just as often I suffered recurring dreams that tore my mind asunder, infinite in the variety of their small details but repetitive in their forms. Always I was struggling to make my way home. Often I was lost and could not find direction; or my destination, once arrived at, turned out to be abandoned. In the worst of these I would arrive nervously at the home of Catherine's family, and the scene would play like this:

A man I know answers my knock on the door. His face is tight and severe.

"I'm home," I say.

"You are not welcome here," he answers.

"Where is Catherine?" I ask.

He shuts the door and slides a bolt to lock it. Quickly I walk to a window, through which I see Cate sitting beside a man of my own age. They are seated together on a settee, where I had often sat. I shift my eyes to a pane of glass with better clarity and see her holding an infant, which she sets into a cradle. She walks toward the door, opening it only wide enough for me to see her face.

"Leave this place," she says, her voice filled with anger.

"You did not wait for me?" I ask, dismayed.

"How could I?" she cries. "You are a traitor!"

Over and over this dream came, in one form or another, and when in time its theme became less frequent, I worried over what its disappearance portended. The green silk gloves I'd bought for Cate in New York I had kept in my possession, holding on to them as if they were a talisman, a tangible demonstration of my faith that this episode would soon end and I'd put them on her hands. Now they lay in the bottom of my knapsack where I was afraid to touch them.

I went about my business as Arnold's personal scribe, but suspended, as best I could, the natural inclination for camaraderie with the soldiers and sailors. I got along with them as necessary to fit in, but I could not bear to learn small human details about the lives of these soldiers and expect to fight against them. In war, I believed, you must love something enough to defend it with your life, or hate a thing enough to kill; there is no middle ground. Every contradiction, every antagonism in this idea was embodied by Arnold, and I could entertain no other. I waited desperately for the day to come when we would sail back north.

When at last we returned to New York in early June, I was afforded a day of shore leave before eventually being quartered again in the city. I walked to Peck's Market by the wharfs at the end of Ferry Street, passing twice by the Underhills' boardinghouse. On the second pass I saw Amos tending his garden in the side yard. There was a narrow alleyway beside it that led to a stable, and it provided some privacy from Queen Street. I stood next to the low white fence. Amos was on his knees, facing away from me, pulling weeds.

"It's good weather for a garden," I said loudly.

"Yes," he answered, without looking over his shoulder. I wondered if he had seen my uniform as I had rounded the corner.

Although confident there was no one within earshot, I lowered my voice.

"Does Miss Dell reside here?"

Amos spun around, still on his knees; he looked me over, then picked himself up and brushed off his breeches.

"God Almighty," he said.

We determined quickly that he had received all of my dispatches, and none had raised suspicion. The important information had got his attention, and he had delivered it somehow to his contact, who I suspected was Tallmadge.

"Where do you go next?" he asked.

"I don't know. I will send a letter."

"This must be difficult—do you want to give it up? Do you want to escape?"

"Every day," I said. "But escape is no easy thing. Both sides have cause to hang me."

"Come to this house," he said. "Come at night, and I will hide you, for as long as it takes."

My breathing quivered, for here, it seemed, was my only friend. I thanked him, and told him that I did not yet know what I would do.

"So, this young lady," I said, ending our conversation. "Miss Dell—is she a handsome woman?"

Amos looked downward at the soil, then lifted his eyes toward me.

"Helen of Troy's beauty launched a thousand ships," he said. "We'll see how many our Hannah will launch."

4

September came. I was still one of Arnold's legionnaires, and we were at sea again, aboard the thirty-two-gun frigate *Amphion*. The sailors were unknown to me, but I was familiar now with nearly all of Arnold's loyalists and traitors. We were joined by the Thirty-eighth Regiment of the British army. I was nervous because our next destination had been a well-guarded secret; only the day before sailing did I learn of Arnold's target. I hastily wrote a letter to Hannah Dell and buried it deep within the canvas mailbag minutes before it was tossed into the last dispatch boat. There was hardly enough time; but if Providence took a part in this, Amos would receive the letter and rush it to Tallmadge, who would alert an army of militiamen to greet the traitor. Then I would leave this war and find a way home.

On the fourth day of September, soon after sunrise, we set off from our rendezvous point at Whitestone and sailed into Long Island Sound, a fleet of more than two dozen ships and two thousand men, on a mission to destroy the privateers that harassed the British from New London and Groton on the coast of Connecticut, where the Thames River meets the sound. I would be close enough to home. My time had come.

I sat on a trunk at the center of the lower deck, deep in thought, planning contingencies for my escape. The hammocks had been rolled, creating space to gather, and the soldiers who would soon march on New London were animated and jovial in these early hours, although I knew that in a day or two they would become stern and sober when the fighting approached.

"Fresh fish tonight, sir," said a redcoat named MacIntosh. "First night out of port, always the best meal of the voyage. Mackerel and herring, and some bluefish, I'm told—oily stuff."

"A thousand times better than salt cod!" answered a thin-faced redcoat.

"Or stinking meat and maggot biscuits," said another.

"I wish it was salmon and pastry and juniper berries, but I will not complain," MacIntosh rejoined.

Nathan Frink, whose lovesick letters, unknown to him, had not yet earned him the cat-o'-nine-tails, chimed in: "When I was a lad, my father taught me to catch salmon in the Housatonic River . . ."

"What name is that?" said another redcoat, in a thick cockney accent. "H*oooo*s-uh-town-eek!"

"When the rivers ran fast in the spring," Frink continued, "and the salmon came upriver to spawn, they came in thousands! A lad could walk across the river on their backs!"

"Hah! Methinks you're a liar!" the thin-faced redcoat exclaimed.

"Don't believe me," Frink retorted. "We'll ask Mr. Wheatley."

Thus my quiet reverie was interrupted.

"Mr. Wheatley," Frink called out, his voice rising in tenor. "Surely, when you were a lad, your father taught you to fish for salmon?"

I did not hesitate; truth was not important.

"He did," I answered.

"And could you walk across the river on their backs?"

"There were a great many fish," I agreed, "and whereas Mr. Frink was a light and dainty young man, I am confident he could dance across their backs."

There was raucous laughter at this. Frink seemed to take offense, but the joviality of the redcoats overwhelmed his indignation.

Soon, I thought, this will be over. I bowed my head and closed my eyes, letting my mind wander deep into the past, reminding myself of the person I was, so I could reclaim myself.

5

I remembered: The day I shot the bear was cool and clear. The sun settled in the late afternoon and the sky turned orange and crimson, and many times I looked toward the barn where the bear was suspended from a tree limb. My mother and a man from a farm nearby had cut it and pulled out the guts and now it hung, as if descending from the sky above. It was my bear; I had killed it. Inside the house, Mother stirred the embers of the fire, which mimicked the red-orange glow that seared the horizon. We ate. Then, sitting near the fire, she told me about my father.

We had rarely spoken of him, and though I knew there must be some reason for this, I wanted desperately to know about him; he was a mystery that filled my childhood thoughts. There were moments when my curiosity swelled to the point of eruption and I asked about him, but my cautious inquiries were met with silence and visible sadness, so I learned to live with unanswered questions. But on this night she spoke of her own accord, perhaps seeing in me, on this day, something that made it safe: an acknowledgment, perhaps, of the effects of time on us both.

What she said relieved me of a fear that had grown within, that my promise as a son had been insufficient to tether my father to this earth. And even though Mother's recollections were tinged with regret, for they told of desires unmet, her words filled me with gladness, revealing to me my own worth. She told me that my father had dreamed of taking me with him to the Merrimack River, to the oak-shaded basin of Amoskeag Falls, where giant Atlantic salmon fought their way upstream in such numbers that they crowded the river below the falls. He promised that, as I grew, he would teach me to catch them, and how to cure the orange meat with woodsmoke. Once his boy was older he planned for us to hunt together, traversing the woods the way he said the Mohicans did, calling to one another in whistles and birdsongs, and coaxing white-tailed deer into our gunsights. In the fields that surrounded the house we would break the soil, plant together, harvest together, and tend chickens and hogs. No sooner had I learned to walk than I followed at his heels, eager to trail him and running to keep up, and this he loved. Mother remembered vividly a day when he put me on his shoulders so I could pick apples from the high branches, and I would pull mightily, bending the branch until the fruit snapped off, and I would scream with delight, and he would laugh with as much joy as she had ever seen in him.

It pleased me, too, that Mother found happiness telling me this, which I saw unmistakably in her face. But then the gleam and glint in her eyes faded, and they took on the worried look that I knew well. She talked about the war against the French and how my father had been a soldier. He had greater courage than most men, she told me, and he had learned useful things traveling in the wilderness and soldiering among the Stockbridge Indians. He could live on the food he found in the woods. He had a keen eye with a musket and was quick to reload; he made arrows fletched with eagle feathers and stitched a quiver of deerskin. He was a strong man. He felled trees with his axe, and built the hearth of fieldstones. He was a good man, she said, and repeated it, again and again: he was a good man.

But he came home from the war with scars. Mother said his memories of the war were a great burden. She thought about this, and sat quietly for a while. Looking at the embers and the flames that sporadically rose up, her eyes tightened and I could hear her breathing punctuate her words.

She told me that a wild beast of some sort had once been killing the stock at night.

"When was this?" I asked.

"You were just learning to speak," she said. "Your sister was nigh, but not yet delivered."

Father, she continued, resolved to lie in wait for the beast and kill it. He hid himself in the wagon, and the first night slept there. The second night he waited again. Mother said she had fallen asleep when she heard a war cry, as if from a savage, and the footfalls of a man running toward the barn. She roused herself and heard the burst of a musket shot.

"Was it a bear?" I asked.

"No," she said. "Your father had a brother who lived close and came to inspect the safety of the animals."

"Who was he?" I asked. "Did I know him?"

Her head leaned forward and in the flickering light I saw her grief.

"Your father had awakened as if in the war. He saw only shadows, and believed it was an ambush, so he fired at his brother, and put a musket ball through his heart."

My face felt singed, as if the embers had become a furnace, and my thoughts flashed the image of my bear hanging in the darkness outside, and the clearest memory of my father, suspended above the earth and twisting toward me.

She did not cry, I suspect because she had already done so, as much as one could across the years. But I, however much wanting to be a man, wept like a boy.

"The next day your sister was born. She came too early, and we did not think she would live."

When this was said, she reached for my hands and held them between hers and, looking into my eyes, searched for the unknown.

"Do you remember—did he say anything to you, on that day?"

I told her what he said to me, and how I'd walked away, but then had turned and gone back to him.

She took both of my hands and held them to her face, and we never spoke of it again.

6

As the British fleet approached New London and the mouth of the Thames River, two cannon shots exploded from Fort Trumbull, one following the other, just as the first light of dawn lit the sky in scarlet and cast long gray shadows of masts and spars. Immediately, as if lying in wait, a third cannon was fired from the *Amphion*, startling even the soldiers on deck making ready to board landing boats. The two shots from shore were an alarm from a lookout—I had hoped to hear them—to rouse the Connecticut militiamen to battle. The third shot was Arnold's contrivance, turning the urgent two-shot call to arms into an unthreatening three-shot announcement—one that heralded good news, a celebration of an incoming prize taken at sea, and an invitation for Connecticut's fighting men to roll over and resume their sleep.

The fleet—by now some thirty vessels, including the *Lively*, the *Beaumont*, and the *Recovery*, each with twenty guns or more—had arrived a day earlier and waited several miles out in the Long Island Sound, heading for the ports of New London and Groton only after midnight under cover of darkness. The mission called for troops to disembark on either side of the river: Arnold and his troops would advance on the western bank to New London, while Colonel Eyre and Major Montgomery, with the Fortieth and Fifty-fourth Regiments, marched along the eastern bank to Groton. Now a gusty wind, shifting its direction, made it hard for the ships to hold position at the mouth of the river. The wind flapped the blue-gray cloak Arnold wore over his red coat as he surveyed the shore with his spyglass and looked upriver, where fifteen miles north his broken father, his pious mother, and his siblings taken by fever lay side by side in the burial ground. On the streets and in the houses, visible through the round view of his glass, there were people with whom he once did business, played card games, and took friendly meals. Some of them would die today. As he slid his spyglass shut and reached under his cloak, I saw the small pistol, his last defense, protruding from a pocket of his coat.

As the first flatboats carrying units of the Thirty-eighth Regiment skidded onto patches of beach, near the lighthouse on the New London side where the river spilled into the sound, musket fire erupted from a grove of trees and from a warehouse on the riverbank. Several British frigates and two bomb ketches met the muskets with volleys of cannon fire. Projectiles rocketed overhead with piercing whistles as seven hundred men, two dozen horses, field artillery, and carriages were quickly shuttled from the ships to the shore on either side of the river. In the flatboats sixteen oarsmen rowed in unison, while forty redcoats sat facing inward on two rows of long benches, tight against one another, their muskets upright between their knees. A sailor manned the tiller while another called commands to the oarsmen. The redcoats said little, but grumbled and cursed at the crossfire. Near us, a bateau full of Jägers, never comfortable while defenseless and crammed on a boat, sang a hymn. Beside me was a Welshman named Hughes. Twisting his head partly toward me, he spoke from the side of his mouth.

"I hear this is Arnold's own homeland, is it not?"

"Yes," I answered.

He said nothing else, and resumed his steely forward gaze.

On shore, a drummer beat a call to order. The soldiers of the Thirty-eighth Regiment, joined by Arnold's American Legion and a contingent of Jägers, formed into marching order with regular efficiency, emerging from the boats on the coastline like rogue waves. The drummers beat the rat-tat-tat rhythm of an advance, and the marching army took the shape of a red and white serpent, speckled with flashes of sunlight on the silvery bayonets, slithering up the road toward New London. At its head, on horseback, was Arnold, who showed no hesitation as he pointed his sword and hollered commands, sending a column of his army to the left, to a small barricade he called Fort Nonsense, and the rest against the imposing Fort Trumbull on the bank of the river. As Arnold suspected, the fort was lightly defended—the foiled alarm was surely to blame—and the sporadic musket shot that came from the parapets was overwhelmed by fire from British six-pounders that shattered the stockade walls and dislodged the stone that sat atop the earthworks. Two shots from the fieldpieces blasted apart the wooden gateway. A team of Jägers charged in, clearing shards and running to protect the heavy cannons that pointed at the Thames River and the Long Island Sound, saving them from being spiked and rendered useless by the militiamen. When a Jäger reappeared at the broken gate waving an arm and hollering in German, five artillery officers with their gunnery crews marched at quick pace into the fort, followed by an ammunition wagon and two fieldpieces drawn by horses.

Arnold ordered a division to march to the docks to destroy the ships and warehouses, and another to advance toward New London's center. He rode at the head of this column, and I was close behind him on foot. My assignment was to write orders for Arnold to be dispatched as needed. My fervent hope was to be given an order and to dispatch it myself; I would hurry, with luck on a horse, and fall back to the coastline, routing myself up an empty path where I'd scuttle my red coat and the accouterments of my uniform, and desert—once again, but this time toward home and my American compatriots, to whom I would tell my unlikely story and fight to regain my good name and honor.

As the road turned from the shipyards toward the town, cannons from the captured fort erupted in a volley that crashed into the hull of an escaping American brig. I turned my head in time to see crewmen leaping overboard, not wanting to be casualties of the next shot. A sloop at the end of a dock caught my eye as blazing orange flames shot skyward from the center of its deck, its foresail raised but not set, flapping in the wind and pulling the ship into the river as it billowed black smoke. I saw skirmishing at the dock and heard the sharp cracks of musket fire, but the ships tied there were engulfed in flame in quick succession. Scattered in the center of the river, clusters of rowboats moved at a rapid pace, ferrying men—militia, I presumed—across to Fort Griswold, upriver on a hilltop on the Groton side, which would surely be attacked later in the morning. Their oarsmen—two or four per boat—strained mightily, and all onboard kept their heads low, fearing the carnage that would come from a single cannonball. The British ignored them, having plenty of larger ships to target, as every brig, sloop, and schooner frantically raised sail and struggled to get upriver. When the great cough of a cannon punched the air, a second or two would pass before a bloodcurdling crash shattered wood, metal, and—God help the sailors—bone.

The rhythmic clunking sound of the marching army changed tenor, sharper now as men, horses, and artillery carriages crossed a wide wooden bridge over a jut in the river that marked the entrance to the town. Here we came upon the stores and shipyard offices that lined the main street, and the cross streets adorned with the houses of merchants and sea captains. Servants had hastily piled family silver and furnishings into wagons and were snapping the long reins and cracking whips as they looked over their shoulders. Young boys sporadically raced between buildings, carrying terse messages to their occupants, sometimes catching sight of the advancing army and retreating to a hideaway. Women ran, pulling children by the hand, the smallest hoisted on their hip. Dogs barked. Behind us, cannons continued to blast from the fort, splintering ships in the river, and farther away the British frigates could be heard firing on ships that tried to make a getaway into the open water of Long Island Sound.

A squadron of Jäger marksmen scouted ahead and watched around corners for ambushes. Gunshots erupted from an alleyway on a cross street and hit a Jäger square in the chest, knocking him hard on his back to reveal a swelling bloodstain above his heart. Another Jäger dropped his rifle and went down on his knees. Then a cascading volley snapped from the other direction and two redcoats fell hard to the ground. Arnold's horse pounded its rear legs as if to run, but was quickly brought to rein. Arnold's voice rose above the commotion, directing a volley of return fire at the hidden militiamen that cracked the air like lightning.

A grizzled sergeant, with a pink scar running from his left ear to his chin, reached into a box affixed to a carriage and raised a stick the length of an axe handle, with thick oily cloth wrapped tightly around its far end. He held it forward as if offering it to Arnold, waiting for the general's attention.

My stomach twisted. *These are his own people*, I thought.

Arnold's eyes locked on the sergeant. He gave a decisive nod.

"Burn it," he commanded. "All of it!"

The sergeant barked orders as a half-dozen redcoats pulled torches from the same box and an artillery gunner produced a bucket of fire. A haze of white heat and orange flame suddenly enveloped the oil-soaked rags. Three of the redcoats moved quickly to the warehouse while the other three crossed the road to where the lifeless Jäger lay on the ground. Two more redcoats charged the front of the nearest house and smashed the windows with the butts of their muskets. The sergeant reached his torch inside and pressed the fire against the long curtains, which immediately ignited to create a wall of flame.

The Hessians, eager to avenge their fallen mate, quickly surrounded the adjacent house and broke every window within their reach. A woman ran screaming from the front door, her hands raised in front of her, palms outward to push them all back, shouting desperately at a redcoat approaching with a torch.

"Don't burn this house!" she yelled at him, frantic and crying. "Children live here! This is my house!"

Another redcoat stepped in front of her and swung his left arm against her head, knocking her to the ground, then pointed his bayonet at her chest.

"Begone—or die," he commanded her in a thick cockney growl. She picked herself up, gathering her skirt, and ran back into the house, where by now bright orange flames leaped up behind the shattered windows.

I saw a boy of fourteen or fifteen and young girl run from the backyard to an alleyway, urgently pulling two smaller children by their hands. I wanted to see the defiant woman join them, running to safety, but she did not exit the rear of the house.

I looked at Arnold, who gave a passing glance at the burning houses before returning his gaze to the center of the town ahead and ordering his army forward. The warehouse was engulfed in flame, whipped by the wind and fueled by something stored inside it that burned hot and billowed blue-black smoke. The redcoats marched quickly past it, but more shots came from the side streets that led to the docks; commands were shouted and several platoons cleared those streets with overwhelming volleys of musket fire. A fieldpiece was pulled up from the back by a team of jittery horses that yanked at their bits, tossing their heads up and down in the smoke.

I paused amid the disorder at the fringes of the marching column, insisting to myself that I must see the woman leave the burning house. In a moment she did, again through the front door, but this time there were flames climbing her skirt, burning on one side below her knee but rising quickly as she ran, futilely trying to avoid the fire that was part of her. The Jägers and redcoats did nothing to help her; they surely set eyes on the burning woman, but they turned away from her, and continued to smash and burn the row of houses.

From a garden across the street, beside a house not yet consumed by fire, a black man ran to the woman, grabbed her, and pulled her to the ground. Lifting himself onto his knees, he beat on the burning dress with his hands and arms. The redcoats ignored him. He stood and grabbed the woman's arms with his burned hands and led her up the street, leaving a trail of dirt and dust and a few red embers dying in the swirl.

I heard my name. A lieutenant on horseback hailed me and I ran forward to Arnold, who leaned down from his horse to hear a report from a local loyalist. Instinctively I withdrew a half-sheet of paper from my pocket and a wooden lead pencil.

"Wheatley," the general said. "Tell Colonel Eyre across the river to move as far upriver as he can, quickly, to hold back the procession of retreating ships."

I wrote this within seconds in the style of orders to which he was accustomed, then handed it to him for his mark. When he reached an empty hand toward me I gave him a second sheet, on which he wrote:

Take Sgt. Wheatley across the river at once. B. Arnold, Brig. Gen.

Arnold pointed toward the river, jabbing his finger into the air. "Too many goddamn ships are getting beyond our reach," he said. "Take whatever men you need. There are boats with oarsmen at the docks. Make haste."

The lieutenant who had hailed me sat upright in his saddle and eyed two of his men. "Take the sergeant to the docks," he ordered. "Find a boat. Make certain he gets to Colonel Eyre."

The three of us backtracked toward Fort Trumbull, moving at quick time against the current of marching soldiers filling the main street like a flood. The smoke of burning pitch and tar from a flaming warehouse blew across our path, and the advancing redcoats coughed and blinked and turned away their eyes, but still marched resolutely forward into the town. Cascades of gunshots echoed against stone buildings, resounding at startling angles, while the low roar of burning homes and warehouses seethed and crackled, amplified by the swirling winds whipped up by the fires. We turned toward the river and hurried through a low cloud of smoke and ash that stung our eyes. Instinctively we headed to the dock farthest from the fighting, from which the burning ships had already been pushed into the river. One of the redcoats spotted a whaleboat—a long narrow craft with pointed bow and stern that moved much faster than the flatboats—coming from Fort Trumbull, staying close to shore. We signaled to it from the foot of the dock. Two soldiers disembarked with a crate of torches, fulfilling an order Arnold had sent after the first warehouse was lit on fire.

We gave Arnold's order to the helmsman, who told the four men at the oars to row with all haste to the opposite shore. The men glanced at one another, having no more desire to row into the maelstrom than we did. The river, a half-mile wide, was littered with the burning carcasses of American schooners and sloops. Those that did not burn were desperately tacking upriver, harnessing the wind against the tide and current. Dozens of small boats zigzagged while rescuing sailors, or shuttling supplies, redcoats, militiamen, or messages. Over their heads musket fire and cannon shot flew from every direction, as the British fired at the ships sailing north and Connecticut militiamen in Groton shot across the river to harass Fort Trumbull, both filling the air with unseen rounds that rattled every nerve even if they missed the flesh.

Keeping our heads down, avoiding lethal hazards we sensed but could not see, we steered past the burning hulk of a two-masted schooner that was minutes from submerging and turning its fire to steam. I directed the helmsman toward a stony outcrop on the riverbank that would give us some small bit of cover.

"I can go alone from here," I told the two redcoats who accompanied me.

"We will go with you," one of them answered.

"Go back—I don't need you."

"Our orders, sir," he said firmly, "are to take you to the colonel."

The three of us jumped onto the rocky riverbank and scrambled over some scrub brush, taking our bearings while the helmsman let his crew rest. The two redcoats carried muskets, and fixed their bayonets once we were ashore. I led them up a short, steep hill, heading straight ahead and due east, believing Colonel Eyre and his soldiers to be to my right, and the Connecticut militiamen to my left. I wanted a confrontation with neither.

"Sir!" said the redcoat who'd insisted on his orders. "This path on the right will lead us to Colonel Eyre."

"It's too exposed," I answered. "Wait here—let me go forward and see what lies ahead."

The two redcoats stood in place, alert and defensive, their muskets lowered as if to charge, while I walked quickly toward a cluster of scrub pine and shrubs on a sandy rise. I had to decide whether I would play along with my escorts, or run. I was already winded from climbing up the bank, but another chance might not come.

The voice of a boy screamed behind me. Before I could fully turn around, three musket shots cracked so loudly and so close that I fell backwards against the rise, unsure if I'd been hit. My hands searched my chest and I raised my head to look at my legs. There was no wound; I hadn't been the target. Below me on the hill both redcoats lay on their backs, their white waistcoats soaked with blood.

Beside me, something moved. I turned my head and looked into the barrel of gun.

7

For months I had designed my escape, my desertion back to American lines. It consumed my nights in the dim hulls of British warships, and gripped my imagination during the rhythmic marches with Arnold's army in Virginia. I envisioned every sight and sound, wanting to see and know the lay of the land, the time of day, the people who would assist or confront me, and how I'd read their expressions and answer their questions. I dreamed of this to sustain me through my long and dangerous masquerade, but also to anticipate every contingency I could conceive so that I would be prepared when the moment came.

I thought of André and his captors, knowing I could face a decision like the one that surely haunted him at the gallows: confronted by militants in common clothing—militiamen, loyalists, bandits—I would not know which details of my two identities to disclose, or what evidence would save my life. With only seconds to observe his captors, André had revealed his British loyalty. From there it was a straight line to the hangman.

As I lay on my back, a young militiaman—hardly more than a boy—stood above me on the path I'd been climbing, aiming his musket at my head. Below me, one of the redcoats was struggling for breath and coughing blood; the other was clearly dead. From another path to the right came several armed men, heading toward me. Past them, in the river, I saw the oarsmen of the whaleboat heaving mightily against the waves, making their own escape.

"Give him water," one of the men said, pointing to the gasping redcoat. Another, notably older than the rest, swung a tin bottle with a cord strap off his shoulder and bent down on one knee. Then, for a moment, everyone held still, because the gasping had stopped.

"He's dead, James."

I looked at the young militiaman holding the gun on me. The long musket barrel trembled while his hands shook nervously.

"I am an officer in the Continental Army," I said, breathing quickly, my own voice shaking. "General Washington himself will vouch for me."

The man called James looked at me, his eyes narrowing.

"Why, he's a liar!" said the young one holding the gun.

"I served in the Third New Hampshire," I said. "Major Tallmadge and Henry Lee both know me."

"You are a loyalist," James said, uncertain if it was a question or a statement.

"I am not," I insisted. Two dead redcoats lay on the ground behind my captors. I heard the drumrolls of a marching army nearby.

"I'm an officer in the Continental Army, sent by General Washington to spy on the enemy, and I'm trying to escape."

James took his eyes off me and looked south, to where the advancing British army was, at most, a half-mile away. The drumrolls that paced the advance seemed louder than they had been just seconds ago.

"Tie his hands," he ordered. "We'll take him to the fort."

As the older militiaman bound my hands with a strap of leather, James pulled the orders from the pocket of my red coat.

"Is this Arnold's doing?"

"It is," I answered. "All of it."

"He is the Devil's bastard son," James said, clenching his jaw.

"Arnold is across the river, in command," I told him. "Colonel Eyre is leading the Fortieth and Fifty-fourth Regiments up this side."

"To where? How far?"

"Not far. His intention is to destroy the ships sailing upriver."

James looked out at the smoldering vessels that slowly spun in the crossways of current and tide, across to the flame-engulfed docks of New London, past the black smoke of the burning warehouses, and farther to the torched houses with orange flames whipping up from where the roofs had been, tongues of fire spitting from their windows.

He seethed. "I would kill Arnold with my own two hands," he said.

My captors took me quickly north on a footpath close to the riv-erbank, across patches of swampy sand, over large flat rocks, and weaving between tangled trees. I knew this landscape would slow the march of the British regiments, but still they would not be far behind us. For ten months I had been absent from my rightful brothers-in-arms. There was much I was eager to say, to recount my record as an honorable soldier, but little of it would serve me if they believed I was a loyalist or deserter—which, on its face, stood to reason.

I kept the rapid pace, but with my hands tied behind me I could not climb a crag of jagged stone.

"Dobbin!" James called, addressing the young one. "Grab his arms and pull him up."

Lifted onto the crest, I again made my case as we hurried across the rocks.

"Sir, I am a captain in the Continental Army. Major Lee and Major Tallmadge—do you know them?—they will both vouch for me. General Washington himself is acquainted with my mission, and he—"

"Be quiet," James barked, agitated but not angry. "I have no idea who you are. We'll deal with you later."

From atop the crag I could see the bastions of Fort Griswold. Its walls were earthen, topped and reinforced with stone, with a dozen or so eighteen-pounders pointing toward the river, and lighter field-pieces arrayed around the fort. As we drew closer, other men ap-proached the fort from all directions, men both young and old, in groups and alone, all of them in haste. They carried muskets, car-tridge boxes suspended from shoulder straps, wooden canteens and tin water bottles. Most wore the everyday clothes of farmers, labor-ers, or tradesmen, out for a day of work. They hailed one another as they arrived, and the men already on the bastions called out greet-ings, underscored with reassurance, in the spirit of those who know they are about to be outnumbered.

Thick clouds of black smoke draped a curtain above the river, obscuring the inferno that enveloped New London, until the wind ripped the curtain and revealed, for moments at a time, a seascape of burning ships, or the customhouse ablaze, or a long contiguous line of flame consuming row upon row of warehouses. Through briefly opened portals in the churning smoke, I could see carts loaded with people and household possessions fleeing up the hills to the north, and the town center—its stores, the printshop, clusters of houses— glowing the hot red of burning cinders, and the tall steeple of a church wrapped in fire as if by the Devil, spitting shards of flame toward the heavens.

Clusters of shots echoed over the rocky crags and cedar swamps from where we had come, and these were returned with rapid cascades of British musket fire. Skirmishers, like James and his crew, were harassing the British regiments, buying time for the men to gather at the fort and prepare for battle. Next to a redoubt on the hillside, below the fort on a plateau facing the river, we scrambled into a covered way, a waist-deep ditch that gave some protection to soldiers moving between the redoubt and the main fort, barely wide enough for two men to pass. On the rampart above us, from behind the high parapet, several men stopped their work, turning their tormented gaze away from the cataclysm across the river and staring directly down at me.

"Who's the wicked scum?" one yelled.

"Prisoner," James called back.

"Cut his throat!" shouted another.

James and his men led me through a slim entryway at the fort's southern wall. Inside the fort, at the edge of the parade ground, a group of soldiers faced us in a semicircle, inspecting me with eyes reddened by the wafting smoke borne by the wind, and by the anguish carried with it.

"Colonel Ledyard," one called, turning his head toward the center of the fort. "A prisoner!"

A large, tall man, of imposing bearing and obvious strength, stepped in amid the group. Someone called him "Captain."

"Where'd you get him?" he asked.

"Came ashore by the gray rock," James answered. "We killed two others, but this one was unarmed."

Several men stepped aside and an officer—Ledyard, the colonel—stepped forward.

"Says he's one of us, sent to spy on the British by General Washington himself," James continued.

The colonel looked me square in the eye.

"Prove it."

Quickly, I began reciting my credentials, my history, and those I knew who could vouch for me.

The colonel raised his hand, signaling me to stop.

"What force is headed to this fort?"

"Colonel Eyre and Major Montgomery, with the Fortieth and Fifty-fourth Regiments," I repeated.

"How many men?"

"Three to four hundred, on this side of the river."

The colonel made no reaction, but I knew he was rapidly calculating the strength of his force against theirs, and that his calculation would bring no comfort.

"On the other side of the river?" the colonel asked.

"At least four hundred."

"And who has wrought this destruction?" he asked. A cloud of gray and black smoke was passing overhead, spreading out like fingers and casting narrow shadows over half the fort.

"Who is in command of all this?"

Every man looked at me but James, who knew the answer and set his eyes upon the colonel.

"Arnold," I answered. "Benedict Arnold."

Amid the splintering shadows that spread over the fort, an oblong ray of light penetrated the haze and moved east across the parade ground, as if the black fingers of smoke swept a lantern overhead. The light settled on the group of men for an instant, illuminating in vivid detail the faces of the colonel, of the militiaman James, of young Dobbin, of the hulking captain, and of each of the dozen or so men who stood before me.

By that light, I saw that they were resolved to fight.

8

"Put him in the cell," the colonel said, aware that a battle was imminent and there was no way to guarantee that I was either friend or foe. Dobbin, the young militiaman, took my arm and we followed James quickly toward the southeast corner of the fort, where a rounded rise of earth and heavy stone made plain that we were headed for the magazine, where barrels of gunpowder were stored and protected from the incoming fire that could explode it and reduce the fort and its occupants to a charred crater. It made no sense to imprison me there, but a quick look left and right revealed how primitive the fort was, with little more than the protective earthworks, the arrays of cannons, and a simple wooden barracks, hardly more than a long barnyard shed, built beside the eastern rampart.

My eyes focused on the magazine's heavy oak door when James pulled me suddenly to the left, and I saw my cell. Next to the reinforced wall of the magazine, no farther than the length of a musket, was a narrow cave-like portal dug a foot or two deep into the earthen bulwark, with a short wooden door no higher than a man's waist set back within the portal.

"Damn it," James cursed. "There's no lock." He looked quickly along the ground where it met the stone wall. "Wait here with him, Dobbin," he ordered, and hurried toward the barracks.

"Don't worry—I won't run," I said to the young militiaman.

"You wouldn't get far," he answered.

"They call you Dobbin?"

He nodded.

"Well, Dobbin, I ask you to trust me in this: If the fighting becomes fierce and you need another man, know that I am willing to fight. Let your commanders know that."

Dobbin looked me in the eye. "I will, sir."

Across the grounds of the fort, James had gone inside the barracks, looking for a lock and key.

"I was ordered by General Washington to be a spy. It is a dirty business—I'm sure you know that—but I want nothing more than to put aside the deceit and be who I am: an American soldier."

Then, as if speaking to myself, I added, "I am an honorable man."

Dobbin looked over his shoulder, then back at me. "An honorable man is worth something."

From the swarm of men who hurried about the fort, James suddenly reappeared.

"Here's the lock," he said, breathing quickly as he handed a lock and key to Dobbin.

"Get in there," James said to me. "God willing, we will figure out who you are when all this is done." He told Dobbin to lock me up, then hurried away.

I bent down, then settled on my knees and put my hands on the dirt to crawl like a dog through the squat portal into the earthwork. The small wooden door was pushed shut behind me, and I heard the smack of the metal latch.

Inside the cell was dark, except for a square patch of light from a window the size of an orderly book cut into the door, with three black iron rods that blocked the passage of anything more than light and air. I extended my arms and felt for the walls on either side and behind me, and figured that three men could fit within, seated side by side. I could stand only if I bent my knees and hunched my back. Crouching, I swept my hands along the dirt floor, and up and down the walls. The chamber was empty and barren, and I was alone.

Suddenly, while I was still looking about, waiting for my eyes to adjust to the darkness, a violent punch hit me, pounding my core like a mallet on a drum. My arms flew up instinctively, covering my head as I dropped down unsteadily onto the floor. For an instant I thought I'd been ambushed by some unseen vigilante, but knew a moment later that a cannonball had hit the rampart somewhere close and caused the earthen wall to quake. The sounds of incoming cannon fire, the explosive cough from a distant gun and the whistle of the ball cutting through the air—these sounds came as whispers into my buried cell. But the concussion made the earth shudder, and there was earth all around me.

I sat on the dirt floor facing the door and the shallow notch that was the anteroom to my cell. On my knees I crawled to the small barred window, pressing my face against it to observe the thrust and parry of the fight. I could see the north side of the interior field, called the parade ground, or the place d'armes. Also within view were several of the eighteen-pounders perched on the western rampart and aimed at the river. Past them I could make out most of the corner bastion, where the wall expanded and extended outward like an arrowhead. Two big guns were visible there, but I knew there were others I couldn't see, aimed at Fort Trumbull. Straight across the field from me was the sally port, the main entryway into the fort, where half the stockade door was closed and two men held the other half open only enough to admit the last of the gathering militiamen. To my right, my view ended at the midpoint of the sparse wooden barracks.

Sounds passed into my cell in muffled echoes. Voices shouting commands and requests, and the encouragements hollered among men arming themselves against fear, were deadened as they hit the earth and funneled through my window. There was so much to be done, yet nothing I could do, and still my heart pounded rapidly in my chest. I knelt, then sat on the ground. Through the window and its vertical bars I could see the top of the fort's stockade door swing closed, and above that the sky, a background of blue muddled by gray haze, streaked with feathering trails of black smoke from the fire consuming New London. Through my portal, as if through a spyglass, I watched the smoke swirl, twist, and billow, splitting apart and merging into new forms, changing again and again, passing from my sight but always replenished, born anew of the burning city. In those shapes I saw a hammer drive a nail, and it became a house, small and rectangular; from it grew the pitch of a roof, and it was my father's house; and the door opened and with that it became my mother's house; and the wind blew and the shape became the hearth where we would talk and work and she would teach me to read and add numbers. A gust broke it apart but a column of ashen cloud whirled, and I saw in it a face, one that I longed for, but the wind churned and then there was nothing I could recognize, and I thought, *Make me to know mine end, and the measure of my days, what it is: that I may know how frail I am.* A shroud of black smoke curled over the bulwark and settled in the hollow in front of my cell; I covered the window with the palms of my hands, protecting my damp, heavy air.

When I pulled back my hands I saw Ledyard—the colonel—and the captain, and a dozen or more officers and men huddled at the center of the fort. The colonel selected three of them and they walked to the gate, waited as it was pulled open, and passed through. Outside the gate, I suspected, standing between the poised regiments and the fort, there must be a delegation of British officers under a flag of truce, prepared to offer terms of surrender: the typical hard choice of capitulation or conquest with no quarter, with its implicit promise of death. As militiamen peered over the ramparts to observe the formality with which the officers communicated, the burly captain ordered his men to quicken their preparations. Men checked their cartridge boxes and spoke among themselves in clusters.

Within minutes the three officers returned, and the colonel ordered every man to the parade ground, where he held a council of war. With my ear turned to the window I heard a mix of words amid mumbled voices: "attack," "bastards," "reinforcements," "families," "die," "honor," an inventory of artillery shells, and several times "Arnold." Then hands were raised, and it seemed that they were all raised, and the three officers walked again to the gate. The men hurried back to their positions, buoyed by righteousness tempered with defiance, and I wanted them to fight, but I feared I was to be a spectator to a harvest of death. I hoped, indeed I prayed, that at the end of this day I would have the opportunity to convince the colonel of my true identity. If the battle went badly, I would have no choice but to continue my masquerade as a loyalist soldier, captured and imprisoned by the Americans. But I believed it more likely that my body would lie on the ground, punctured by ball or bayonet, my lifeblood having spilled from me; or the magazine would blow, and I would be consumed by fire and the shattered earth of this cave-like cell. It is a pity, I thought; all of this is a pity. I glanced left and right into the darkness of my grave, thinking, *The days of our years are threescore years and ten; and if by reason of strength they be fourscore years, yet is their strength labor and sorrow; for soon it is cut off, and we fly away.*

Then at once came the crash of cannonballs pounding into the ramparts, each one smashing against the earth like a massive felled oak tree. Volleys of British musket fire blasted outside the walls, which triggered the explosive return of artillery fire—deadly grapeshot—from the bastions of the fort, and the popping of muskets, sporadic but constant, and the hollers of men at war, and the screams of men dying. I rose to my knees, pressing my face to the barred window, where the acrid smell of gunfire, of steam and sulfur, defiled the air. A boy wearing a light blue cap ran from the far bastion directly toward me—maybe coming to get me, I thought—but steered himself just to my side, to the magazine, then passed before me again, but I could not tell where he went. I leaned my face against the window and pressed my hands against the door, straining to see farther toward the corner of the fort, when I heard a clank—the slip of a latch—and the door moved an inch, as if to open. I pushed against it, meeting some drag, as if a heavy stone were holding it shut. But it was unlocked: Dobbin, the young militiaman, had believed me, I realized. He had seen some truth in me, and left me a way out if the battle turned to cataclysm. This generous act by my young captor caused in me as much sensation as the cannonballs that pounded the fortress wall and rattled my dark cell.

I pulled the door shut, and it stuck tightly against its wooden frame. Seconds later a commotion arose outside the door with loud commands and the legs of soldiers visible through my window. They surrounded a fieldpiece as it was pushed and pulled up the ramp of the bastion nearest me. A giant of a man lifted the trail of the carriage and the others pulled on ropes or pushed the carriage from its front end. As they pushed and pulled, a cannonball struck the barracks at the far end of the parade ground, shattering the wood into splinters that ripped through the air like harpoons. Across the field near the bastion was a well, and I spied the boy in the light blue cap again, with two more boys, hiding behind the well when the barracks shattered, then carrying buckets of water up the slope to where the cannons fired grapeshot and canister down onto the British regiments. Men descended from the ramparts to reload, jumping or sliding on the slick dirt slopes, while others scrambled up to take their place and fire on the enemy. The militiamen were good with their guns and shot quickly, raining a steady fire on the redcoats. A soldier in his shirtsleeves ran to and from the magazine again and again to retrieve powder cartridges for the cannons.

Teams of men—two or three together—carried the wounded and the dead from the bastions to a patch of earth near the barracks, a place I could not see, then hurried back to their positions. Men from the northwest bastion came running toward the magazine with their muskets as a cannonball tore into the wall behind me, so hard that I thought it most surely had penetrated into my cell. Shots were fired rapidly from positions over my head, and more artillery fire hit the wall I was encased in, at times with an earth-quaking thud. Other shots tore the top of the bastion to pieces, blasting earth and shattered stone onto the field and barracks, and knocking men off the rampart, some dead before they hit the ground.

A soldier in a white-fringed hunting shirt stained with blood pointed to the sky above the magazine and yelled: "The flag! Raise the flag!" At that moment there seemed to be a lull in the firing, as if both armies, on either side of the fortress walls, were looking at the empty space where the flag had flown, but had been shot down. Then I heard, carried on the wind from outside the fort, a distant chorus of "Huzzahs!" and I thought, *Have we surrendered?* Quickly I realized that the British regiments, believing the flag had been lowered, must have thought this as well, and were cheering and charging the fort. But their cheers were met with a deafening crackle of musket fire, as if all the guns in the fort ignited at once, and there were screams from without, so loud and anguished that they seeped through the soil.

Two militiamen appeared on the parade ground with their arms around a bundle of sharp wooden pikes, spears with which to stab at the redcoats scaling the walls. They hesitated at the center of the fort, not sure which point of attack needed them most; then each went to a separate bastion. From a stone firepit near the barracks, two men carried a cauldron on a crossbar hoisted across their shoulders, filled with hot water, oil, or shot to pour over the parapets.

The men above me on the rampart, and the redcoats on the far side of my earthen barrier, yelled and cursed, and the wounded screamed. A cannon on the bastion above the magazine fired grape-shot down the length of the wall, clearing it of invaders. I waited for another burst, but the shots from the fort slowed, and became too few. The hulking captain appeared on the parade ground, hurrying awkwardly, carrying a small lifeless body as a light blue cap fell to the ground behind him. Farther on, above him on the bastion, I saw men in red and buff and green coming over the parapet.

The colonel saw this too, and gave the order to cease fire and sur-render the fort. There was confusion as orders were shouted. Sporadic shots rang out, but they dwindled, and with surprising quickness the chaos of battle gave way to stillness. A drumbeat rattled outside the fort. As ordered, the men within the fort grounded their arms, laying their muskets in piles on the packed dirt. Several scrambled to fill their wooden canteens from a bucket, hoping to take this one thing with them when marched to a prison ship. There was no regimental order to these militiamen, but they formed into two columns, several rows deep, and stood quietly. The columns separated up the middle, and through this corridor I could see the colonel, standing in front of his soldiers, facing the door of the fort. The back of his blue coat was spattered with streaks of mud, but the white and silver epaulettes on his shoulders momentarily caught the sun, and matched the silk cockade on the black felt of his cocked hat. He held his sword in both hands, ceremoniously, its brass hilt extended slightly forward, ready to be offered in surrender to the British commanding officer.

On his order, two men slid the beam that barred the fort's heavy stockade door, then pulled the doors back, opening them to the enemy. Outside, a cluster of officers in scarlet and white, with glim-mering silver regimental gorgets, waited fifty feet away. Behind them, several columns of infantry stood in formation, shouldering their muskets, the long guns extending high over their heads, tipped by polished bayonets.

Three British officers walked forward as an order was given for the columns of redcoats to follow, marching until the first column was com-pletely within the fort. Squinting through my portal, I saw that Colonel Eyre was not among the officers; nor was Major Montgomery, which could only mean that they had been killed or wounded in the battle.

The order was given for the redcoats to halt. Colonel Ledyard took two steps forward, extending the hilt of his sword to be received by the British commanding officer, in the formal act of surrender. The officer reached for the sword, wrapping his fingers around the hilt, and withdrew it toward him, to where his hand was even with the gold-buttoned pocket of his scarlet coat. For an instant he held perfectly still, and all the soldiers of both sides were still, and the war itself seemed at a halt.

Then, in an instant, he cocked his arm, bending it at the elbow and pulling the sword back, such that it appeared like an arrow drawn taut in a longbow. With a slight twist of his body, and stepping for-ward on his opposite foot, he thrust the sword into the gut of Colonel Ledyard. He held it there, the point of the sword lifting the colonel's coat behind him before tearing through it, and when he withdrew the blade with equal violence, the first line of the British column dropped to one knee, leveled their muskets, and fired a volley at the unarmed militiamen. I spun my body away from the small portal of my cell and threw my back against the earthen wall beside the door. Another volley, from the second line, exploded in the fort, and the screams of men dying were met by the hollers of those still alive and running for bayoneted muskets to meet the charging redcoats, and for swords and pikes and unloaded guns to use as clubs.

Next to my squat, obscure cell, men threw open the door of the magazine and seized tin canisters of powder cartridges. A cascade of shots at close range killed them all in an instant, and more than one ball drilled into the oak door of my cell. I wrapped my arms around my head, waiting for the kegs of powder in the magazine to blow the fort off the hillside, and heard a British voice shout, "*Stop firing!—You'll send us all to hell together!*" I heard the clash of metal on metal, and wood on bone, and the flaming cough of musket fire; and I heard defiant curses screamed in anger, pleas for mercy, and calls begging for water.

I pressed my hands over my ears, pinching my eyes closed even though there was nothing in the dark cell to see. With my knees drawn up against my chest, I huddled in the blackest corner of my cave, wanting to be blind and deaf, knowing only the rapid, insistent beating of my heart, racing as if in battle, when all I did was hold still.

Thus I stayed for hours, embedded in the earth, reluctantly listening to the moans of the wounded being lifted into carts by the survivors, who in turn were marched to prison ships; to the redcoats scavenging from the bodies they'd slaughtered; to the hammering of iron spikes into the touchholes of the cannons; to the orders of the British officers to dig graves for their dead in the field outside the fort, and the curses they uttered and the prayers they said; and the forlorn cries of the widows who came when the British were gone, who hadn't been widows in the morning; and the boys and old men who spoke quietly, who looked at the eyes that stared back at them, unblinking, who had come to find their fathers and their sons.

I could not tell the time, but it was deep into the night when the fort seemed still at last. Slowly, and tentatively, I pushed open the door to my cell. I had shed my soldier's coat and waistcoat. Lifting myself from a crawl on the wet ground, where I plunged my hand into a sticky puddle, I emerged into the night in my breeches and shirt, dressed only in white. Accustomed to the dark, I made my way furtively alongside the interior fortress wall, not certain that I was alone. In the corner, where the injured had been taken during the battle, coats, boots, and shoes lay on the ground against the barracks, every piece a shade of gray in the darkness. I took a coat because I was beginning to shiver. It was too big, but I could tell it was not from a uniform. I picked up a cap that had been lying on the coat, but it was too small. I thought to take it anyway, for I did not want to leave it on this pile, but I put it down.

From behind the barracks I pulled myself up the earthen slope of the rampart. I discerned an empty field on the other side, and a grove of trees to the right. I slid down into the ravine that surrounded the fort, and bending low, I ran to the trees. I ran through forests, and brush, and grassy fields to the coast of Long Island Sound, and then I followed the rocky waterline and the beaches for several miles east. When at last I sat down, on soft sand in a shallow notch of stone, my troubled thoughts were overcome by the rolling tumult of small waves breaking on the beach, and my eyes closed.

It was just before dawn when I awoke. Pale rays of yellow and orange light shone from across the sound. In the haze I could see the color of my coat: it was green. There was a hole ripped in it above the pocket, and a dark red stain spread across it, shaped like a cluster of seaweed on the sand. The knees of my white breeches were caked with red-brown mud, and dried blood stained my hands.

I lifted myself up and dropped the coat on the sand. Pulling off my shoes, I staggered toward the sea, which still held the summer's warmth, and trudged into the rippling surf that broke upon my knees. The hues of the sky intensified, spreading the colors of fire over the blue-gray heavens. I bent down and splashed my hands in the seawater, shaking them, scraping them, reaching for the sand beneath me, desperate to cleanse them. Collapsing upon my knees, I let the sea take me in. My shirt billowed at the surface until the water drenched its fibers and dragged it down. I pressed my face into the brine, and pushed deeper, and deeper still. Opening my eyes beneath the surface, I saw nothing. Then, as I pulled my head from the dark water, the sun broke over the horizon. At the distant edge of the sea a long thin line ignited, brilliant like a flame, marking the place where the heavens and earth collided, and it seemed to be burning.

PART 4

New England & London
1799–1801

At his house in Gloucester place, Brigadier-general Arnold. His remains were interred on the 21st, at Brompton. Seven mourning coaches and four state carriages formed the cavalcade.

THE GENTLEMAN'S MAGAZINE,

London, June 1801

1

On the last night of the year 1799, well after the sun had set and the cold darkness of winter had turned everything still, I heard an uneven beat of drums, and going out my door to witness the commotion, saw two dozen torches, held aloft among a parade of women and men bundled against the cold. There were children among them, too, who jumped up and down and flailed about as in a dance or a game. Walking close together, with a few stragglers hurrying to keep up, they marched down the road in crosscurrents of shadows and light, perhaps a hundred people, and though my eyes strained I could not see a face that I might know. Nearly all of the revelers sang, some of the men with unusual exuberance—their talents unlocked, most assuredly, by warmed cider and rum:

> *Now like the snake cast off your skin*
> *Of evil thoughts and wicked sin,*
> *And to amend this new year begin:*
> *God send us a merry new year!*

As they rambled beyond me, toward the road that would take them back to town, the singing and the cacophony of talk and laughter blended into a fading chorus, paced by an ebbing echo of the drums. Soon I could no longer see the marchers themselves, but only the ethereal fire that rose from the tops of the torches. When they were completely gone, and there was nothing to see but the gray silhouette of my familiar world, I felt unnerved by their absence. I looked behind me, through a window, at the table where I had been sitting. There was a candle there, and though it burned, it hardly seemed to cast any light.

Time was passing from one age to another. I had waited years for redemption. It had not come.

2

When Henry Taggart had walked down the hill from the Albany hospital, awkwardly waving to me, lifting his one remaining arm while keeping his knapsack from slipping off his shoulder, I was confident that I would see him again. But twenty years had come and gone, and I knew nothing of him. I had thought, every year, to go find him, to find his farm and meet his wife and son. I wanted to see the boy grown to manhood, and his father in good stead: the high-spirited one-armed farmer. If the rumors of my desertion and treason hadn't got to him, or if he had kept faith in my character despite them, I would push the plow for him, and hunt deer with him, and tell him what had happened, the whole thing: how General Greene had summoned me; how Washington himself had appealed to me to feign my desertion; how I had ridden with Champe and outrun our own dragoons; and how we had come so close to bringing Arnold back across the river. I would tell him of our plan and how it was foiled, and how I could have run my knife across Arnold's throat, but followed the imperative of my orders. I would tell him how I was a spy, and not a traitor, and how Champe escaped in Virginia, and I in Connecticut.

I had told this to no one, but I could tell Taggart. Though I hadn't ventured to search for his farm, I often wondered if I might see him, a one-armed man, on the back of a horse, or riding a wagon full of hay, or standing in a road, facing me, ready to grant me absolution.

I never saw Taggart, anywhere. But now it was time to go find him.

All that I knew, from our conversations in Albany two decades earlier, was that he had planned to leave his rough plot in New Hampshire to farm some family acreage near a town called Lebanon, in the fertile soil of southern Connecticut, near Pease Brook before it runs into the Yantic River, which runs into the Thames. Taking a leap of faith, I would go there and seek him out.

In good weather it took four days to ride to Willimantic Falls, but I laid over at an inn for a day when a bitter wind whipped an early spring snowfall into cold wet swirls. In the afternoon of the fifth day I saw the town ahead of me. At a sawmill beside the river I asked where the mail was posted, believing the local postmaster would know of a one-armed farmer. I was given directions to Young's Tavern, a long two-story brick building on the south side of the river.

"Do you know of Henry Taggart?" I asked the inn's proprietor, a thin old man with a scarf around his neck, who received the town's mail. "He lost his arm in the war."

He looked at me, then to the corner of the room, squinting.

"I'm looking to get to his farm," I told him.

He shifted his jaw to one side, the facial mechanics of deep thought.

"Which arm?" he asked.

The innkeeper was full of curiosity, but of no use. I asked the same at a gristmill, and then walked my horse back over the bridge to where a cluster of shops stood, and inquired of the shopkeepers. But no one knew of Taggart.

I asked if there was an inn at Lebanon, and if I could get there before dark. I rode due south some seven or eight miles alongside fields waiting to be tilled, passing no more than a handful of riders and wagons.

At Alden Tavern I paid for a bed and a meal, and a stable for my horse. On a wall inside hung an engraving of Washington, browned by years of sunlight and tobacco smoke, with a well-worn black leather cartridge box on a peg beside it. I asked the innkeeper if he had fought in the war. He, in turn, inquired if I had, and when I told him about Saratoga and pointed to the scar on my forehead, he sat down to tell me about the battles he'd seen, and how his father had horsewhipped a captured British general who'd tossed his corn and beans on the floor in defiance of his captors.

"I'm looking for someone I knew in the war," I told him, and described Taggart as I had to the others in the previous town.

He paused. The exuberance with which he'd been speaking dimmed, and he nodded his head slowly.

"I know where you can find him," he said.

3

In the morning, following the innkeeper's directions, I rode north again, then west, for several miles, and found the red clapboard house he had described, and the dirt path just beyond it that led to a large sycamore tree near a hillside. Beneath the farthest reaches of the tree's branches was a shack, beaten by years of weather into a dull, lifeless gray.

I dismounted, and held the reins of my horse. The ground was soft from rain and melted spring snow. Weeds and grasses grew around the shack, as far back as the hillside, where the remnants of a stone wall separated the field from the trees on the hill. There was a mud-hole in back, surrounded by a rail fence and a hogpen on one side, but I didn't see any hogs. I lowered my eyes and looked at the sun's glimmer on the patches of tufted grass. My horse shook his head, unsure why I stood so still. Ahead of me, impressions of a man's shoes went here and there with no certain direction.

"Henry!" I called toward the shack, and then called again, "Henry Taggart!"

There was silence, and nothing seemed to move.

"Taggart!" I called out. "It is Gideon Wheatley. You knew me in the war, after Saratoga, at the hospital in Albany."

I waited, and sensed a flicker of motion behind the window. Then the door opened, and a man stepped onto the slab of bluestone at the foot of the door. His head was uncovered, exposing a bald top with a ring of gray and white hair that descended, unkempt, onto his shoulders. He wore the heavy cloth trousers of a farmer, and a woolen coat that was soiled and worn. I could see by how they hung upon his frame that he was underfed. He raised his one hand to shield his eyes from the sun, and looked at me. The sleeve of the other arm hung empty at his side.

"Wheatley," he said plainly, in a voice I recognized. He looked intently at me, and I at him, until his image became distorted and opaque, and I had to rub my eyes.

"Did you travel far?"

"A fair distance," I answered.

"Well, my God," Taggart said, coming to life. "This is a good day."

He was alone, as the innkeeper told me he would be. We sat on a couple of stumps by a stack of firewood. We talked about hogs and crops, the winter that had just passed, and the death of Washington, only months earlier. In that way we came to talk about the war, and of coming home. I told him that I learned the fate of his wife and son from the innkeeper, who, despite the years that had passed, still seemed pained when telling me. I detected the faintest relief in him, that the burden of recounting their deaths had been lifted.

Years ago, when I had first set eyes on Taggart, when he was feverish in the hospital bed, with strips of bloodstained cloth wrapped tightly around the stump of his arm, he had talked desperately about his boy, fearing his son would be deprived of a father should he die.

"My boy Robert still needs me," he would insist to anyone, and often just to himself.

After Taggart was reunited with his wife and son, and after they'd harvested their first crop on their Connecticut farmland, Robert enrolled in the militia. He was hardly past boyhood, but full of a young man's vinegar, and angered by the injury done to his father.

The innkeeper had known Robert. "He was young, but strong, like his father, and a fine soldier," the innkeeper told me. "A keen shot, and the first to turn out for any skirmish."

Near the end of the war Robert answered an alarm, to ward off an incursion by the British. The fighting went on for hours and, in the end, Robert did not come home.

"The bloody bastards shot him dead," the innkeeper said, clenching his fist as it rested on the table.

Taggart's wife, Eleanor, died a few months later when a winter fever savaged the town. "The sickness came to nearly every house," the innkeeper remembered. "But still a lot of people thought she died from grief."

The innkeeper had gone into his kitchen then, behind the tavern room, and returned with two loaves of bread. "Give these to Taggart," he said.

Now I gave the bread to Taggart, who decided we should eat some of it. In town I had purchased raisins, pickles, and a dozen apples, which I did not want him to think of as charity, so I presented them for our meal.

We sat on the stumps. I broke pieces of the bread for Taggart, and the food and the warmth of the sun awakened our memories and encouraged our colloquy. Two tin water bottles hung from a peg by the door to the shack, joined together by a length of rope. I filled them at a well down the path toward the red house, and returned with them draped across my shoulders. Taggart, sitting on the stump with his hand on a knee, closed his eyes for a moment and gently nodded his head. He seemed contented.

"Do you remember Arnold?" I asked him.

"One does not forget Arnold," he answered.

In the distance I heard a cow bellow. A breeze rippled through the branches of the sycamore tree.

"I have wished him dead," Taggart said. He spit the seed of an apple at the woodpile.

"I could have killed him," I said suddenly, surprising myself. Taggart's eyes invited me to continue.

I told him my story, describing every detail that was singed in my memory. As I recounted the days and months I spent talking with Arnold while he lay broken and helpless in the hospital, Taggart again recalled his march in Canada, when Arnold helped him as he sat ill at the side of the road, and how he carried the wounded general away from the butchery in Quebec. But his words this time were inflected with disdain. In Taggart's voice I heard what had become of his esteem for Arnold, how it had withered, and then rotted, and how his words now hissed like embers in a fire.

"On the last night in New York," I told Taggart, who listened with rapt attention, "the townhouse was nearly empty. I stood at the top of the stairs and saw a light coming from the room below. I knew it was Arnold. I had the blade that Mulligan had given me, and I descended, without a sound, to where I could see Arnold writing at his desk, under faint candlelight.

"My orders were that I could not kill him," I continued. "But still I ask myself, and it troubles me: How many lives might have been spared by a quick cut to his throat?"

I was arguing, I realized, as if before a jury. Taggart sat still, silently focused on my words.

"I could have stopped him," I said, shaking my head. Taggart leaned forward, listening, seeming to share my anguish.

"But I did not," I went on. "You and I knew a different Arnold, and that memory shielded him. And yet, every day since, I think of how it could have been different had I used the knife."

Taggart stood up, stiffly. He looked across the field, his eyes darting here and there, squinting, and scratching his chin with his thick, gnarled fingers.

"Walk with me, Gideon."

I followed him as he walked behind the woodpile and through a well-worn path in the coarse grass. On the other side of the sycamore tree, in the shade of its wide trunk, were two grave markers made of bluestone, cut square but with softly curved tops, on which no lichen grew. In front of me, I saw the name *Robert Taggart* carved into the stone.

"Eleanor is here," he said, pointing to the grave farther from the tree.

"I wish I could have met her," I said to Taggart.

"And here is my boy, Dobbin."

My breathing paused as I recognized the nickname.

"You called him Dobbin?" I asked.

"Yes."

My eyes fixed on the name carved in the stone.

There's no lock.

I won't run.

You wouldn't get far.

A sound that lived in my head echoed again, and I heard a thousand musket balls piercing the air and a hundred footsteps charging with bayonets.

An honorable man is worth something.

"Dobbin," I said. "He died at Fort Griswold."

Taggart, too, was staring at the gravestone. He nodded his head.

4

On the fifteenth day of March in 1801, when the gales of winter still bore down on the Atlantic, I took my berth on the brig *Aurora*, in Boston harbor, crowded with a cargo of lumber, iron fittings, barrels of rum, and fourteen passengers, all bound for London.

I found the *Aurora* nearly at the end of the Long Wharf, which stretched for half a mile into the harbor. A boy from the boarding-house pulled a wagon with my one trunk. It was morning, when the work of the day is most energetic, and we made our way through a gauntlet of bustling commerce. Wagons full of cargo were pushed and pulled by burly dockers, to and from the warehouses built on the wharf. Winches lifted and swung pallets of crates, bricks, and lumber. On either side of the wharf were tied eight or ten schooners, brigs, and barques, their yardarms suspended above our heads by webs of tar-covered rigging. Lines from the vessels were tied to pilings and thick cleats on the wharf. As we navigated our way up the wharf, the first sight of the *Aurora* pleased me; her cargo had been loaded, and her appearance was one of good order. Some of her sailors, uniformly attired in duck cloth trousers, checked shirts, and pea jackets, hauled the trunks of the arriving passengers up the gangway, where, at its foot, a crowd was assembled. Each passenger seemed to have brought a party of well-wishers to send them off, and there was much hugging and handshaking, and long looks and several kisses. I approached a neatly attired man who carried a stack of papers, and after finding one with my name on it, he directed two sailors to carry my trunk aboard.

"Is that all you have, sir?" asked one of them, a tall, thin young man, with an accent I didn't recognize.

"The others got three or four apiece," said the shorter sailor, motioning with his chin toward several passengers at the top of the gangway, who were still waving to those below.

"I'm not staying as long as they are," I explained. I gave the boy with the wagon a copper coin embossed with a woman's head and the word *LIBERTY*, and followed the sailors and my trunk onto the ship.

In the middle of the afternoon the *Aurora* was untied and brought about, and with some fanfare the captain showed his skill by setting top gallants to catch the faint land breeze and glide away unaided from the wharfs, helped along by a falling tide. A pilot boat scuttled ahead of us, and the crew pushed hard against the ship's capstan, winching up a chain that pulled the *Aurora* to a mooring buoy in the crowded harbor, where we spent the night. The tide would favor our departure in the morning, but the day saw a torrent of rain and fitful winds, so the captain waited. The second day brought clear skies, a steady breeze, and a high tide that welcomed a string of ships into the Atlantic. Late in the day, just before sunset, I looked to the west and saw the last trace of land slip below the horizon.

It took the *Aurora* thirty days to cross the Atlantic and sail up the river Thames to London, the first of which were met with some degree of interest, while the remaining days were beset by the gnawing tedium common to captivity. The first three days out of Boston saw a light steady breeze, very nearly dead aft. The ship had a great many sails upon her, both light and heavy, and the sight of this canvas against the blue sky and the surging, powerful motion, of which one is always aware, gave the passengers hope for a rapid, comfortable voyage. Half of the fourteen passengers were merchants, men bound for London to negotiate trade, almost all of whom had made the journey before. There were two women among us, both accompanied by their husbands. One couple was older, and possessed of means; they were making their way to France, eventually. The other couple was young, and planned to live in London for a year or more. The husband, tall and lean, had traveled recently to the new federal city on the Potomac River, and was sailing to London for government work. His wife, younger than he, had an adventuresome spirit and frequently walked the deck to marvel at the ocean, but one could hear her trepidation at times when she spoke.

"Have you been to sea before?" she asked me. Only along the coast, I told her.

"Ever in a storm?"

Yes, I told her, but without details. "The *Aurora* is a fine ship; you needn't worry."

"I have never been to sea," she said. She told me that she had prayed repeatedly, twice a day for a month, beseeching the Lord for an untroubled voyage of good breeze and calm seas.

Despite her earnest prayers, the seas did not stay calm. On the fifth day the crew was ordered to trim the yards, as the wind was getting ahead. Dark clouds were coming from windward, on track to converge with our course. Soon enough we were in a heavy sea and strong gale, with frequent squalls of hail and snow, driving on under close-reefed sails. The deluge sometimes found a way through the deck and the walls of the cabin, and trickled into puddles, small and cold, that smelled of brine and oakum.

Nearly half the passengers became dreadfully seasick, including the young lady, and I saw little of them for three days, during which time they did not eat. More than once I put my own head in the bucket, which usually provided immediate relief. The small cabin was a forlorn spot on such days. The swinging lamp accentuated the roll and pitch of the ship and did little to dispel the gloom, so the only thing to do was lie down. At times this was difficult too, especially at night. The seas would crash against the hull and the ship would rise and fall, demanding some effort not to fall from one's berth.

In between tempests, when the wind was steady, I ventured onto the deck and found some sailors amenable to conversation. One was a barrel-chested Scot who'd been raised in the Leeward Islands and had twice sailed around Cape Horn. He wore a silver crucifix round his neck. Off the cape, he told me, he once spotted an albatross asleep on the water, all white, its head tucked beneath its wings, rising and falling on the rolling waves. When the vessel drew near it, the bird lifted its head and looked at him with large, staring eyes, then lifted its wide wings and climbed into the air. His crewmates on that voyage later caught an albatross with a baited hook they floated on a shingle. The cook served the great bird for dinner, and asked them to catch more if they could. As he told me this, lightning flashed in the distance, and low grumbles of thunder cracked and rippled. He kept his eyes on the water, both the near distance and the faraway, and every time he saw lightning he made the sign of the cross.

When this string of squalls was at last behind us, I arose before dawn to see the first gray light on the horizon toward which we sailed. The sunrise at sea arrives in silence and surrounds the ocean; it is not accompanied by the cock's crow or the singing of birds, nor do shadows grow as they do when sunrays are cast upon the trees of the forest or the spires of town. At times the sea mirrors the rising light, and it is barely perceptible where the burgeoning glare of dawn meets the unknown depths; rather they combine into a chalky gray-blue wash, engulfing everything but the vessel, making one's ship seem at once both insignificant and almighty.

Colors emerge as the sun climbs the sky, and the details of the sea all around take shape. One morning a sailor on watch called out, "Dolphins!" I looked aft and saw them, swimming inches below the surface and leaping into the froth just ahead of the bow. Their long, high dorsal fins appeared dark blue and green, and their backs were colored in pigments of brilliant silvery blue. They arced and curved through the water, revealing their mother-of-pearl flanks amid the splash that caught the sunlight and cast all the hues of the prism.

Two sailors opened a chest on deck and pulled a harpoon from it, cleating the line and promising a dinner that didn't come from a salt barrel. On the second throw the lance dug deeply into a dolphin that swam only yards from the hull. They gaffed it and brought it aboard, where it beat its flukes against the deck and shuddered. The shades of silver, blue, and green were vivid and rich, and seemed to change with every movement of the dolphin; but as the writhing decreased, the colors diminished and faded into a bland yellowish gray, and the only remaining tincture was a red puddle beneath the carcass.

For eight days we had fair breezes and clear skies. The passengers who traveled for business frequently played long games of cards or checkers. The captain's small library was adequate, although it revealed no great erudition. Some moments aboard ship were invigorating, as when a loud smack on the water jarred us from our idle pursuits, and was soon followed by the breaching of several whales. Three times on our voyage we set eyes on other ships passing, sailing westward. Crew and passengers huddled at the rail to see the vessels. But their white sails, billowing in the distance, did nothing to dispel the sense of solitude felt among the passengers, and only stirred the desires that brought loneliness.

The days were mostly wearisome, and became more so as my interest in the captain's books waned. Conversations were pleasant, but the longer the voyage, the more spiritless they became. The crew could entertain with stories, but they, for the most part, left the passengers to themselves, unless a sailor could be found at rest, or on a quiet watch, and drawn out by my interest. Stopping in the galley to get a light for my lamp, I came upon the cook in a talkative spirit. Offering a piece of raw onion, which we both ate, he told about a sailor on a voyage to South America who was hardly able to open his mouth because of the scurvy, and had nearly surrendered himself in despair. The cook had pounded raw onions and potatoes in a mortar, extracting the juice, which the sailor sucked by teaspoons, holding the liquid in his mouth as long as he could, even though the smutty flavor made him gag. But soon he was eating the onions and potatoes whole; within days he ate foods that restored his strength, and soon after was back at his labor, furling sails and winding the capstan.

"It was his resurrection," said the cook, holding up a piece of onion and biting into it.

For several days in the middle of the Atlantic, the winds were barely a whisper and the sails hung limp or merely fluttered. The crew spotted sharks and dumped scraps of fat overboard to draw them close. Two sailors stood by with harpoons, and the first shark to come near was hit by the third harpoon thrown. The shark drew the line tight and flailed wildly, but the barbs stuck. It was gaffed and held alongside the hull while the Scot who wore the crucifix reached overboard and cut its flesh with a long-handled boarding knife. Its blood in the water drew other sharks nearby, and these were lanced with harpoons. This hunt continued for two hours; six sharks were killed, but not a single one was lifted aboard.

"Why don't you eat the shark meat?" I asked the cook that night.

He leaned against a wall of the galley, half-sitting on a low shelf, and drew a drag from a long clay pipe. The smoke added a sweetness to the odors of brine, broth, and charred hardwood that infused the galley.

"The first time I ever sailed," he said, "I was a lad of fourteen years. We'd been to sea two weeks when a burly sailor named Knox, who was sometimes a cod fisherman, was stricken in the belly, as if, he told us, he was cut with a knife. He laid up in the forecastle, moaning all day. At night he screamed in pain, and when the sun rose he was dead."

The cook moistened the stem of the pipe with his lips, and drew on it again. He tilted his head and blew the smoke straight upwards.

"Every sailor paid his respects, and then the first mate and the cook—of all people—wrapped the corpse, and several of the sailors stitched the shroud tight, and filled the foot of it with heavy stones from our own ballast to pull the corpse quickly to the bottom. The captain read from the Bible and called on God to save the soul of poor Knox."

The cook was looking into the dark corner of the galley, away from the dim light that seeped through a hatch above our heads.

"I was the youngest on board, and took my place behind the sailors. I stood against the gunwale, letting the sea distract me from the sad ritual, looking overboard and watching the waves lap against the hull, when suddenly, in a flash of white, I saw the shrouded corpse plunge into the waves, straight and nearly without a splash; and in the same instant, before the corpse had vanished from sight, it was hit broadside by a long missile of gray and silver. In another moment I saw the blood, the ripped shroud, and a second shark, and maybe a third before I covered my eyes so as not to see, but still I heard the sailors yell and holler and scream the Lord's name in such a way that for many nights I lay awake, face-to-face with the terror."

He looked at me, holding the pipe in his hand.

"They are man-eaters, come from hell."

So we did not eat the shark meat. Twice more on the voyage the sailors harpooned sharks. The blood drew more of the species, and the sailors slaughtered them.

Seven days out from sighting the English coast, the sailor at watch called out to the helmsman, who adjusted his steering. The sea was calm, and the sun bright; the passengers on deck, eager for any interruption of the daily tedium, gathered at the starboard bow in the hope of seeing whales breach or some other sea life. What they saw instead was a scattering of debris: first a dozen or more barrels, saturated and heavy but still buoyant, bobbing just above the surface; then odd boards and broken beams, and a panel of wood planks that seemed to contain windows, as if from a captain's cabin; and a long mast, trailing its rigging and a patch of white sail that descended into the deep, twisting below the surface like the giant squid of rumor. The passengers looked but said little, while the sailors fixed their eyes on the debris, and the first mate and captain both peered at the wreckage through spyglasses, to find its name or some distinguishing feature.

A week later, as boredom showed in the drab, sickly faces of the passengers, excitement enlivened us all when several fishing vessels were spotted and the first mate declared them evidence that land was near. Late in the afternoon the captain ordered the crew to heave to by backing the main topsail, so the *Aurora* would make headway very slowly, awaiting new daylight for our approach to the rocks and shoals of the English coast. Before leaving the deck on this last evening at sea, as the darkness draped over the vast ocean, I set my hands on the rail and watched a ruby-red glow shimmering on the water from the east, miles away but coming at our bow with rapid speed. This I had not seen on our voyage, and yet the sailors on deck said nothing. I watched it spread and approach, and then rise slowly into the sky, obscured at first by a bank of billowing clouds that passed quickly to unveil a blood-red moon, unnaturally large and nearly complete in its circular shape. The black silhouette of the bowsprit and the rigging of the foremast marked it like a series of scars.

When the moon was well above the horizon, and its blood-red color changed to orange, as if the orb were a simmering ember, I hastened to my quarters and opened my trunk to remove a small leather portmanteau, of the kind that cavalrymen attached to their saddles during the war. Freeing one of its buckles, I slipped my hand inside and removed a small dagger, like the one Hercules Mulligan had once given me. I pulled it from its sheath to examine the razor-sharp edges of its blade, laying it flat in the palm of my hand.

I reached into the portmanteau a second time, touching two small glass vials wrapped in cloth, each the size of a thumb and sealed with crimson wax. I held them under the pale light of the swaying lantern so I could see in both the pale grayish-white powder, pernicious yet full of promise: a quantity of arsenic sufficient to kill a man, with enough left over to kill him yet again.

In the morning we sighted the distant coast of England. After two days sailing up the channel, the captain ordered the gun fired to call a pilot boat, to take us up the Thames to London.

5

The river Thames below London Bridge was a forest of tall masts, and the number and proximity of vessels gave the impression that a leaping frog could hop from one to the next and travel for miles. A heavy mist hung over the river, blackened by particles of soot that hovered in the moist air. The sharp smell of burning sea coal infused every breath I took, but it did not wholly obscure the stench of the dung and night soil that spread across the water's surface like floating lesions. When a breeze kicked up and broke the fog, spires could be seen rising from dozens of churches, revealed in clusters as the fog rolled slowly from east to west. When I spotted the great dome of Saint Paul's Cathedral, ringed with thirty-two Corinthian columns, I no longer smelled the soot and shit, for I was seized by awe and my breathing stopped altogether.

A crowd of hackney carriages, wagons, and men pulling hand-carts hurried about the docks, conveying disembarked passengers and their trunks. Several ships were unloading at the same time. Coachmen called out their fees in shillings and pence to engage a fare from the neatly dressed men and women who came down the gangplanks a bit unsteady on their feet, followed by the sailors who heaved the trunks upon their shoulders, showing their own strength to the London dockworkers. I employed a boy with a bag barrow af-ter quizzing him on nearby lodging houses. He hurried me along, explaining that all nearby beds were typically filled by midafternoon, and took me to a long, narrow coaching inn, several stories tall, with a courtyard and covered outdoor galleries leading to the bedchambers.

Indeed, the innkeeper sold me his last bunk, in a room with one large bed and a small cot against the wall. An Irishman with a sunken, pockmarked face had claimed the cot, and in the evening it was necessary to share the bed with another traveler, a tall man with a sharp nose and lengthy beard. When I spoke to him, merely to suggest I was a courteous bedmate, he responded in a language I did not recognize. We both nodded to each other, and then climbed in beneath the blankets. The bed was not sufficiently tight, and gravity drew me toward the center; thus I slept fitfully throughout the night with one arm clinging to the bedstead. The next day both men departed, and I put my things on the tiny cot, claiming it for however many more nights I would sleep here.

In the morning I asked the innkeeper how I might find the address of a business associate. He directed me to the General Post Office building on Lombard Street, a short walk across London Bridge. Once inside the stately building, at a long clerical desk behind which were many rows of cabinets, I made the same inquiry of a clerk, who walked to a set of books propped on a lectern at the far end of the long desk. I gave him the name of my alleged associate, expecting some reaction, or just an inquisitive look, but the clerk gave none. He opened one of the books, which he identified to me as the Post Office annual directory, found the name, and pointed to it.

"Shall I write it down?" he asked. I handed him a lead pencil and my pocket notebook, opened to a blank page. He wrote:

62 Gloucester Place, Marylebone.

I asked him by what direction I could get to this address. We moved to a tabletop beside a window where he opened a large portfolio, revealing pages of maps that divided the city into quadrants, carefully detailed with street names, and with parks and public squares designated by orange or green wash. The clerk pointed to my destination, several miles to the west. With his finger he traced a direct route past Saint Paul's to Oxford Street, which I would follow to Portman

Square, and then turn north onto Gloucester Place. I hastily copied these instructions into my notebook, and thanked him.

I headed there straightaway, and as I walked on the cobblestone streets and the crowded footpaths, London revealed itself. I was eager to find my destination, but every sight was a distraction. Quick-stepping men and women passed around me, with a "By your leave, sir" or a cautionary "Have care!" The buildings that lined the main thoroughfares were several stories tall and built of elegantly carved stone blocks, and even down the smaller streets, the shops and residences—built of stone, brick, or timber—stood in orderly rows. Large, ornate shop signs, full of color, hung from numerous walls and protruded over the footpaths, announcing the commerce engaged in within. Soot-blackened brick chimneys emerged from every rooftop, and their spiraling trails of black smoke drew my gaze to the dome of Saint Paul's. Often I stopped and craned my neck to look upwards, to study the colonnade, the balcony and ribbed dome, and the stone lantern at the top, rising in stages to an unimaginable height. The grandeur of the cathedral captivated me, and I hastened to remind myself, standing in the shadow of its holy purpose, that it was not an innocent man I intended to kill.

Once past the cathedral I walked at a quickened pace toward Oxford Street, amid a river of carriages, wagons, and people of every sort. Horses traveled in every direction, their hoofs clattering in a fanfare of unregulated drumbeats, and iron wagon wheels rumbled on the cobblestones. I stepped gingerly past pools of horse piss and dung, and tried to wave away the coal smoke that never subsided. Collectors for the penny post rang bells to entice readers, while vendors cried out appeals for their fish, fruits, and a beguiling variety of medicinal potions. Milk women announced their supply with a high-pitched yodel, and knife sharpeners appeared on nearly every other corner, whetting iron and steel against their grindstones.

By the bells that rang from any number of belfries, on church spires and public halls, I knew I'd been walking briskly for more than an hour and a half when I came upon Portman Square, which occupied an entire square block with a circular garden in the center.

I hurried around the manicured hedge that enclosed the varied shrubbery and made for the far corner, which I determined to be Gloucester Place. Without pause I marched up the street, beside a long row of handsome townhouses distinguished by an elegant repetition of design: a continuous ground floor of white sandstone, with each residence denoted by an arched double door capped by a fanlight window, and a continuous iron-railed balcony that separated the sandstone from the red brick and white-trimmed windows on three upper stories. Many of the doors bore numbers signifying their address, and when I spotted number 62 on a heavy black door, I walked faster still and passed it, crossing the street and stopping only at the next corner, where I could discreetly look it over and take it in, this singular spot on the map that I had crossed an ocean to find.

I walked around the nearby blocks to capture the lay of the streets and the location of shops and taverns; then I determined to return to my inn by taking a series of perpendicular short streets, down and over, down and over, as if descending steps, till I was again on Oxford Street. On this route, a short distance from Gloucester Place, a sign offering lodging hung on a brick house on Marylebone Lane. Favoring its location, I inquired of a white-haired woman who answered the door, and following a short interview and a deposit of one week's rent, it was agreed that I would return the next day and live for an indeterminate period of time in Mrs. Baxter's house.

6

"My Dear General," I wrote, seated at a writing table in my chamber in Mrs. Baxter's house.

Although much time has passed, it has not diminished the esteem in which I hold you, forged in the difficult months at the Albany hospital, and strengthened further during my service in your American Legion. Business has brought me to London. It would be the utmost favor to me to have the pleasure of your company for a brief visit.

His reply, I advised, should be sent to the post office on Cavendish Street, where it would be held for me. I paid a boy to take it to his door, for I was too impatient to send it by post.

Then I waited for his response.

Patience is a hard-wrought virtue, but to my benefit the city of London beckoned me to explore it, and whenever I was done with finding distractions on the city streets, Mrs. Baxter's house proved to be a pleasant haven. Upstairs, I had a small room of my own. In the room next door was another boarder, a man named Van den Berg, a wine merchant from Amsterdam who spoke English with a heavy accent. Van den Berg and I took our meals in a room at the front of the house, while Mrs. Baxter spent much of her day in a large kitchen, where I would see her eating in the early morning with a young man, handsomely attired, who spent little time at the house. A young woman whose long brown hair was pulled back behind her head, but was often draped forward over a shoulder, brought tea and bread and our meals to Van den Berg and me. The first thing I noticed about her was that she was very much with child. I assumed she was the young man's wife, and at my first breakfast I asked her name.

"My name is Louisa," she replied. Van den Berg nodded, as charmed as I was by the small intimacy of being told her first name. "And you may call me that," she added. I returned Louisa's smile, and noticed that her eyes were the same grayish blue as the sea.

On my second visit to the Cavendish Street post office, a building no bigger than a typical shop, the clerk returned from the sorting bins with a letter addressed to me. I broke the seal and read:

Dear Mr. Wheatley,

I did not know if you survived the war. I recall conflicting reports.
It pleases me that you did, and that you are here in London. At
this moment I am not in good health. As soon as this malady has
passed, I will write again. I look forward to our meeting.

B. Arnold.

Having nothing to do but wait, I spent nearly a week walking about,
taking repose in the gardens and public squares, and in the coffeehouses. There were many of these in London; upon leaving a coffeehouse,
one need walk only a few blocks to find another. I entered a good number of them, and if they were uncluttered by men meeting for business
or gambling, I would find a seat and review the news and gossip as
told in London's newspapers. When not eating at Mrs. Baxter's house,
I found the fare at the coffeehouses to be satisfactory. On the other
hand, the coffee that Londoners drank was unappealing; it languished
in the cup like a syrup of soot, and tasted like an old shoe. When
I ventured into the Chapter Coffee House on Paternoster Row, I asked
one customer, as he came out the door, how the coffee was, to which he
replied, "Black as hell, strong as death, sweet as love." But like so many
others who drank the brew, I found that it quickened my mind; thus
I got used to it, and made it a part of my daily routine.

I roamed the city, walking to the Tower of London and paying
ninepence to view the Royal Menagerie, where I watched monkeys
mimic the behaviors of men, and a baboon pick insects from its hair.
I saw raw meat thrown to leopards, a hyena, and a pack of wolves.
In a stone pit a tiger paced back and forth, which I studied for quite
some time while other visitors came and left, and then after seeing
the monkeys I returned to watch the tiger again. I walked across
the bridges—the London Bridge, Blackfriars, and Westminster—
and took note of the ships anchored in the Thames. I passed by

without entering most of the churches, but went inside Saint Paul's and Westminster Abbey, where I found the tomb of Geoffrey Chaucer. Staring at it, as if in a trance, I recalled an afternoon at Yale, in Connecticut Hall, hearing Chaucer's fourteenth-century English read aloud. The next day I searched for booksellers, and found a small volume of *Troilus and Criseyde*, bound in red leather, for which I paid dearly. I read it in the coffeehouses, and while seated on a bench in the fields at Lincoln's Inn. It was there that I found the passage:

> *The noyse up roos, whan it was first aspyd*
> *Thorugh al the toun, and generally was spoken,*
> *That Calkas traytor fled was, and allyed*
> *With hem of Grece; and casten to ben wroken*
> *On him that falsly hadde his feith so broken,*
> *And seyden, he and al his kyn at ones*
> *Ben worthy for to brennen, fel and bones.*

From my seat on this cultivated lawn, adorned with sculpted ornaments, where I could look past the gates of Lincoln's Inn and see black-robed barristers schooled in law, I read aloud to myself, whispering, of the ancient punishment for traitors, that *he and all his kin, at once, are worthy to be burned, skin and bones.*

Eventually, having seen enough of this soot-dusted city, I grew impatient and took to studying Arnold's house several times each day, standing in the shadows at a nearby street corner, where someone looking out a window could not discover me. I looked for any sign of his whereabouts, or some indication of his condition. Although I noticed changes in how the curtains were drawn from hour to hour, no one seemed to come or go. Eagerly I waited for his summons. Having learned the habits of the mail, I went twice a day to the Cavendish Street post office, where the clerk understood that I waited for a single item, and would often acknowledge me as soon as I stepped in the door, and shake his head in the negative.

I grew anxious, wondering if I should communicate with Arnold again, until one morning, while pacing about the garden at Cavendish Square, I saw Louisa coming from Mortimer Street, carrying a wide wicker basket laden with carrots and cabbage. I hurried over to greet her, and took the basket, telling her, "You have quite enough to carry already." As we made the short walk along Wigmore Street and up Marylebone to the house, I asked her about the markets, and how often she went to them.

"Every day," she said. "The best time is midmorning, especially if you go to the market at Covent Garden, after the farmers from Middlesex, Surrey, and Essex have brought in their vegetables. By afternoon they are picked over. But the chicken, Mr. Wheatley," here she looked at me, grinning, "the chicken that you complimented the other evening, that is best gotten in the early morning from Fleet Market."

"Yes," I said. "A fine chicken, that was. And where does one get fish?"

"Well, the fish is best at Clare Market, in Saint Clement Danes."

"And meat?"

"James Gibbs's Oxford Market."

"So much work to feed Mr. Van den Berg and me."

"A pleasure," she said, looking at me, smiling. "And also to feed Mr. Baxter—my husband, you know—whose appetite knows no end. And Mrs. Baxter—his mum. And me. Food for us all." Putting the palm of her hand against her belly, she added, "And some for the little one, too."

From that day forward, putting myself to use, I accompanied Louisa to the markets whenever she went, carrying the basket and all that was put in it. I knew little or nothing of childbirth, but I worried that the child could be born at any time. I looked after her well-being, making way for her in the crowded markets and on the streets, standing between her and the riders and hackney carriages that passed too close.

"What is your intuition?" I asked her one morning, as she sorted through various roots and greens at Covent Garden. "Is your child a boy or a girl?"

"Some of the ladies look at me," she answered, "and think they can tell, but it's hardly a mother's proper business to think one way or the other."

She sniffed a long sprig of rosemary and set it in the wicker basket.

"Surely, Mr. Wheatley, you must have children back in America?"

"No," I said with a short shake of my head.

"Well, then," she continued, reaching for a bulb of fennel. "You must have a fine wife, I'm sure."

"No, I don't," I answered. And then, wanting somehow to explain myself, I said, "She was a casualty of the war."

Louisa turned and looked at me, the happiness gone from her face.

"I am sorry," she said. "I am so sorry."

"No, no," I said quickly. "I was not clear. Nothing happened to her. But the war put many miles between us, and a misunderstanding."

"Well, then, I hate the war for that," she said.

I reached for the fennel and set it in the basket.

"I suspect you weren't even born then."

Her smile came back, gently. "I was a very small child."

Louisa's husband, Mr. Baxter—who introduced himself to me as Edward—was employed by a quadrant and compass maker, and also ground lenses for scientific instruments. On a day he spent at the house—an infrequent occurrence—he invited me into the kitchen. On the long table stood a tall wooden spindle that held, from two upward-extending arms, a circular glass lens. Behind the frame that held the lens, bent on a diagonal, was a mirror—as if the lens and mirror were pages of a book, held open at a forty-five-degree angle and set facedown upon the spindle.

"It's a *vue d'optique*," Edward Baxter told me, and when I opened my eyes wide, he smiled. "Some call it a zograscope, or simply an optical diagonal machine."

There was a stack of engraved prints on the table. Edward placed one underneath the mirror while I looked at the glass lens. Moving

my face forward and back to find the perfect distance, I was pleasantly astonished at the heightened perspective the glass brought to the
enlarged image.

"The Colosseum in Rome!" I declared.

He placed another print beneath the mirror.

I paused to study the image of a triumphal arch and a bank of
classical columns.

"The Roman Forum," I said quietly, hearing the sense of wonder
in my own voice.

"The Arch of Titus and the Temple of Saturn," Edward said. "It's
my dream to travel to Rome with Louisa someday."

I studied the rest of the prints, of Saint Peter's Basilica in Rome
and the Duomo in Florence; of the old London Bridge, crowded with
the shops that were built upon it; of the great cathedral in Salisbury;
and the ruins of Kenilworth Castle.

Responding to my enthusiasm, Edward told me of the spyglasses
and telescopes he helped to create, and the navigational instruments
favored by the ship's masters who came to Mr. Clarke's store, where
he was employed, near the wharfs. When the voyages of Captain
James Cook gripped our conversation, Edward went to a cabinet and
produced a bottle of brandy, and for some time he told me about
sextants, chronometers, and the calculation of longitude. We talked
about traveling the world, and in so doing, Edward revealed something of his dreams.

On the day we walked to the spice market, Louisa brought with her
a bag of small glass bottles and vials. The market was a feast of aromas,
of sweet herbs and exotic spices. Louisa went about filling her bottles
with purpose, while I meandered through the merchants' stalls, sniff-
ing here and there, matching smells with memories and questioning
those that were unfamiliar to me. We left the market with bottles of salt
and kitchen pepper, lemon peel, parsley, and mint, and with smaller
vials of ginger, coriander, and anise seed, each plugged with a cork.

Returning to the house, Louisa walked slower than usual, the
strain of her condition becoming apparent. We stopped at the post

office on Cavendish Street, as was my habit. The clerk saw me and waved his hand for me to come over. While Louisa waited by the door I hurried in and received the letter. I thought to break its seal immediately, but put it in the pocket of my waistcoat instead.

At Cavendish Square, a block from the post office, a crowd was gathered, hooting and cheering at a puppet theater, a rectangular wooden box taller than a man by half, decorated with colorful paint and covered on its front by a blue curtain. In the stage above the curtain a Punch-and-Judy show was underway. The puppeteer behind the curtain spoke his parts through a tin squeaker, which added to the humor, and the glove puppets he held on his upraised arms had painted wooden heads coifed with horsehair and preposterous hats. Louisa leaned against a wall by the gate that opened to the square, eager to enjoy the merriment.

Punch was in trouble, as he so often was. The Constable had put him in prison—for murder! A small coffin sat on one side of the stage, and the puppeteer's left hand produced Jack Ketch, who placed beside it a gibbet, with a hangman's noose. The crowd quieted its laughter to hear every word of the drama:

> JACK KETCH: You've got one bone in your neck, but that shall soon be broken.
> PUNCH: Mercy! Mercy! I'll never do so again!
> JACK KETCH: Now, Mr. Punch, no more delay. Put your head through this loop.
> PUNCH: Through there! What for?
> JACK KETCH: Aye, through there.
> PUNCH: What for? I don't know how.
> JACK KETCH: It is very easy; only put your head through here.
> PUNCH: How so?

Punch poked his head to the right of the noose, avoiding its center, inciting laughter from the crowd.

> JACK KETCH: No, no, here!

The crowd laughed and cheered as Punch poked his head around the left side of the noose, and Jack Ketch shouted, "Not so, you fool!"

> PUNCH: Mind, how you call fool; try if you can do it yourself. Only show me how, and I'll do it directly.
> JACK KETCH: Very well, I will. There, you see my head, and you see this loop: put it in, like so.

Jack Ketch put his head through the loop, and Punch shouted, "And pull it tight, like so!" pulling the body down and hanging Jack Ketch.

"Huzzah! Huzzah!" shouted Punch, and the crowd joyfully cheered "Huzzah!" with the puppet, which then began to sing:

> *They're out! They're out!*
> *I've done the trick!*
> *Jack Ketch is dead—I'm free;*
> *I do not care, now, if Old Nick*
> *Himself should come for me.*

Back at the house, Mrs. Baxter was glad to have the spices. She and Louisa took them into the kitchen. I went upstairs to my chamber to open Arnold's letter. I peeled off the button of red wax and recognized the handwriting. He thanked me for my patience. Although he was still suffering from gout, he revealed, he had essential business to attend to near Trafalgar Square, and proposed that we meet in the midafternoon on June 12, at Old Slaughter's Coffee House, at 74 St. Martin's Lane. I should return post only if the proposed meeting was inconvenient.

It was to be done. I had two days.

An afternoon cloudburst dashed cool wind and a needle-like rain against the windows. With a tinderbox I took hot coals from the kitchen stove and lit a fire in the parlor, where Louisa was sitting with a woolen shawl across her shoulders. I sat in an armless chair beside the fireplace, tending the embers and glancing at Louisa. She sat quietly, looking toward the window at the fleeting watery shapes made by the dripping rain, and the shimmer on the glass that came and went.

"I hope it clears soon," she said, and her eyes dropped to where her hand rested, on top of where her child slept, waiting to be born.

At my feet, the fire breathed and crackled. A single flame announced itself, grew and climbed upward, casting an aura of firelight. I looked at Louisa, as if seeing her through the *vue d'optique*, vivid and sublime and held gently in the hand of time.

The next day I excused myself from breakfast, explaining that the business I had awaited now called upon me. I walked to the short streets near the wharfs, stopping at the offices of the shipping companies. By afternoon I found imminent passage to Boston when a textile merchant suffering from a gastric fever decided not to cross the ocean, and gave up his berth.

The following morning, on the day of consequence, Mrs. Baxter went to the market with Louisa. I sat at the table in the kitchen, clearing a spot beside an empty pot and a basket that held the glass vials of spices. I laid a sheet of paper on the table, and with a pencil wrote a note:

> Dear Edward and Louisa,
>
> Please accept this gift. Save it for when you go to Rome, or use it
> to some advantage for your child, whose beauty is assured. Your
> hospitality has meant more to me than you can know.
>
> Gideon Wheatley

I put the letter in a small sack with a portion of the money I had brought with me, having anticipated the possibility of a long stay in London. In another bag I left a note to Mrs. Baxter, apologizing for my hasty departure—a necessity of business, I told her—and advanced two weeks' payment for lodging as a token of my appreciation and regret. I left both packages on the table. From under my arm I took my small portmanteau, placed it on the table, and emptied its contents, inspecting the tools of my task: a sufficient amount of money, a sheathed dagger, and two sealed glass vials of arsenic. Once consumed, a single vial of the powder would gnaw at Arnold's gut like hungry rats. He would die overnight, or slowly, in agony, within a day or two.

At that moment I heard the front door open, and quickly reassembled my things into the portmanteau. The footsteps passed by the kitchen and climbed the staircase. It was Van den Berg. I carried my trunk out the door and hailed a young man in the street with a hand-cart. We walked south to Charing Cross, and then along the Strand and Fleet Street to an inn by the wharfs, where I found a narrow room for myself, alone. I sat in the public house next door well into the night, where I drank of London's gin.

7

But for his limp, I would not have recognized him. From inside the coffeehouse, where I sat at a small booth near the large bowed window, I saw a man much thinner than I expected, clearly worn by age. He climbed slowly from a hackney carriage, dressed as a modest merchant, in a black coat with a cutaway front over a dark waistcoat, with black breeches and white stockings. I was not certain it was Arnold until he stepped forward, with a cane, and the left side of his body dipped in an unusual gait. I met him as he entered through the door.

"General Arnold," I said, extending a hand. The other hand stayed in the pocket of my coat, protecting its contents.

"Hmmph," he replied, adding with mild exaggeration, "Don't say that too loudly in this town." His eyes surveyed the room, which held only a handful of patrons at this midafternoon hour.

"So, Mr. Wheatley," he continued, looking deliberately at my forehead to examine its round scar. "Is it really you?"

"Many years have passed," I said.

"Yes, many years . . . many years," he agreed. "And look at me," he added, with a hint of annoyance, or disappointment. "Dropsy, gout, and some days I can hardly breathe." Opening his arms and bending slightly at the waist, as if formally presenting himself, he harkened back to the Albany hospital, and the words that had passed between us then:

Non sum qualis eram.

I remembered that Arnold's father had inscribed those words on the leather packet that held locks of hair from his children, the four who lay in the cemetery. *I am not what I once was.*

"Nor am I," I responded.

Arnold grinned wryly, and we took our seats at the booth. He seated himself with a bit of difficulty, bothered by his ailments but trying his best to disguise his discomfort. His face was bloated and seemed a maze of chafed redness and pale white blotches; the skin beneath his chin drooped. As he placed his hands on the table, I saw that his knuckles were swollen, a sign of the gout.

With little prompting Arnold took up the conversation, filling in the years. His eldest son had died of fever in Jamaica, six years earlier, while the other two boys from his first marriage were well, though they remained in Canada. For a few moments he regained something of the spirit I was once familiar with, during his better days at Albany, as he talked about two of his later children, Neddy and James, who were both engineering officers in the British army.

"James has been at Gibraltar for two years," he told me, "and the officers all speak very highly of him. Neddy is in Bengal, in India, beloved and respected by his men."

He paused to take a breath; I noticed his breathing did not come easily.

"If he retains his health . . .," Arnold continued, but did not finish the thought.

When I had stood in the stairwell with Mulligan's dagger in my hand, it was Neddy whom I had heard, an infant crying.

"Parting from them is a trial for both of us," he said.

There were younger children as well, which surprised me: two little boys, George and William, and a daughter, Sophia.

"Peggy is a good mother," he added, "and cares well for the children." He offered this with no sense of satisfaction, but rather with a vague hint of disappointment, as if his own success in this matter was in question.

"London is a hard place to do business," he told me. "Not every man is honest. And the memories of the British ministers are woefully short. To have been a general in the American war . . . You would think I had fought with Caesar, two thousand years ago. Gone and forgotten."

He went on about this, wheezing as he spoke, his face reddening: about how his sea captains had made handsome profits for themselves but cheated him; about how the prime minister had lost the papers Arnold sent for compensation of monies owed him. I nodded and winced in sympathy, but I was paying no attention to his complaints. Beneath the table, I put my hand into my coat pocket, reaching for a vial of arsenic. There was one vial loosely wrapped in cloth, just as I had placed it. I searched with my fingers to find the second vial, but it was gone. A surge of panic gripped me, demanding that I search my mind for it, that I remember where it was, incensed that I might have lost it. By force of will I composed myself, knowing this distraction could foil my purpose. One vial was more than enough; the second was merely a spare.

"And you, Wheatley," Arnold said, shifting his posture against the straight backboard of our booth. "What have you done? There was a woman, whose name I forget."

"She did not wait for me," I told him. "I was gone too long, and word got to her that I was a traitor."

Arnold's jaw stiffened. "You were a patriot," he insisted. "The French have been no friend to America. I was right about that. All you have is factions and discord. Jefferson's election was nearly stolen by Burr! The United States will come apart. It is already coming apart."

"I was indeed a patriot," I said. He did not seem to hear me.

"They are fools, out for themselves, whose only means of self-promotion is to ruin our reputations." Arnold grimaced. "Have I been forgotten, or am I still the bastard son of the Revolution?"

"Both," I answered. "You are remembered only enough to be despised."

He shook his head, rejecting the premise.

"To hell with them," he declared. "I am man enough for damnation."

I drummed my fingers on the table, agitated and nervous.

Arnold looked squarely at me. "I grieved for you. I thought you were dead."

"I crossed the river and walked into an ambush," I told him.

"I know. The soldiers who went with you were found dead."

I nodded.

"Were you taken to Fort Griswold?"

"Yes."

"I was told there were no prisoners there."

"I was the only one."

"And you survived."

"I escaped."

"During the battle?"

"After the battle. After all of it."

"Then you can tell me what happened."

"What happened? The militiamen put down their arms and surrendered the fort. Then they were slaughtered."

Arnold squinted, and for a moment bit his lip.

"Those were not my orders."

"You won't remember the name Taggart, but he fought with you in Quebec, and lifted you up when you were shot. I saw him last year. You did him a kindness during the march in Canada that he hasn't forgotten."

"Tell me," Arnold said.

"I will," I replied, lifting myself from my seat. "But let me get us coffee."

Arnold nodded.

I walked to the back of the long room where a coffee cauldron hung in a large brick fireplace behind a square bar partially enclosed by spindles that reached to the ceiling. Beneath the cauldron was a stack of simmering embers, and above it a plume of steam carried the coffee aroma into the air. I put coins on the bar, and the barman filled two white porcelain cups, both decorated with delicate blue drawings of garden flowers. He set the cups in front of me. Then he turned around to face a bucket, where he was washing pots. I pulled the vial of arsenic from my pocket and held it in my hand, ready to pinch off the red wax that sealed it and pour it in a cup, as if it were sugar.

This was the moment I had long contemplated, for which I'd boarded a ship and sailed across the ocean, and thoughts of revenge and my own redemption pressed upon me in a whirlwind of visions. I recalled Dobbin yet again as he declared to me the value of an honest man, a short time before dying, and Taggart at his son's grave, nodding his head to confirm Arnold's great crime against him. I pictured orange flames winding violently upward on church spires, and the woman in New London whose clothing burned as she ran from the Jägers. I remembered, too, the young boy in the light blue cap at Fort Griswold who ran toward me across the parade ground, and how I had found his hat in a pile of bloodied clothing and almost took it with me, but did not. The blue cap disoriented my thoughts: it brought to mind the dolphin that had been harpooned alongside the *Aurora*, and how its vivid silvery blue had faded to a bleak gray as its blood drained onto the deck. I recalled the story told by the cook, of the prayers said for the dead sailor and how sharks had torn apart the corpse. "They are man-eaters," he'd said, "come from hell." I envisioned the ocean in its enormity: for thirty days and nights I had studied the waves, large and small, how they surged and climbed, reaching upward, then slipped and slid, to be absorbed into the depths of the sea. Behind them, new waves ascended, and I had watched them, over and over, again and again.

For only a moment these recollections caused me to pause, but I shook my head to regain clarity and refocus on the task at hand. Across the room, in the booth, partially hidden from my sight and waiting for me, was Arnold—the warrior, the traitor, the unrepentant broken man.

The coffee was hot. I carried one cup carefully, so as not to spill a drop, and set it down in front of Arnold. Then I returned to the bar for the other cup, sipped from it, and brought it to our table.

"Taggart . . .?" Arnold said, shaking his head, unable to recall the name.

"He was shot at Saratoga. Dr. Thacher sawed off his arm."

Arnold blew on the hot coffee.

"He told me how the soldiers were in the throes of hunger on the march to Quebec, when a farmer fed them meat. Taggart filled himself, and got sick. He was bent over on the side of the road when you rode up on your horse. He thought he'd be kicked, or hit with a sword and made to march—but you took him to the riverbank and hailed a farmer on the other side, who rowed across. You paid the farmer to take care of Taggart, and told Taggart to catch up when he recovered."

Arnold nodded. It was not clear that he remembered Taggart, but I saw that he remembered how his soldiers revered him.

"And then, as fate would have it, Taggart was beside you in the chaos when you were shot on the Sault-au-Matelot road. He lifted you, put your arm across his shoulders, and pulled you from the maelstrom."

"I remember," he said. "You saw this man recently?"

He sipped his coffee.

"I did. He lives like a pauper."

"He has no family?"

"His son was killed."

"Where?"

"At Fort Griswold."

Arnold's expression changed; the glimmer of spirit, of the general beloved by his men, disappeared.

He sipped again from his coffee cup.

"I'm sure he fought nobly, as did his father."

"He had put his gun down," I said. "They had all put their guns down. They had surrendered. And *your* army—*your* soldiers—shot them down."

"I told you," Arnold replied, tension rising in his voice. "Those were not my orders."

As he breathed I heard a gurgle coming from his chest. He leaned toward the cup to drink from it, then raised his head and looked straight at me.

"Any of us could have been killed," he said. "It comes with the business of war."

"Would you have killed Washington?" I asked.

"There was no—"

"If the British had captured Washington at West Point, according to your designs, would they have hanged him?"

He lifted his cup and drank from it, swallowing twice.

"I suppose they would have," he answered.

"You feared the noose. Didn't you fear dying that way?"

"You should know that I did not fear dying. I was never a coward."

"Washington wanted you to hang for treason."

Arnold's face twitched.

"I'm sure he did."

Two merchants came through the door, loitering by the entrance for a minute, until two others joined them. One of them said something about the cargo of a ship. They walked past us, taking no notice.

"Did I ever tell you that I watched John André hang?"

"And then you deserted, and joined my legion."

Arnold lifted his cup and drained it, swallowing the last of the coffee. He set the cup on the table in a way that suggested our conversation was coming to an end.

"I did not desert," I said.

He looked at me, but our eyes did not meet.

Slowly and deliberately he said, "I do not know what you mean."

"Washington sent me. He sent me, and Sergeant Major Champe, to find you in New York."

"To do what?"

"To capture you, to bring you back, so he could put a noose around your neck."

Arnold's head and shoulders were shaking, and his quick breathing amplified the gurgle coming from his chest.

"An assassin," he said, his voice rising.

"No. I was to bring you back . . ."

"An assassin," he repeated.

". . . to be hanged," I said.

"I knew he would send assassins," Arnold said, more to himself than to me.

"No—here you are," I said, pointing a finger at him. "An assassin would have killed you when he had the chance."

Arnold breathed deeply and tried to calm himself. Now he felt the sting of betrayal, even though he had long ago escaped the noose. His gaze hovered along the tabletop as he searched his memory for missed clues and details. Then, for a moment, his eyes locked on to his white coffee cup, empty but for a scattering of grounds. He straightened his back and looked at me defiantly, half his mouth smiling wryly, as if he'd figured out the game.

"Am I murdered now?" he asked, both alarmed and full of contempt.

My hands, set flat and gripping the edge of the table, rolled outward, turning my palms toward the sky. I looked at Arnold as if the answer was self-evident, and thought to taunt him with silence. But a cold pity made me answer:

"We are all murdered."

8

I returned to southern New Hampshire—to my house, and the place of my birth—at the end of July. The crossing had gone without incident; the brig *Stockport* was larger than the *Aurora*, and was fitted more for passengers than for cargo. The summer winds were mostly steady, except for a few days of doldrums, and though the voyage west took longer, the good weather and the fact that I was headed home brought tranquility to the passage.

I'd been away for more than four months, and now it was too late for planting, and most of my money was spent. But I was full of hope, more than I had been for years. I had sought redemption, at great effort, and I believed I'd found it. Many years had passed since the end of the Revolution, when rumors were spread and my loyalty was whispered about with suspicion. Children in this town knew nothing of my past, and some of the people who lived here now had come from elsewhere. There was no more whispering. I wanted to become a schoolmaster, to teach again, an idea manifested by the half-dozen books I'd bought in London and carried home. I resolved to do this, to revisit an ambition, as if it were a crate hidden away in a dusty attic, to open it again, and to start anew.

Until that day came, when I'd stand before a room of students, or until the winter snow, I took work driving a market wagon on a circular route between several towns and the mills on the riverbank. The millworkers stacked the wagon with barrels of flour or cornmeal and secured them with ropes. Oftentimes other merchants shipped their goods on the wagon when there was room, so that the day's cargo might include a hogshead of wine or beer, or a crate of axe heads, ploughshares, hoe blades, or cowbells—or once, a tin crate full of oysters packed in ice.

Shortly after I'd begun this work in early August, during days that were warm and dry, I ended my deliveries at the Red Oak Tavern, where hogsheads of beer were in demand. After I unloaded the barrels with the proprietor and one of his sons, I went inside to look over the newspapers that were stacked on a table. On the top of the pile was the *Columbian Centinel*, printed in Boston. As was my habit since returning home, I looked first at the death notices. There I was confronted by a single sentence, as if it had traveled across the ocean looking for me:

DIED—in England, Brigadier-General ***BENEDICT ARNOLD***; notorious throughout the world.

The proprietor, noting the heat, came to the table over which I was bent, staring down at the paper. He handed me a glass of water, and when I took it, and thanked him, his eyes settled for a moment on my hand, which was shaking as it held the glass.

9

In September, all good fortune attended me. I gained the acquaintance of Mr. Samuel Appleton, who was one of the proprietors of the academy in New Ipswich, which trained boys in Latin and Greek languages, literature and writing, music and the art of speaking, geometry, logic, and geography. Circumstances required another teacher. After several conversations and letters, and a day spent at the academy, I was hired for the remainder of the term. For the next four days I completed my obligation driving the wagon, and as the wheels rolled on the familiar roads and the two horses nodded their heads, I found myself singing.

On the last of these days, when all the barrels and crates were delivered, and all that was left in the wagon were the lengths of rope that had tied the cargo down, I stopped in the square and entered the post office, a white clapboard building that was newly built, checking for any correspondence from the academy. There was one letter waiting for me, carefully folded and sealed with red wax. My name and the address were written in a fine hand that I did not recognize. It was from London.

The gold light of autumn spread across the square. As I walked to the wagon and stood beside the horses, I realized the letter was likely from Louisa, with news of her child. I broke the seal and opened it.

It was from Edward. As I read the letter, I leaned against one of the horses. The horse raised its head and pushed back, and both horses shook their reins.

"Dear Mr. Wheatley," he wrote, "I am without words . . ."

> . . . but to tell you that, soon after your sudden departure, Louisa became ill. She suffered for two days, and on the third morning did not awaken. Our child, too, is lost. The kindness of your gift was remembered at her funeral, to which it was applied . . .

I read it, all of it; then I read it again. I looked at the sun, and at the shadows at my feet, and at the chestnut hair of the horse, and around the square at the buildings and carriages and carts, and the people walking. I climbed into the wagon and rode toward home, but passed it by, and drove the wagon into the woods.

Epilogue

New Hampshire

October 1801 & April 1802

1

The last few minutes of the night are silent and still, but this is an illusion. A field mouse rustles, an owl blinks its eyes, water in a stream glides against rocks. The wind, though light at this hour, touches the smallest twigs and the needles of the pines, and they twitch like unsteady hands. Imperceptibly, something changes; the owl turns its head. The heavens begin to fade and disappear, and out of the gray-black darkness faint colors emerge. Then comes the full light, which gradually, inexorably, unveils the forest. Lengthy shadows appear, and slowly retract, while thrushes and warblers nod their heads and sing, announcing themselves. A goshawk finds the mouse.

Hours pass; the shadows are nearly gone. Worms and beetles burrow in the soil, warmer now than it was. Three white-tailed deer step over fallen branches, then pause, then step again, foraging. They come upon the dirt road and cross it, leaping into the brush on the other side. In the canopy of trees, sparrows dart from branch to branch, and from somewhere distant comes a pulsating echo: a woodpecker beating on a hollow tree, drilling into tunnels of ants. All the while there is the sound of water in a stream, slipping among stones and swirling into pools. The shadows stretch, and in time grow long again, advancing toward evening. They spread across the road, and over the ruts from the wagon wheels, and I walk, stepping on the shadows, and through the shadows, as far as I need to go.

I lift my arm and press my fingers against the oak tree that still stands near the side of the road. Even in the dusk, I know where to find it. Many years ago, a boy claimed the tree as his own, and carved his initials—my initials—into the bark. I find them there, recognizable to no one else, a gray scar on an old tree trunk.

I hold my hand against the tree, and wait, and it comes back.

"What are you doing?" the boy asks.

"Go home," says the man, who is standing on the wagon.

But the boy waits there, looking at the eyes of the man, looking at him with all of his attention, and the man looks back at the boy, with all of his.

From high on the wagon the man speaks again, saying words that, to the boy, have no meaning, yet seem to echo in the forest:

"Blow ye the trumpets."

Then, for a moment, there is silence.

"Go home."

The boy walks away, hitting his stick on the ground. When he reaches the edge of the woods he turns and goes back, quietly, wanting to be with the man. But as he comes upon the wagon, the boy drops his stick and runs for home.

2

Near the stone wall, away from the barn and the icehouse, I built a fire, stacking kindling and split logs that had dried all summer, crisscrossing the wood at the bottom, then leaning tall dry sticks over the pile, the way we had stacked our muskets in camp, crossing their bayonets.

Inside the house, from the hearth, I filled a tinderbox with hot embers, carried them outside, and dropped them into the stack.

The embers flared, the kindling caught fire, and the dry wood popped. The flames wrapped around the split logs, and sparks swept upward and spiraled on a rising current of hot air, till they disappeared. I sat on the stone wall and felt the heat, watching the wood burn, and the flames dance, and the smoke rise into the night air. I watched the fire breathe, and the heat flare and rise, wrapping around the sticks, burning them and breaking them down.

When the fire was at its hottest, when it became a bed of luminous orange-red coals and blazing chunks of burned-over logs, I went back into the house. I returned with the leather portmanteau I had taken to London. I stood in front of the fire, feeling its heat and seeing its light reflected on me. From a small compartment within the traveling bag I took two glass vials and lifted them in front of my eyes. Both were sealed in red wax, tight and unbroken, unchanged from when I had acquired them, carried them to London, and brought them back across the ocean. Against the firelight I saw the poison powder within the vials.

One step brought me to the edge of the fire, and leaning over it, above the scorching heat, I dropped the two vials into the center of the radiant coals, and stepped backward. The vials hissed, followed for an instant by a flash and rising flame, and then the red-hot coals burned down to embers, and the embers down to ash.

3

It was an afternoon in late April, the following spring. I stood in a room paneled with chestnut, looking out a tall window that faced a grassy commons, and across it, a stately two-story inn, with four fluted Doric columns supporting the second-floor balcony and overhanging roof. Atop the cupola was a weathervane: a copper eagle grasping an arrow. I watched it swing into the changing breeze. I had spent the day reading aloud to boys who were mostly attentive, whose youthful energy was tempered by careful manners, and who possessed ambition of that laudable kind—to improve themselves. I had read to them from Chaucer, from one of the books I had purchased in London.

At day's end, as I walked to my quarters, four of the boys approached me. Upon my greeting them, the eldest, young Mr. Quincy, whom the boys called Quince, spoke on behalf of the group.

"Mr. Wheatley, sir," he began. "We have heard it told . . ."

"In our history class," one of the boys added.

". . . that you fought in the war, at Saratoga—"

"And other things," the boy named Edward interrupted.

"That you were . . .," began another.

Here they all became silent.

"Go ahead," I beseeched them.

"That perhaps you were a spy," said Quince.

"For General Washington," Edward said, clarifying the suggestion.

Quince continued, explaining that the war was of great interest to them, and that they were particularly interested in spies. He wondered aloud if I had ever seen the traitor Benedict Arnold, and would I tell them all about it.

How my fortunes had changed, I thought, as the chaos of war, and its aftermath, had settled over the years. I agreed, but warned them that the story, if I told it fully and truthfully, would take some time. If they wanted to hear it, I suggested that we meet the next day—a day without classes—at noon, at the south end of the commons.

This seemed to please them.

"May we bring guests?" Quince asked, at which I laughed, and agreed.

Attending to errands in the morning, I returned to the academy at half past eleven to get a stool to take to the commons, on which to sit and address my small coterie of inquisitive historians. But a few tasks captured my attention, and I was unprepared when the town bells sounded noon. I closed my books and put away my papers, seized the stool in one hand, and left the building to walk across the commons.

I hurried at first, until I turned and looked down the yard and stopped, suddenly needing to think of a new location where I could sit with the boys. Something else was happening at that end of the commons. Forty or fifty boys—nearly all the students at the academy—were seated on the grass, joined by twenty or more girls and young women. Behind them were an equal number of townspeople, men and women I'd never seen before, and teachers from the academy.

In my confusion I turned away, wondering if I had forgotten some public meeting, when Quince approached, running.

"Mr. Wheatley," he called. "We're all waiting for you."

The boys had indeed invited guests; many more people than I had imagined appeared eager for a story, to hear something revealed about the late Revolution. I walked with Quince toward the crowd, where a scattering of conversations drew to a halt, and all heads turned toward the two of us as we approached. A hundred faces were looking at me, and quickly I thought of how to begin.

For an instant, my own beginning came to mind:

Blow ye the trumpets.

And I remembered: When last I spoke to so many, it was to a company of soldiers, who answered with shouts of "Huzzah!" They cheered "Huzzah!" a second time, still louder, and repeated it again. The other companies joined the call, and all down the line their cheers resounded. With the fury of a windstorm their voices gathered into one, swelled by the echoes of history and myth. The sound swept over us, and those who were tired drew strength from it; those who were fearful gained courage; and those who were uncertain found conviction.

As his peers made room for Quince to sit, I took my place, facing the crowd.

"The boys asked me for some stories," I said loudly, so all could hear. "They asked if I knew any spies."

The faces nodded.

"A few of them seem to think I was a spy—for General Washington."

The boys in the front stared at me, enthralled.

"Yes, I have known spies," I said, "more than I ever thought I would. But none were the daring masters of concealment and subterfuge you're thinking about. More often they shuddered at the very idea."

Briefly I told them how Mary Underhill had hung a red towel on her clothesline; how Hercules Mulligan extracted military gossip from his British clientele; and how Mr. Townsend, the dry goods merchant, conveyed secret messages among spies.

Quince, who sat front and center, raised up his hand. "But Mr. Wheatley," he said, "were *you* a spy?"

As he asked his question a swirling breeze came up the commons, whistling and droning through the trees behind me. I took my hat from my head and held it against my chest. Coming and going on the wind I heard the whispered chatter of a thousand voices known to me, and thousands more unknown.

When I blow with a trumpet, I and all that are with me, then blow ye the trumpets. . . .

I looked at the people assembled. In the life of the republic, so much would depend on them.

I lifted my voice.

"By some measure we are all spies, of one kind or another," I said, casting each word to the far corners of the crowd. "Some play bit parts in grand schemes and swallow the risk like a bitter drug. A few will travel behind the lines to gauge an enemy's strength, or befriend a double-dealing rogue to unmask a secret treason. But I've learned this: that every honest man spies upon himself foremost, to see what hides in his own dark alleys. A bloody war can oust a king, but the skirmishes we fight alone, in silence, also make their mark on the world."

"I was a soldier in the Revolution . . ."

Author's Note

Gideon's Revolution is a work of fiction, but the story is based on things that really happened.

As both a lawyer and a historian, I've been studying the law of treason and the life of Benedict Arnold for over two decades. The fact that the Treason Clause is the only criminal law in the US Constitution caught my attention in law school, resulting in a law review note that spurred my continued interest in the implications of loyalty, allegiance, betrayal, and treason in a democratic republic. These ideas came together in my PhD dissertation and a subsequent book on the meaning of treason in the United States. As I surveyed the legal and cultural landscape of disloyalty, one character appeared everywhere: Benedict Arnold, who, with his act of betrayal at West Point in September 1780, became the face and name by which we recognize and condemn disloyalty, even to this day.

At some level, every mention of Arnold's name hints at a basic question: Why did he do it? What compelled George Washington's best battlefield general to betray the cause to which he had shown such devotion?

Following that inquiry, a second line of questioning arises: How do we make sense of betrayal, when the thing betrayed is not just an individual but a foundational idea? If the first question concerns the fall of *a man*, the second implicates something closer to the fall of *man*, a notion that informs our nation's own origin story: that the delicate balance of self-government requires certain virtues and democratic habits, and if we fail to cultivate them, we risk seeing the whole great experiment come undone.

Our knowledge of Washington's plot to abduct Arnold and bring him to justice is limited; its success or failure, after all, depended on the greatest secrecy, and its players were spies. But we know some of the story and can piece together the details. The rest we can imagine.

Every author I've met who writes historical fiction has heard me ask this question: How faithful must the story be to what really happened? There are many perspectives on this. My professional inclination as a historian was to find every available fact I could and stick with it, and try to imagine it into life, as it were. But I also wanted to explore the two questions we have asked about Arnold for well over two centuries: Why? And how do we reckon with betrayal, both individually and collectively? For that, too, I've relied on imagination.

Many hours of reading and research brought the facts to light, but the imaginative work was quickened by retracing the footsteps of Benedict Arnold on battlefields and city streets, from the Plains of Abraham to Ticonderoga and the rolling hills of Saratoga; from the cobblestone streets of old Quebec City to lower Manhattan's Bowling Green and Golden Hill. One late summer afternoon I wandered through the colonial-era burial ground in Norwich, Connecticut, circling back again and again to the headstone of Hannah Arnold, Benedict's mother, who rests beside a son and two daughters, each of whom died in childhood. I was a guest that night in a nearby house built in 1745, in which the teenage Benedict had lived while apprenticed to an apothecary. Sitting quietly in a dimly lit room where the boy had once walked about, where I thought I could almost see him, I began writing *Gideon's Revolution*.

I'm grateful to the many people who walked with me on those adventures, engaged me in conversation, or read the manuscript and enhanced it. I look forward to sharing this finished story with them.

A special thanks, however, goes to Michael McGandy for his keen editorial eye and his enthusiasm for this novel; and also to the talented people at Cornell University Press, who bring books to life.

Reflecting on the French Revolution, Edmund Burke observed that, before we can "proceed towards a love to our country, and to mankind," we need first to "love the little platoon we belong to in society." For this reason, I dedicate this novel to Kerry, Owen, and Nathaniel, knowing that my membership in this little platoon is the best thing that has ever happened to me.